Sylvanus Cobb

The Fortunes of Conrad

a novel

Sylvanus Cobb

The Fortunes of Conrad
a novel

ISBN/EAN: 9783337349356

Printed in Europe, USA, Canada, Australia, Japan

Cover: Foto ©Andreas Hilbeck / pixelio.de

More available books at **www.hansebooks.com**

THE

FORTUNES OF CONRAD

A Novel.

BY

SYLVANUS COBB, JR.,

AUTHOR OF "THE GUNMAKER OF MOSCOW," "ROLLO
OF NORMANDY," "OUTCAST OF MILAN,"
"CONSPIRATOR OF CORDOVA," ETC.

NEW YORK:

ROBERT BONNER'S SONS,

PUBLISHERS.

THE POPULAR SERIES: ISSUED SEMI-MONTHLY. SUBSCRIPTION PRICE, SIX DOLLARS PER ANNUM. NO. 4,
JUNE 1, 1881. ENTERED AT THE NEW YORK, N. Y., POST OFFICE AS SECOND CLASS MAIL MATTER.

THE FORTUNES OF CONRAD.

CHAPTER I.

THE COT AND THE CAVERN.

In a quiet, lovely valley, among the Nord Mountains in Brittany, close by the head-waters of the Meu, stood a small cot, with wooden walls, and a sharp roof thatched with straw. Attached to the cot were a few small outbuildings, and a sheep-fold. A large, noble-looking dog lay upon the grass before the door, ever and anon moving his head, and changing his position, as though he were waiting for some one to come out. The scene from this spot was wild and grand. A few acres of open, grassy space, was bounded by a dense wood, broken here and there by crags of rock ; while in the distance the dark old mountains, crowned with heavy forests, arose against the blue sky ; and all the while, by day and by night, the waters of the river, speeding down from their hill-side sources, sent forth a rolling murmur, making vocal the Spirit of that forest haunt.

Within the cot, in the apartment which served as a sitting and eating-room, sat a woman who had passed well into the winter of life. Her hair was gray, and her kindly-fashioned face was marked with many furrows. She was at least three-score-and-ten ; but her form was erect, and her eye was bright ; though care had left some traces upon her brow.

Near to her, upon the stool of the window, leaned a young man, whose life had not yet reached the span of more than three-and-twenty years. He was tall, and fair of form, with gently sloping shoulders and swelling chest. His hair, of a nut-brown color, curled closely about his neck and temples, and his features were formed after the model of the grandest style of Roman beauty. He did not seem to present a very powerful frame, if one only looked at the outline of his form ; but there was a massiveness in his structure—a concentration of power in that firmly-set hand—a flashing of the dark hazel eye—a curling of the finely chiselled lip—and a nervous delicacy in the tapering limbs, that told the keen observer of wondrous force. His costume was simple and neat. He wore a shepherd's frock of blue cloth, secured at the waist by a broad leathern belt, which was fastened with a heavy silver buckle. His leggins were of leather, such as the antelope hunters wore; and upon his feet he wore light hunting shoes. His cap, which he held in his hand, was of red cloth, with a band of black velvet, and adorned with a few eagle feathers.

" Ah, Conrad," said the woman, with a slight show of regret in her tone and manner, " I may as well give up all hope of ever seeing you in the Church."

" Indeed, my dear mother, you speak truly," returned the youth, in a tone of rare sweetness and depth. " If you had meant to make a priest of me you should not have brought me to these mountains. You should not have allowed me to breathe this fresh air, and roam through these grand old forests. These mountains are not the stepping-stones to the cell of a convent. No, no—I cannot renounce the life of a free mountaineer for the cowl and cassock."

Marguerite bowed her head, and smoothed down the folds of her dress.

"I fear," she at length said, raising her eyes once more to the youth, "that our good Francisco has not labored very hard to turn your thoughts away from worldly things."

Conrad smiled, and played with the feathers of his cap.

"I think," he replied, "that Francisco was once a soldier."

"Yes," added Marguerite; "he was, in his early manhood, one of the bravest and most valiant of the warriors of Brittany; but that was many years ago. When he undertook your education, he had renounced the sword, and had resolved to lead the life of a hermit."

"And has he not kept his resolution?" asked Conrad.

"Aye, I think he has; but yet, my son, he has not succeeded in bending your mind as I had hoped."

"Simply, my dear mother, because you hoped for that which is impossible. I tell you, Francisco has done his best; and if he has finally presented you with a young man wholly unfitted for holy orders, be assured he has returned to you a faithful and loving son, who will serve you and protect you with all his power of soul and strength."

He approached his mother as he spoke, and stooped to kiss her. She wound her arms about his neck, and gently murmured:

"Good, noble boy. Heaven shield and guard thee!"

It was early in the day, and when Conrad left the cot he took his way towards a point in the forest where great rocky bluffs lifted their heads above the tops of the trees; and when he stopped it was before the entrance to a cave.

"Ah, my son; I give thee a good-morning!"

The speaker was an old man, past three-score, with hair and beard well whitened, and possessing a form still upright and stalwart. He was habited in a long robe of gray stuff, and carried a staff in his hand. His face was bronzed, and full of hard lines, but they were bluff, honest lines; for his heart was kind, and his soul was above all littleness. Francisco, the Hermit, was known and loved by all who had ever had occasion to seek his hospitality or his assistance. The hardy mountaineers, who saw him often, spoke of him as one who had become disgusted with the world, and who had sought the retirement of the mountain cave that the evening of his life might be passed in peace and quietness.

"Good father," returned the youth, in tones of mingled love and reverence, "I find thee well and hearty, for which I thank God."

Teacher and pupil embraced each other, and then seated themselves upon a broad stone, beneath the branches of a giant old oak.

"How is it with your mother this morning?" asked the hermit.

"My mother is well, and she has spoken again concerning my taking holy orders; but I think she will rest now. She must see by this time that I cannot enter the Church. And, moreover, this morning, after I had announced my fixed purpose not to assume the priestly robes, she blessed me."

"Your mother means well, Conrad; and perhaps it had been better that another teacher than myself had been given thee. Between you and me there are no secrets touching my past life. I am an old soldier, and the clang of steel hath still a charm for me. I found thee apt and strong, with a disposition to manly exercise; and I could not resist the impulse to give thee such education as every free man ought to possess. If I have done wrong, they must blame my head, and not my heart. If you were to have been a priest, you should have been given to the old Abbot of Saint Aubin instead of to me. Dagobert was a priest, and I was a soldier. They made a poor choice. I' faith, when I found of what stuff you were made, I could no more have helped placing a sword in your hand than I could have helped giving bread to a starving man. When I saw the lightning-flash in your eye, and the tower of strength in your broad breast and shoulders, and the steel-like tenacity of the muscles in your wrist, I should have sinned against my own conscience had I kept the use of the sword and buckler from thee."

Conrad's face beamed with pride and joy as the old man thus spoke.

"And am I, father, so proficient in the use of arms as you would lead me to believe?"

"By my life," cried the hermit, with honest energy, "I never met your superior—never. Should the time ever come when your life shall hang upon your sword, you have only to remember the instructions I have given you. Your arm is strong enough; your wrist is like a mass of finely tempered steel; but keep your head cool, and your heart quiet. Keep your head cool—your head cool, my boy. By my soul, you have an eye as quick as the flash of light."

"O, I should like to see a battle!" exclaimed the youth, starting to his feet. "I should like to draw my sword in the defence of some glorious cause!"

"Hush, hush, my son." The hermit trembled, and seemed troubled. "I fear I have done wrong."

"In what, father?"

"In that I have led thee to such desires. Your mother does not know that I have spent so much time in giving thee this dangerous education. Let it rest where it is. Defend yourself always against mortal danger ; but do not seek that danger."

Conrad was upon the point of replying, when he was interrupted by the approach of two strangers. They were two middle-aged, powerfully built men, habited in the garbs of pilgrims. Francisco offered them seats ; but they respectfully declined.

" We are not weary, good father ; for we have left our horses not far away. We do not seek shelter ; nor are we in search for food. Somewhere, to the eastward, beyond these dark mountain forests, in Mayenne, is the Monastery of Saint George. We wish to go thither, and we do not know the way. Therefore we seek a guide. Half a league from here we met a shepherd who informed us that a youth named Conrad, living in a cot by the river, would be an efficient guide. We stopped at the cot, and the good mother whom we found there directed us hither."

" The shepherd told you truly," said Conrad, advancing a step. " I know every path in this forest, and can lead you to every mountain pass."

" And you are the youth of whom the shepherd spoke ?"

" I am."

The pilgrim ran his eyes over the fair, youthful form, and then continued :

" We want a guide, and we will pay well for the service. Will you go with us ?"

" If it please my mother, and my good old friend, the hermit, I will do so with pleasure."

" You will not regret it, my friend," returned the pilgrim. " We will reward you well."

" I think not of reward," said Conrad, shaking his head.

" And yet, a few pieces of gold would not harm you."

" True, sir Pilgrim. If you have gold to spare, and I can fairly earn it, I shall not refuse it."

" Then let us make the contract, so that you shall not depend upon a bounty, while we shall not be expected to give more than may be just."

" That is the true way," said Francisco.

" Then," resumed the pilgrim, who had thus far spoken, " we will give ten crowns to the man who shall guide us safely to the Monastery of Saint George, in Mavenne."

Conrad considered the sum a large one, and was ready to accept the terms. He went up to the cot, where he acquainted his mother with what was required of him, and asked her permission to accept the proposed terms. Marguerite would have shrunk from allowing the youth to expose himself to danger ; but she could see no danger in the service thus required of him. She had a great respect for priests, and monks, and pilgrims ; and there was no place in the world to which she would sooner have sent her son than to a monastery ; so she freely gave her consent, only asking him to go and come as quickly as possible. He promised to waste no time upon the road ; and, having received her blessing, he went down to the hermit's cave, to prepare for his expedition.

From an inner apartment of the cavern, Francisco brought forth a sword and a dagger.

" My son," he said, "you know the temper of this sword, and you know its weight. A better blade was never drawn in Brittany. There may be no need of this in the work upon which you are going ; but its presence can do you no harm. You will not forget the instructions I have heretofore given you. We cannot tell what you may meet upon your road. Remember,

you are never to seek a quarrel. You will never interfere in other people's business, unless it be to protect a
woman, or to assist an oppressed fellow-creature who
may demand your aid. In short—never seek danger
for the sake of adventure ; and never flee from danger
but with honor.

"And now, one word touching these pilgrims. I
would not have you be over-suspicious ; and yet it is
well that you should be ever on your guard against
imposition ; and to this end all suspicious circumstances
must be considered."

"And do you discover anything suspicious about these
men ?" asked Conrad.

"Only this," replied the hermit : "In my day, pilgrims did not usually travel on horseback. But these
men may be true and honest for all that. Nevertheless,
you can keep your eyes open."

Conrad thanked his tutor for these hints, and then
went out and mounted his horse, which he had brought
down from the cot. He sat easily in the saddle, like a
soldier who had seen much service ; and his long, heavy
sword was borne with grace.

"By the life of me," muttered Francisco, as the youth
rode away, "he is the fairest man I ever saw. Woe
unto the man who excites his wrath ; and woe unto the
heart of the maiden who meets the light of his flashing
eye !"

The old man sat upon the broad stone, with his eye
fixed upon the point in the wood where the youth had
disappeared, when he felt a hand upon his shoulder, and
on looking up he beheld Marguerite.

"Ah, my sister, are you lonesome so soon ?"

"No, Francisco, I am not yet lonesome ; but I wish
to talk with you about Conrad."

"We could not converse upon a better theme ; so sit

thee down, and let us commence. You look troubled, Marguerite. Are you afraid that the boy has gone into danger ?"

" I do not think that the guiding of those two pilgrims is dangerous ; but I do fear that danger is before him. Ah, Francesco, you have not done as you should."

" Mercy ! What have I done out of the way ?"

" You have been the boy's tutor ?"

" Certainly."

" And you knew that he was destined for the Church ?"

" I knew that such a consummation had been thought of."

" And yet you have given him an education entirely unfitting him for holy orders."

" Why was he put into my hands ?"

" Because you were thought to be true and faithful."

" Aye—and so I have been."

" You were not asked to teach the boy the art of war."

" Have I done so ?"

" Have you not ?"

" Hold, Marguerite. Let us understand each other. I see your meaning, and I will meet you fairly. Suppose you should to-day bear to me a young, unfledged eagle, and bid me rear it as I would a hen, or a goose. By and by the eye begins to gain fire ; the beak grows sharp and fierce ; the talons become strong and tena- cious ; and the wings spread themselves with mighty instinct of power. What shall I do ? The bird is not a hen ; it is not a goose. Following the law of its life it has grown to be an eagle. I can clip its wings, I can cut off its talons ; and I can mutilate the sharp beak. And what then ? Have I made it anything different from what it was ? I have made it less than it should be ; I have taken away its power, and destroyed its beauty ;

but I can never change its nature. In the time to come the wings may grow again, and the eagle will soar aloft into its native element : and if I have deprived it of its beak and talons, then I have made it a thing to be despised and pitied by its kind.

"Listen to me, Marguerite, Just as well might the fowler attempt to train the eaglet up to herd with geese, as I to train Conrad up to be a priest. I never offered him a sword. He demanded it. He found my old chronicles, and read them ; and from that time his soul was filled with love of bold and daring deeds. And here I am willing to confess my weakness and my fault. When this fire flashed forth in his life, I loved him better than ever before ; and when he kissed the hilt of my old sword, and, upon his knees, begged of me to teach him how to use it, I could not refuse him. And Marguerite, I think I hazard little in saying that the youth whom you destined for the Church is, today, the best swordsman in Brittany."

"That cannot be," said the woman, with surprise.

"And yet it is so," confidently returned the hermit. "Thirty years ago I was acknowledged the champion swordsman of our army. Conrad has not only learned all that I ever knew ; but he possesses such a strength of arms, and a power of bones and muscle in the wrist, as I never saw equalled."

"Well, well," said Marguerite, after some reflection, "I have no desire to lodge blame upon your shoulders Francisco ; but since matters have turned out as they have, we must form some new plan for our charge. He will not enter the Church, and it is very evident that he will not be long contented to remain in this secluded place."

"I agree with you," said the hermit.

"And," pursued the woman, with a slight shudder, "he must not go to Vannes."

"Not at present."

"*Never! Never!*" pronounced Marguerite. "If he leaves this vale, we must send him as far away from the capital as possible."

"Let us wait until he returns from Mayenne," suggested the old man, "and then frankly and freely advise with him ; for I tell you, he is no longer to be controlled against his own inclinations, unless we can show him good cause. If you like, we can send for Dagobert."

"We will wait," said Marguerite. "We will see Conrad first ; and then we will call upon the old Abbot if necessary. O, woe is me if harm come to the child !"

The hermit made no reply, and the woman arose and returned to her cot.

CHAPTER II.

THE VEILED LADY.

At a short distance from the cot, by the edge of the road, Conrad found the two pilgrims, who had unhitched their horses, and were prepared to mount.

"If we are to travel together," said our hero, "it would be pleasant for me to know your names."

"Most assuredly," replied one of them, with a light laugh. "I am called Baptiste ; and this man's name is Adolphe. But, gentle sir, I did not think we had engaged a warrior to be our guide."

"How ?" asked Conrad, as though ne did not comprehend what was meant.

" I alluded to your sword," returned Baptiste.

" O," cried Conrad, with a smile, " this is not mine. It belongs to my old friend, the hermit ; and he thought I had better take it."

" Perhaps you understand its use ?"

" I should like to do so, sir ; but my quiet, retired life has not given me need for such weapons. I have never used the sword except in play with the hermit ; but I can use the cross-bow, and cast a javelin. I slew a wild boar with my javelin only the day before yesterday."

" A good deed, truly," said Adolphe. " You were brought up in this forest, I think ?"

" Yes, sir."

" Have you ever visited the capital ?"

" No."

" By my life, you have been a regular recluse."

" I hope to visit the capital at some time."

" You owe it to yourself to do so, my dear friend."

Thus they talked for an hour or more, during which time they rode two leagues, and reached the bank of a small tributary of the Meu, where they found two more persons ready to join them.

" We did not mention these people." said Baptiste, with a nod to our hero, " because we were not sure that they would join us. They have come from Pontivy, and are probably going our way. Let me ride on and speak with them."

The two strangers who had been thus met could not fail to attract Conrad's attention and arouse his curiosity. One was a man of gigantic stature, mounted upon a powerful war-horse ; and the other was a female, of delicate form, closely veiled, and seated upon a Spanish jennet. The man was armed with sword and spear, and upon his saddle-bow he carried two spare swords.

" Who is that giant ?" asked the youth.

" His name is Goliath," replied Adolphe. " He is the most mighty warrior in the kingdom."

" And who is the female ?"

" I do not know ; but I think she is some lady whom Goliath is conducting to a convent. Let us see what word Baptiste brings back."

By-and-by Baptiste came.

" Conrad," he said, addressing the youth with frank familiarity, " would it disturb you if we should conclude to change our plan somewhat ?"

" Perhaps not," was the guarded reply.

" Do you know the way to the Norman frontier ?"

" Yes."

" Do you know where the Castle of Saint Cyr is ?"

" Aye—I know the old structure. It is a vast pile of wall and tower, in the midst of a deep, gloomy forest, just on the confines of Normandy."

" Well—this man wishes to be guided to that point, and I have consented to accompany him."

" What in the world will he do there ?" asked Conrad.

" O, Saint Cyr is not his final destination ; but, once there, he can easily make his way alone. He is taking with him a nun to convent beyond the border. As for Adolphe and myself, it matters not which way we go. Goliath is our friend, and we wish to please him."

" Since it matters not to you," said our hero, " it surely matters not to me. Saint Cyr is not more than five-and-twenty leagues distant ; and though the way is through a dense forest for the most part, I can take you there as quickly as the lady will wish to ride."

" Then it is settled," cried Baptiste. And with this he rode back to the giant, whom he shortly afterwards brought and introduced to the guide.

" This is Goliath of Vannes," he said to the youth.

"And this is Conrad the guide," he added, addressing the giant.

"A fair youth, truly," spoke Goliath, in a growling tone, and with a smile breaking over his broad, coarse features ; "and, I think, an honest one."

"I will serve you, sir, as I have been requested," returned Conrad, modestly.

"Good ! And the sooner we are in motion the better. You can ride on in advance with Baptiste and Adolph, while I follow with my charge. If you serve us well, I will add something to the sum which has already been promised you."

The young guide would have made some reply to this, but the giant did not wait for it. Conrad viewed him as he turned to leave, and wondered how his horse could bear him up. He must have been nearly seven feet high, and was stout in proportion. His hands were broad and thick, and his neck was like a bull's.

"By my life," muttered Conrad to himself, "I shall have no great love for that man. I do not like him. If he thinks I like his flattery, he is mistaken. Bah ! he is too big. I suppose some people would respect the huge mass of flesh, and fear the anger which might call into action those great arms ; but I do neither one nor the other."

"I think," said Baptiste, speaking to his companion, but loud enough for Conrad to hear, "that we might wear those swords which Goliath has to spare. What say you ?"

"A good idea," replied the other.

Thereupon Baptiste went up to the giant, and brought back the two swords, which they girded to their loins as though they owned them.

Goliath drew up on one side with his charge, to allow the others to pass on in advance, and as Conrad came opposite to the spot he bestowed a searching look upon the veiled female ; but he could see nothing more than he had seen before. He felt sure that she was young ; and he allowed himself to fancy that she was not very happy. Yet in all this he might be mistaken. She might be old, and she might be perfectly contented with her lot. She sat quietly upon her saddle, with her head bowed, the thick, dark shroud that enveloped her reaching from her head to her feet.

It was now a little past noon, and as soon as the narrow stream had been forded, Baptiste rode up by Conrad's side and told him that he might travel at good speed while the way would permit.

"I can lead off just as fast as the lady can ride," replied the guide. "If it be your pleasure, we may reach the Ille before we sleep."

"Good ! It shall be so."

The path was a dark and dubious one ; but Conrad knew it well, and proceeded without any mistakes. Adolphe rode by his side most of the time, while Baptiste remained behind with Goliath and the lady.

As the guide had promised, they reached a ford of the Ille just at dusk, and when the horses had been secured, Adolphe spread out the supper of bread and dried meat, which he had carried in his saddle-bags. Conrad had hoped that the lady might keep them company at the repast ; but it was not so. She took her food apart, and was allowed to remain by herself while her guardian eat ; but the youth could see that she was not suffered to be wholly free ; for, when Goliath could not see her, he bent his ear to keep the sound of her step. And one thing more Conrad noticed : Both Baptiste and Adolphe seemed to feel an interest in the lady's safety ; and, when she had been prepared for the night's rest, it became very evident that a strict watch was to be kept upon her.

When Conrad threw himself down beneath the tree which was to serve him as a shelter while he slept, his mind was filled with doubt and suspicion. He did not like the looks of things at all. The hint which he had received from old Francisco may have served to awake his vigilance ; but, even if the hint had not been given, he could not have failed to suspect. In the first place, he was sure that the three men who were following his lead through the forest, were of one party, and had one interest. He believed that Baptiste had as much interest in caring for the veiled female as Goliath had. And, further, he was convinced that Baptiste and Adolphe were not pilgrims at all ; but that they were soldiers and adventurers. During the afternoon he had heard them converse somewhat, and their language was sadly at variance with the characters they had assumed. Next, Conrad did not believe that they had intended to go to the Monastery in Mayenne. They had calculated, from the first, to go to Normandy ; and Goliath had only remained behind while they came for a guide.

At this point the youth began seriously to reflect.

"Why should they have done this ?" he asked himself. "Evidently," his reason answered, "to blind the hermit. They wished that their destination should not be known to those who remained behind. And why this wish ? I should like to see that lady's face. I think she is young and beautiful ; and I fear that she is taking this course against her will."

As Conrad thus spoke, he raised himself upon his elbow, and looked towards the place where the lady had lain down. He could not see her, but he saw a tall, dark form standing close by where her bed had been made ; and in a moment more he thought he heard a prayerful voice, low and plaintive, making some supplication. The answer was in the growling tones of the giant ; and he seemed to threaten her. Then the voices ceased and Goliath came away.

A little while afterwards Conrad fell asleep, and when he awoke the light of day was beginning to break the gloom of the forest. He arose and cared for his horse, and ere long afterwards Adolphe had prepared breakfast.

"Can we not reach Saint Cyr this night ?" asked Goliath, after the meal had been eaten.

"Not easily," replied Conrad. "With a good road we might do it without harming our horses ; but the way from this point is rough and winding. We will be there to-morrow noon."

The giant was not at all pleased with the reply ; but as he had no power to better the road, he was forced to submit ; though he urged the guide to travel as fast as he could.

As Conrad had assured them, the path was found to be a difficult one ; and when night came they were a good five leagues from Saint Cyr. They were camped in a deep valley, and the same arrangements were made for resting as on the previous night.

By this time Conrad's suspicions had become perplexing and painful. He was sure that the veiled lady was not a willing companion of the three soldiers ; for, be it understood, he had determined that Baptiste and Adolphe were educated and practised men-at-arms. It was late when he lay down by the side of his horse, and for a long time he reflected upon the curious circumstances into which he had been thrown.

"By my life !" he said to himself, "if that lady is being oppressed and wronged, I am a party to the foul transaction. If these villains are dragging her away from her true friends, I am a base tool in their hands! Ye gods! I dislike all three of them! They have tried to deceive me, and they think to use me as they please. They fancy that I am but an ignorant mountaineer, ready for any work that will pay me in gold. By the power that made me, they may find out their mistake!"

He started to his elbow, and looked around. He wished to speak with the veiled lady. He had resolved to do so if the thing were possible. Fortunately the place where he had lain down was between two large trees, so that his movements could not be seen by the soldiers, even if they were awake to watch him. When he had once made up his mind to seek the lady, he was not long in starting upon the attempt. Her place of rest was at some distance, and he was sure that one of the men was close by her; but this did not deter him. He crept, upon his hands and knees, out from between the two trees, up the slope of a bank, to a cover behind some low bushes. These bushes reached almost to the point where the lady lay, thus affording him a safe shelter to within a very few yards of his destination. He stopped when he arrived at the end of the copse, and soon discovered the female upon a bed of moss, with a large mantle thrown completely over her. One of the men was sitting against a tree, not far off, the other two being evidently asleep by their horses. While Conrad crouched there under his leafy cover, the man got up from the foot of the tree, and approached the spot where the lady lay. It was Baptiste. He moved without noise, and when he had satisfied himself that all was right, he glided away down the vale, and was soon out of sight.

"It may be," thought Conrad to himself, "that he has gone to see if I am safe; but I cannot go back now. This is the moment for me, and I must take advantage of it."

Without stopping for further thought, he moved noise-lessly down to where the lady lay, and spoke to her. She started, as though from a dream, and pulled the mantle from her head.

" What now ?" she asked, in a tremulous tone.

" Hush, lady ! Be not alarmed. I am the guide. I may have held unjust suspicions. One word will suffice. Are you in need of help ?"

" O ! in Heaven's name—"

" Hush ! Speak not so loudly. I am here unknown to your guards. Am I right in supposing that you are an unwilling companion of these men ?"

" O, good sir, I am a prisoner ! I have been torn from my friends, and these men are my enemies !"

She had arisen to a sitting posture, and thrown the mantle from her face ; and, by the dim starlight, Con-rad could see that she was young and beautiful ! or, if his sight failed him, his fancy made up the picture. Her voice was soft and musical, and the outlines of her face were delicate and fair.

" They are taking you to the Castle of Saint Cyr," said the youth.

" Who lives there ?"

" No one. It is a gloomy old ruin."

" O, in the name of the great God, who can reward the true and noble, I pray you, save me if you can !"

She clasped her hands, and extended them towards him in supplicating mood.

" Can you—can you save me ?"

" I cannot tell. Hush ! Here comes Baptiste. Down—down, lady, and keep quiet. I will save you if I can."

Conrad sought to regain the cover of the bushes without being detected; but Baptiste was too quick for him.

"Hold!" the soldier cried, springing up the bank. "You cannot escape me. I have been to your resting-place, and found you gone."

It was not in Conrad's nature to crouch before the detection of any of his acts; so he arose and faced his opponent.

"What have you found?" he asked.

"What have *you* found?" returned Baptiste.

Conrad hesitated. If he would serve the lady, he must be careful how he exposed his hand.

"I have found the lady whom you are conducting away," he replied.

"Ha! have you spoken with her?"

"Yes."

"Upon my life, you are curious."

"Aye, Baptiste, I am curious. I am curious to know who this lady is."

"Have you not asked her?"

"I have had no opportunity."

"You have spoken with her."

"Yes, and she would have asked me to help her, I am sure; but before I could find out who she was, you disturbed me."

"Perhaps you would have promised to assist her if she had asked such a service at your hand."

"An unconditional promise of that kind would have been foolish. Still, sir, I should like to know who and what she is."

Baptiste regarded the youth a few moments in silence, and then replied:

"In the morning you may ask Goliath. He knows all about it. For the present I advise you to return to your place of rest. We must be early astir, and you may need your sleep."

Conrad walked away, and had just sat down between the two great trees, when Baptiste again approached him.

"Look ye, my brave youth,—I have a question to ask; and you may rest assured that you cannot deceive me in your reply. You have heard enough to make you believe that yonder lady would like to be free from our company. Is it not so?"

"It is," frankly replied Conrad.

"And I believe you would like to help her."

"You do not misjudge my disposition."

"Then tell me: Do you mean to guide us to Saint Cyr?"

"Such is my intention."

"And the words of the lady have not led you to a different conclusion?"

"Most assuredly not. I promised to guide you to the Castle of Saint Cyr, and I shall do so, unless you prevent me. But I am at a loss to comprehend the drift of your questions. If I wished to serve the lady, I do not see how I could further the object by leaving you and her in the depths of this forest."

"Never mind," said the soldier, with a shrug of his shoulders. "I do not think you will harm us; nor do we mean to harm the lady. Good-night."

Baptiste went away as he thus spoke, and afterwards Conrad lay down upon his grassy bed—but not to sleep. He may have dozed a little during the remainder of the night, but he did not so far lose himself in slumber but that the falling of a leaf would have awakened him.

CHAPTER III.

DRAWN SWORDS.

As soon as it was fairly light Conrad was up, and while he changed the position of his horse, so that the animal might feed to better advantage, he noticed that the three soldiers were standing by some bushes only a few yards from him, engaged in conversation. He listened, while he attended to his horse, and heard Baptiste relating the adventure of the night. The fellows were conversing in the Spanish language, evidently thinking that the simple mountaineer could not understand them; but in this they were mistaken. Old Francisco had been faithful in the discharge of his duties, and his pupil could converse well in French, Saxon, Spanish and German. The youth had been a diligent student, and he had taken a pride in learning.

Goliath, when he had heard Baptiste's story, uttered a round oath, in Spanish, and then added:

"What shall we do? The boy may know too much."

"How can he know too much?" asked Baptiste.

"He may escape us, and make his way back with the story."

"But we will not be so foolish as to allow him to escape."

"Suppose he should slip away into some dubious path while we are on the road?"

"He will not do so. He will guide us to Saint Cyr. I fear him not."

Goliath still hesitated.

"I pledge you my word," insisted Baptiste, "that he will not leave us. I have made myself sure of that."

"Then," said the giant, "all may be well. Still, it will do no harm to watch him. If he conducts us to the castle, his meddling will have amounted to nothing. Should he seek to leave us——"

"He will not," repeated Baptiste.

"But," pursued Goliath, unwilling to give up his point, "if he should, we will serve up his carcass to the vultures, and make the rest of our way alone."

What did all this mean? As soon as Conrad was alone with his own thoughts he reflected upon what he had heard. What meant Baptiste by saying that the guide could not know too much?

"By my soul, there is a deep plot in this ; and, I fear, a deadly one," said Conrad, to himself. "I cannot know too much, because *I am not to be allowed to return to Brittany with my story.*"

He paced up and down by the side of his horse a few times, and at length he stopped, with his hand upon the hilt of his sword.

"I see it all," he muttered between his closed teeth and tightly compressed lips. "I am to be sacrificed to their secret ! I am to conduct them to the Castle of Saint Cyr, and when they want me no more they plan to put me to death. Gentlemen, I understand you ! I will guide you to the castle as I promised ; and beyond that my work remains to be planned."

He drew his sword half way from its scabbard, and then thrust it back with an emphatic movement. He was certain that the three men meant to kill him as soon as he had led them to the end of their journey. They were upon some business which must not be known in Brittany. The story of going to St. George, in Mayenne, which had been told in the hearing of the old hermit and Marguerite, had been only a part of their plan to keep their whereabouts a secret. They had fallen upon a poor mountaineer, who would not be much missed, and they meant to use him as a sorely pressed, retreating army uses a bridge—cutting it away when it has served their turn. And yet the youth had not the slightest emotion of fear. So much reliance had he upon his own prowess, that he rather courted the adventure—not for the sake of the conflict, simply ; but for the sake, in part, of the mysterious lady. While the men-at-arms watched him, he could also be watching them. As for surprise, he did not fear that ; for he was assured that he would be suffered to proceed to the end of the journey before they attempted to harm him ; and when once there he could look out for himself. Of course there was danger—he realized it fully—but this only served to excite him to sterner resolve.

When they were ready to start, the guide took his place at the head of the party ; and after they had proceeded a league or so, Goliath rode up by his side, seeming more pleasant than usual, and opening the conversation with a smile. Many questions were asked touching the country, and the forest, and also in relation to the different paths which led around among the mountains. Conrad soon saw the drift of the giant's interrogations, and his answers were given frankly and without hesitation. The stout man-at-arms had simply come to assure himself that their guide did not mean to give them the slip ; and when he fell back to the lady's side again he seemed to be fully assured that all was safe and right.

The sun had almost reached its meridian height when

the party arrived at a deep, rocky glade, entirely shut in by frowning crags and towering old trees. They had entered by a narrow pass, and at the other extremity of the glade was the way of egress, by a pass full as narrow ; and Conrad knew that when the next defile had been cleared, the walls and battlements of Saint Cyr would be in sight. He drew his rein with a more nervous grasp, and instinctively cast his eyes down upon the hilt of his sword. During the forenoon he had watched the signs ot his companions most narrowly, and his suspicions of the morning had been strengthened even to confirmation. The purpose of the men-at-arms touching himself was not to be misunderstood. There was, to them, a weighty reason why their course should not be known in Brittany, and why the footsteps of the veiled lady should not be followed ; and they considered their secret fully worth a human life !

As they came near to the extremity of the gorge, Goliath again rode up to Conrad's side, and addressing him in Spanish, asked :

" How much further have we to travel ?"

The youth was not to be caught, for his wit was as quick as was the flash of his eye. He turned, and looked into the giant's face.

" Did you speak to me, sir ?"

" Yes," answered Goliath, still in Spanish. " I asked you how much further we had to travel."

Conrad shook his head.

" Perhaps you don't understand Spanish ?"

" How should I ? Spaniards are not plenty in the Nord Mountains."

" I did not know but that you had had some opportunity for learning it."

" We poor mountaineers consider ourselves fortunate

if we can learn to speak the language of Brittany so as be understood by men from the court."

"Well—never mind," said the giant, in his own tongue; "I asked you how much further we had to travel."

"Not much, sir. The Castle of Saint Cyr is not far beyond this gorge. We can take dinner there, if no accident happens to prevent it."

Goliath fell back and rode by the side of Baptiste. Conrad did not appear to watch him, and yet he regarded his every movement, and kept his ears open.

"I think the castle is near at hand." Goliath spoke thus, in Spanish, to Baptiste.

"I am of the same opinion," replied the latter.

"And," pursued the giant, "when we come in sight of the walls, we can dismiss our guide."

"Certainly," responded Baptiste.

"It would be a little cowardly to strike him—"

"Hush! He may overhear us."

"There is no fear. He does not understand Spanish. I was saying, it would be rather cowardly to strike him in the dark. I don't mind his life; but we are soldiers, and I would not like to murder him outright."

"What will you do?" asked Baptiste.

"We must give the shadow of honorable combat to his death. I would provoke him to a quarrel; but that would seem monstrous. The combat would be rather too unequal." And Goliath, as he spoke, drew himself up as though he were absolutely invincible.

"By the mass, you are right," cried Baptiste, who now fully comprehended his companion's meaning. "I will take him upon my own hands. The combat cannot be a very equal one even against me; but it will be better than to crush him beneath your ponderous arm."

"Then we may consider that matter settled."

" Yes," said Baptiste. " I will deliver us of the guide. Ha, ha,—the youngster shall find use for his sword, after all."

Conrad heard every word, and from that moment he felt easy. In fact, he felt anxious for the moment to arrive when the double-dyed villain should provoke nim to draw his sword. The time was about to come when he should test the value of the instruction he had received from Francisco, and when the prowess of his arm should be fully tried. He knew that his old teacher could not speak falsehood ; and that teacher had assured him that his sword was perfect.

The sun had been turned from its highest altitude not more than half an hour when the party entered the deep, narrow defile which led from the gorge, and when this was passed, they came out into a broad valley, between two ranges of forest-crowned hills, upon one side of which, on a broad swell of gray rock, stood the crumbling walls and ivy-mantled towers of the old castle of Saint Cyr. Conrad had been here once before with Francisco, but the place had not looked so grand and gloomy then as it did now. The sun had hidden its face behind a mass of cloud, and the wind was sighing loudly through the branches of the great old trees. The rocks seemed to have grown older beneath their covering of gray moss ; while the massive ruin, like a giant spirit of the past, presided in solemn majesty over the place. Even the men-at-arms were moved by the scene, and Goliath fairly went into raptures.

" I' faith," he cried, " our master hath wonderful taste. He will here enjoy his mistress without fear of interruption. "

" He hath taste and wit both," said Baptiste. "'Sdeath ! the lady will not treat him so tartly in this place. I fancy she will be glad to earn his friendship when she finds that this old battle-scarred ruin is to be her home. Heavens! what a haunt it must be for ghosts."

"Gentlemen," said Conrad, turning in his saddle, and pointing to the old pile, "yonder is the castle of Saint Cyr. I will serve you further if you wish."

"You have come with us far enough," replied Goliath; "and I will pay you the sum I promised."

The giant drew forth his purse, and counted out ten crowns, which he handed to the guide.

"Let me settle with you also," said Baptiste. "Here is the sum I promised."

While Baptiste was engaged in counting out his money, Goliath and Adolphe had withdrawn to the rear, where they took up their position at the entrance of the pass through which the party had just come.

"Aha," muttered Conrad, to himself, when he saw this movement, "this smacks of business. Those two fellows mean to cut off my retreat, while their companion tries my temper. We shall see."

"I think," said Baptiste, weighing the money in his hand, after he had counted it out, "that you will find the sum complete."

Conrad took it, and placed it with that which he had received from Goliath; and then slipped the whole into his pocket.

"I am strongly tempted," he said, "to cast this money upon the ground; but I may meet some needy person whom I may bless with it."

"Ha! do you spurn our gift?"

"Not at all, good Baptiste; for, you see, I have put it into my pocket."

"Very well," said the man-at-arms, slipping from his saddle. "Now that the matter of money is disposed of, I have another subject to introduce. Suppose you should come down, and let your horse feed while we talk."

"Anything to please you," answered Conrad, suiting the action to the word. "Here I am. Now speak."

"Easy, young man. You may find yourself in trouble before we get through ; so be careful. What I have to say is concerning your last night's adventure."

"And what of that ?"

"I wish to tell you that you then did what you ought not to have done."

"Go on, sir," said Conrad, as coolly as though he had been receiving some commonplace instruction.

"You gained more intelligence from the lady than you have confessed," continued Baptiste, growing red in the face.

"I have confessed but little, good sir, for I heard but little. But do not burst yourself in your effort to find fault with me. If you have any questions to ask, ask them."

"What I seek I shall *demand!* Do you understand that ?"

Conrad felt that the crisis was coming. His nether lip began to contract, and there was a nervous movement about the fingers of his right hand.

"You need not make any demands of me," he said, quietly. "What you seek you can ask for, and I will answer as I feel inclined."

"What I *demand* is this," retorted Baptiste, insultingly ; "you shall not mention to that drivelling old hermit either that you conducted us to Saint Cyr, or that we had a lady with us. Will you promise me this ?"

"Never !" answered the youth. "When I leave you my tongue is my own, and I shall tell what I please. In all probability I shall tell the hermit just what I have done, and what I have seen."

" Then, by the gods ! you must overcome me before you leave this place ; for, I swear by the heaven above me, that I will not let you pass with that avowal in your mouth !"

" Do you attack me ?"

" Aye. Defend yourself, if you have the courage."

" Easy, good Baptiste," said Conrad, drawing his sword. " You rush into this quarrel hotly. Do you know wherefore you fight ?"

" Aye—to silence your insulting tongue !"

" And I," added the youth, with perfect calmness, " fight to defend myself."

He spoke calmly ; but yet there was an anxious expression in the contraction of the lips, and in the light of the eye. It was his first essay at mortal combat—the first time that life had ever hung upon his sword. And, further still : Behind the stout soldier thus opposed to him stood two more—one of them a giant in stature and in strength. If he overcame Baptiste, what then ? Could he overcome both the others ? And could he pass from that scene alive if he did not overcome them ?

What wonder, then, that his heart hushed its beatings, for the moment that these thoughts were flashing through his mind.

———————

CHAPTER IV.

A CHANGE OF GUARD.

Baptiste, be it remembered, was a large, strong man, and an experienced warrior. By the side of his gigantic leader he did not show to so good advantage ; but he was taller than Conrad, and much heavier ; and he

flourished his sword with the air of one supremely confident of his own prowess.

"Poor boy!" he said, advancing his right foot, and
twirling his sword to a favorite guard, "you have
brought this upon yourself."

"I ask no pity," replied our hero, glad of an opportunity to speak, for it gave relief to his breathing. "If
you have work to do, set about it at once."

"I thank you for the hint," returned Baptiste. "I
will finish my work, and then go to my dinner. Take
your own method of defence."

The man-at-arms swept his point to the right and
to the left, and then made a direct and furious thrust,
evidently intending therewith to finish the play ; but
his mark was not reached. The point of his antagonist
had kept even pace with his own, and when he made
the thrust his blade only glided harmlessly under the
mountaineer's arm.

Baptiste recovered himself quickly, and commenced a
new attack—a thrust—a sweep to the right—to the left
—then back to the right—a feint at the neck—with a
final push at the breast ; and yet his point only cleaved
the open air. He recovered himself, and stepped back.

"Your old hermit must be a marvelous teacher," he
said.

"He has been a kind and attentive one, at all events,"
replied Conrad.

"If I ever see him again, I'll tell him how well his
pupil bore himself. Come—we will play no more."

The swords crossed again, with a clang that spoke of
sharp work. The man-at-arms had found his opponent
better than he had expected, and he concluded not to
expend more time in fancy fencing. It was now a cut, and
a thrust—a step backward—a step forward—a feint—a
lunge ; and yet the young guide was not touched. Now

Baptiste shut his teeth, and commenced a new move-ment. Presently he caught Conrad's blade with a twisting movement of his own, as though he would wrench it from its owner's grasp ; but such was not his intention, as the youth could detect by his eye. The aim of this was, to cause Conrad to clutch his hilt so nervously as to paralyze, for the instant, the nerve of the wrist ; and, during that instant, to slip his blade away and push it home into the body of his antagonist. The mountaineer, however, had been thoroughly trained in all those movements, and when he felt the sword of his adversary thus winding about his own, he simply leaped backwards without breaking his guard ; and at the same instant Baptiste, from the impetus already given, took a step forward. As he did so, Conrad struck a smart blow upon his upper guard, causing him to clutch his hilt for fear of losing it. The man-at-arms felt his error, and tried to leap from it ; but he was not quick enough. Ere he could disengage his sword from the circle of his opponent, his point was thrown vigorously aside, and on the next moment the blade of the fore-doomed guide had found his heart.

Conrad stepped back, and rested his reeking point upon the greensward.

" I am a dead man !" gasped Baptiste, sinking to the earth, with both hands pressed upon his gushing bosom.

" It is your own work," answered Conrad.

"O—you lied to me! I am the best swordsman in——"

His speech failed him, and he fell back dead ; and very quickly afterwards Goliath reached the spot, and leaped from his saddle.

" Dog ! What have you done ?" cried the giant, drawing his sword

"You see what I have done," replied Conrad, drawing back a pace.

"Aye,—you have, by some foul chance of trick, sent Baptiste to the world of spirits ; and I'll send thee right quickly to join him."

Conrad had béen taught that mere brute strength could not. make a swordsman. The possession of physical power was a necessity ; but it needed to be coupled with elasticity of muscle ; quickness and steadiness of nerve ; delicacy of touch ; litheness of limb ; instantaneous perception of sight ; and perfect coolness of head. Even the different members need to borrow, for the time, each other's qualities. The eye must feel before it can see, and the fingers must "see and think." All these things our hero understood ; and his passage with Baptiste had served to assure him that he had not forgotten the lessons of his tutor. He had found his late antagonist an expert swordsman, and yet he had not been called upon to exert his utmost skill. Two of the most subtle attacks which Francisco had taught him he had not used at all.

Goliath did not wait for extended preliminaries. He came as an avenger, and at once set about the work. He swept his heavy sword about in a circle, and then aimed a slashing blow at the youth's neck. Conrad simply leaped aside from the stroke, and as he did so he wounded Goliath in the left arm.

"'Sblood !" cried the giant, his eyes flashing fury, "you are venomous."

He would have spoken further, but at that moment he found his sword in a perplexing situation. His youthful adversary had caught it by a twisting lock, and he was forced to lower his hand to keep the grasp of his hilt.

"I have you now !" he muttered. His eye had

caught the position of the two blades—each point under the other's guard—and he knew that, if he was quick enough, the strongest wrist would win the chance. As he spoke he lowered his elbow, and sought to raise his hand; but, to his astonishment, he found that he could not do it. His sword was held as though by a vice; and now he sought to do what he might have done before—to withdraw his blade; but he had lost too much time. The discovery that the youth's wrist was stronger than his own seemed for the moment to paralyze him, and before he could so far recover from his astoundment as to draw back his arm, his weapon was borne down till his wrist fairly cracked. Conrad saw the painful clutching of those huge fingers, and he knew that the hand must be weak. With a quick movement he disengaged his sword, raised the point to the giant's heart, and lunged forward with all his might.

Goliath saw the fatal blow even before it was fairly aimed, and he tried to ward it off with his left hand; but his fate was sealed, and his huge carcass soon lay close by that of his fallen companion.

Adolphe saw his leader fall; and his sword, which had been half drawn from its scabbard, was pushed back again. His first thought had apparently been of assisting Goliath; but he hesitated alone to attack the man who had displayed such wonderful prowess; so he remained by the side of the lady whom he had been left to guard, leaving it for the guide to approach him when he thought proper; and he did not have long to wait.

"Now, Master Adolphe," cried Conrad, coming towards him, with his sword still drawn, "what demand have you to make?"

Adolphe hesitated. He surveyed the young mountaineer from head to foot; he saw the reeking blade still held with a firm, confident grasp; and he met the flashing of an eye whose light was like a sunbeam. At length he replied :

" It is for you to demand of me. You have overcome the two men who were my superiors, and I shall not contend against you. You have deceived us well."

"How have I deceived you ?"

" You professed that you knew nothing of the sword."

" Easy, sir. I professed no such thing. What I told you was the truth. I said that I had only used the sword in play with old Francisco ; and such was the fact. But know that Francisco is an old soldier, and that he has been one of the best swordsmen in Brittany. But you do well to talk of deception ! How did you deceive me ? By heaven, sir, you will not accuse me of that ! I have a most serious charge to lay upon thy shoulders. You led me upon a base errand, and sought to make me a tool for the consummation of a most foul conspiracy. You professed to be a poor pilgrim seeking a passage to the monastery of St. George ; whereas you were a soldier and an adventurer, engaged in a cruel work."

" How can you make that out ?" asked Adolphe, trembling.

" Ask the lady by your side. She can tell you. Aye —and she shall tell you. And now I make my first demand. The lady shall choose with which of us she will go. If she chooses to go with you, I will depart in peace and leave you with your charge. If she prefers to go with me she shall do so. What say you ?"

. The man-at-arms seemed at loss for a reply. He gazed from the lady to the guide, and then from the guide to the lady.

" Hark ye, master Adolphe," said the youth, taking a step forward and raising the point of his sword from the ground ; " if you mean to offer resistance, let me know it quickly. Come down from your horse. Down I say."

The soldier slipped from his saddle, remarking as he did so :

"I am not thinking of resistance.; I am thinking how I shall answer my master if I freely and voluntarily give up the lady."

"You need not give her up voluntarily. Let her make her own decision. If she decides to go with you, you will not give her up at all. If she decides that she will go with me, I will sustain her decision with my sword."

"No, no," quickly replied the man-at-arms ; "I have no desire to put you to that trouble. And, as far as the lady is concerned, I can already imagine what her answer will be."

"Let us have her answer at once," said Conrad. He advanced to her side as he spoke, and would have asked her the question ; but she anticipated him. She glided from her saddle, and sank upon her knees before him.

"O, noble sir, take me to thy protection and save me from the hands of this soldier ! Do it, and Heaven will bless thee !"

The veil had floated away from her face, and her features were exposed. Conrad was for the moment entranced. He had never even dreamed of such beauty as he thus beheld. She was not more than eighteen years of age ; of slight, sylph-like form ; and possessing every charm necessary to a picture of angelic loveliness.

"By Saint Michael !" muttered Adolphe, as he beheld the two regarding each other ; "here is a pretty piece of mischief. If our young mountaineer thinks the damsel is beautiful, what must she think of him ? By my faith she hath never beheld so fair a youth before.

If this does not prove to be the commencement of trouble, then I will never prophesy again."

In the meantime, Conrad extended his hand to the maiden and lifted her to her feet.

"I am your servant," he said, "and you may command me. Whithersoever thou wishest to go, thither will I conduct thee."

"Take me to my home, brave, noble sir. O, conduct me in safety to my father's arms, and all blessing shall be thine."

"Adolphe," said the youth, turning to the man-at-arms, "you have heard the lady's request—what say you?"

The fellow had been busy with his own thoughts, and when he was thus addressed, he started and gazed into the face of his interlocutor without speaking.

"Answer me," continued Conrad. "Will you dare to interpose against the wishes of the lady?"

Adolphe laid his finger upon Conrad's arm, and drew him a few steps away, where his low tones could not reach the ear of the maiden.

"Young sir," he said, with seeming honesty, "let me talk to you soberly and earnestly. I have no disposition to oppose you by any force, for I have seen enough to assure me that you are my superior; but you must permit me to give you a word of warning. It is not against me, a poor man-at-arms, that you are about to raise your interposing hand. You are conspiring against the interests of the most powerful man in the kingdom."

"Ha," cried Conrad. "Has the King—"

"Not the king," interrupted Adolphe.

"And who is more powerful than the king?"

"The prince is more powerful. The king is old and broken; while the prince is in the full flush of youth and vigor. The prince is really ruler in Brittany."

" I have heard that Theobald was growing weak ; but I thought him still king of Brittany."

" So he is, in name ; but prince Bertrand wields the power, nevertheless."

" Well—and suppose all this is so—what then ?"

" For your own safety," said Adolphe, " I will tell you that which, perhaps, I ought not to tell. We three men-at-arms were sent by the prince to conduct this lady to the Castle of Saint Cyr. Bertrand will not be likely to look very favorably upon the man who thwarts him. His enmity is fatal, sir."

" What more have you to say ?" asked Conrad.

" I have said all, sir. If you pursue the course you have decided to adopt, you will bring down upon yourself the sure vengeance of the prince."

" I thank you for the information you have given me, Master Adolphe ; but I cannot allow it to alter my determination. I shall take the lady under my charge, and conduct her to her home."

" Do you dream where her home is ?"

" I have not the least idea."

" Has she told you her name ?"

" No."

" Then you know not with whom you have to deal. Allow me to inform you, Sir Mountaineer, that you are mixing yourself up in a dangerous matter. The lady is the daughter of Casimir, Duke of Rennes ; and perhaps you are aware that he stands next in power to the prince."

" So much the more need is there that the honor of his daughter should be protected."

" But what if he were a party to this removal of the lady ?"

" Then he is a most unnatural father ; and I will espouse the cause of his daughter against his tyranny."

Adolphe shrugged his shoulders.

"Go your way, sir. And, in the meantime, I hope you will allow me to go mine."

"You are at liberty to go where you please."

"First," said Adolph, "I would pay some little attention to the remains of my fallen companions. We cannot very well dig graves for them; but if you will assist me to lift the bodies to the backs of their horses, I will carry them to the old castle, where I may find vaults in which they can be properly deposited."

Conrad saw nothing objectionable in this arrangement; so he went and helped the man-at-arms as he had requested. It was a difficult matter to lift the body of the giant; but the feat was accomplished; and when the two corses had been secured upon the backs of the horses, Adolphe mounted his own beast, and set out for the castle upon his ghostly errand.

When he was gone, Conrad returned to the lady. The look of terror had gone from her face, and the youth felt his heart bound with new and strange emotion as he now gazed upon her. She was very beautiful; and there was a softness and depth in the tone of her loveliness that appealed directly to the soul. There was no haughtiness in her manner, no sharpness in the angles of her face; but all was pure and good; and the music of her voice sweetly harmonized with the soft, mild light of her eye, and the entrancing smile of her lip.

"Dear lady," said our hero, "I am told that you are the daughter of the Duke of Rennes."

"Yes, sir; and my name is Rosaline," she replied, with confiding frankness. "And," she added, "since you have done so much for me, and plan to do so much more, I ought to tell you my true situation. The story will be very short."

"I should like to hear it, lady."

"My father," she commenced, "is, as you already know, Duke of Rennes, and his home is in that city—or in the castle close by it. Prince Bertrand, the son of our king, sought my hand. My father was at first anxious that I should accept it ; but the prince was so loathsome to me, and his proposition of marriage so repulsive, that I could not think of it but with horror. My father is an honorable, virtuous man, and when I had convinced him that the prince was a debauchee, and a bad man in other ways, he listened to my protest. I went with him to Vannes, where the royal court is held; and there he learned for himself the character which Bertrand bore ; and my hand was refused. The prince came to see me ; he went upon his knees, and vowed, and swore, and begged ; but I would not listen to him. His very presence was painful, and I could not help exposing my feelings. When he had heard my final refusal, and seen the coldness of my bearing towards him, he glared upon me like a tiger, and swore that I should be sorry for what I had done. At first I had no fear, for I thought his threats were only the result of. sudden wrath, which would soon pass away. And further, I did not think that he would dare to raise his hand against the daughter of the most powerful duke in the realm. But I did not know the reckless daring of the man. One evening, as I walked alone in the garden of the house where I was stopping with my father, two men jumped out from behind some bushes, and seized and bound me, and stopped my mouth. They were Baptiste and Adolphe. They carried me to the wall, where they were joined by the giant, who took me in his arms and bore me swiftly away. I don't know how I came from the city, for excessive terror took away my senses. But, while I was recovering, and before the three men were aware that my consciousness was returning. I heard some words from their lips which gave me assurance that they were employed by the prince to carry me away.

"A night and a day we were on the road; and then we stopped to rest. Goliath swore that he would kill me if I tried to escape. We rested during the night, and on the following morning Baptiste and Adolphe went in search of a guide. You came back with them; and Goliath again threatened me with death if I spoke to you. O, when I saw your face—when I saw how kind, and true, and noble you looked, I believed you would help me if you could; but I dared not speak. The rest you know. You will conduct me back to my father; and your reward—"

"Will be already ample when I have performed my duty," finished Conrad, taking the small white hand which she had extended towards him. He held it but a moment; and then turned away to look after the man-at-arms; for, since he had heard the lady's story, he had conceived a great desire to speak with the fellow once more.

"Rest a while," he said, speaking to Rosaline, after the soldier had disappeared beyond the outer walls of the castle with his ghostly load. "There are one or two questions which I would like to ask of Master Adolphe before I lose sight of him for good. I fancy he will not remain long in the old ruin."

CHAPTER V.

Conrad spoke truly when he said that he wished to speak with Master Adolphe ; and yet he did not tell the whole truth. If he had simply wished to see the man-at-arms, there would have been no need of hurry ; but, the fact was, he wished to hide his face from the lady Rosaline. He was under the influence of a spell which he could not break while her eyes beamed upon him. He was being mysteriously entranced—charmed by a magic power.

"O, my soul !" he murmured to himself, when he had turned away, "this opens to me a new sense of life ; it strikes upon unused chords in my bosom. But this entrance to heaven is not for me. Be still, my beating heart. Let me do my duty. I must return the maiden to her father, and then I must forget her."

While Rosaline ate her dinner, the youth watched for the return of Adolphe ; but no Adolphe came. At the end of an hour he concluded to go to the castle and seek the soldier ; but as he was about to speak with the lady upon the subject he saw a peasant coming towards him from the ruin, with an axe upon his shoulder, and a rope in his hand. He was evidently going into the wood after faggots. Conrad hailed him, and the man came up without hesitation. He was an honest looking fellow, and gazed with a curious surprise upon the mountaineer and his lovely companion.

"My good man," said Conrad, "I think you came from yonder old ruin."

"Yes, sir," replied the peasant; "but I don't live there. My home is more than a league beyond."

"Did you see a stranger at the castle?"

"Yes, sir."

"What was he doing?"

"He was coming up out from the vaults when I first saw him."

"Do you know what he had been doing?"

"No, sir. He didn't look like a man who would answer impertinent questions; so we didn't ask any."

"You say *we*. Had you a companion?"

"Yes; I had two."

"Where are they now?"

"They have gone with the stranger. He had two extra horses, and they rode away with him leaving me to work alone."

"Do you know whither they have gone?"

"Yes, sir; to the capital of Brittany."

"Ah, they have taken another road?"

"Yes. They will strike the Ille north of these hills, and then keep down the valley."

"Very well," said Conrad, putting his hand into his pocket, and taking out a silver crown; "I shall have the pleasure of returning alone. Here, my good man, take this for your trouble."

The peasant took the crown with sparkling eyes.

"Did the stranger seem to be in much of a hurry?" asked our hero, carelessly.

"O, yes, sir. He wanted my brothers to ride with all their might. It seemed as though his life depended upon his speed."

Conrad thanked the peasant once more, and then allowed him to depart.

"Lady," he said, after a little reflection, "would you prefer to go to Vannes, where you left your father, or to your home in Rennes?"

"Why do you ask, sir? You have heard something from that peasant. There is some new danger."

"No, lady. Danger ceases to be danger when we can avoid it. But I will tell you what I have learned from the peasant. Master Adolphe has found new guides, and has set off for the capital with all possible speed. As he is in the employ of the prince, he will command fresh horses where he can find them; and, if his own strength does not fail him, it is not impossible that he may reach Vannes before morning."

"So soon as that?" said Rosaline, in surprise.

"Ah, lady, when fresh horses are at hand to take the places of the jaded ones, long distances may be performed in a few hours. That which we have been two days in accomplishing might be done in eight hours, with proper exchange of horses. So, if we go to Vannes, we run the risk of being met on the road; for Adolphe can carry word to his master, and have a fresh force sent against us."

"But, good Conrad," cried Rosaline, in a tone of relief, "I would rather go to Rennes. I shall be safe when once with my father's people."

"Then all is right, lady. We will start at once, and make the best of our way. The distance to Rennes is not more than fifteen leagues; and, if your strength holds out, I think we may make the journey without much delay."

"Fear not for me, sir. I can bear all that my horse can endure."

Conrad assisted the lady to her saddle; and when he

had mounted to his own seat, they put their horses to a gentle gallop, and were soon speeding away through the deep glade. They kept on thus till late in the afternoon, when they stopped by the bank of a small stream to allow their beasts to rest. Conrad sat down upon a fallen tree, and Rosaline, of her own accord, took a seat by his side. She plainly showed that she trusted him as she would have trusted a brother ; and her gentle smile, when she spoke to him, was calm and confiding.

"Can we reach Rennes before morning?" she asked.

"Yes, lady. If you can keep your eyes open until midnight, I think you may sleep in your father's castle before the rising of another sun."

The promise gave the maiden new hope, and called new light to her face. A little while she gazed down upon the grass at her feet, and then raised her eyes to her companion's face.

"Your name is Conrad," she said ; "and your home is among the mountains."

"Yes, lady."

"Do your parents live there?"

"My mother lives there ; and he who has been all that a father could be, has his home close by us. The story of my life is very simple."

Rosaline asked, by her look, that he would tell it.

"I never knew the face of my father. He was an old soldier, as my mother tells me, and was killed in battle, when I was an infant. My memory does not go back of the cot in the forest, where my childish steps were guided by my mother's hand, and where my youthful mind has been trained by the old hermit who has been my teacher. Francisco is the hermit's name ; and he was a soldier with my father. He has taught me well, and I trust that I have not been an idle scholar. My lessons have been such as my good teacher could safely expound, and to him I owe more than I can ever repay. He taught me Spanish; and my knowledge of that language served me in learning the intentions of our enemies."

"But you have served in the army, sir?"

"No."

"You have had much experience with the sword!"

"Only what I have had in exercise with old Francisco. Until this day I never drew my sword in mortal combat."

"It is wonderful."

"Not very," said Conrad, with a smile. "Francisco is a most accomplished swordsman; and I have been a most eager pupil. And then you must remember that I had all the advantage of incitement. I had something of Right upon my side—something of sacred, holy duty. You were to me the embodiment of a great principle; and I am proud that my first battle had so noble a cause."

The lady Rosaline gazed up into Conrad's face, and the language of her look was grateful and tender. A close observer—one skilled in reading the signs of the human face—could easily have divined the feeling that moved the soul of the maiden. The romance of the youth's mountain-life—his orphanage—his strange tutor —his free and simple manners—all had a charm for her, a charm far deeper than could have been given by a story of noble birth and grand family advantages. With true womanly instinct, she prized the daring-qualities of the hero because their first effort had been made in her behalf. And, further than this, it might have been seen that the youth's calm, fresh beauty made a deep impression upon her. She could not hide the signs that told the story of opening love. Her heart bounded and fluttered with its own impulses; and all she could do was to dwell in the light of those tenderly-beaming eyes, and listen to the deep music of the manly voice.

There is a language not written, and there are words not spoken. There is a sense more subtle than sight; and a conviction more sure than speech. There is a language of sympathy; a mystic bond between two congenial souls; an electric flow of sense and perception from spirit to spirit; whispering of love and faith, which the ears do not hear, and which the eyes do not read. It is a sense which reveals to us that the spirit is not always dependent upon the body for its sources of information—a sense catching its perceptions from the Spirit itself, and communicating with a kindred spirit without the use of outward sign.

Strange feelings came upon Conrad's heart.

An echo was in the heart of Rosaline.

Their hands met, and the thrill was electric. From soul to soul—from heart to heart. What was the language! not of earth, but of heaven.

Conrad was the strongest, and he was the first to break from the ecstatic trance.

"Our horses have rested enough," he said. "We had better be on our way."

Rosaline started as though she had awakened from a dream. She had meant to speak some words of gratitude in answer to her companion's remark touching the battle; but her tongue was slow, and the words were not spoken. She allowed her companion to assist her again to her saddle, and they were soon speeding along through the dark wood.

In half an hour they struck the right bank of a branch of the river Ille, and from this point the road to Rennes was plain and direct, following a smooth valley the whole distance. But as the road became better the darkness of night came on, and the maiden rode closer to her guide and held her rein more tightly.

"How far is it now to Rennes?" she asked.

"Not more than eight leagues. At an easy pace we can accomplish the distance in four hours; and that will bring us to the end of our journey very shortly after midnight. If your horse can stand the trial we shall be all right."

"My horse has a light load," replied Rosaline; "and moreover, he is strong and enduring. But I am not in such a hurry as to put the poor beast to any unwonted exertion. I do not think there can be any danger on the road."

"Not at present," said Conrad. He reflected a moment, and then added : "As far as my own comfort is concerned, I could ride by your side across the continent without tiring; but it is not impossible that Master Adolphe may find some help on the road and think of turning his attention to you."

"But he has gone to Vannes."

"He started for Vannes; but something may arise to change his course. Have you any idea if the prince intended to follow you directly to Saint Cyr?"

"I think he did."

"Then it is not impossible that he may be on the road. It is not impossible that he may meet Adolphe. If such should be the case, they would very easily comprehend that you had gone to Rennes."

Rosaline trembled with apprehension.

"I did not mean to alarm you, dear lady; for there can be no occasion. I am well acquainted with the roads that wind about among these mountains, and in no way can Adolphe overtake us; unless, indeed, it should happen that he had turned from the course laid down by the peasant and followed us. I have thought that he might have done such a thing."

"But why should he do so?" inquired Rosaline. "He could not hope to overcome you."

"Certainly not; but he may wish to meet the prince. If the prince followed us by the same road we traveled to Saint Cyr, he would strike the road we are now in not more than two leagues behind us. So, if Bertrand had planned to follow you immediately, Adolphe, knowing the fact, may only have started off on the northern road to blind me; or, at least, to escape me; and, having seen us start on our return, the thing was easy for him to follow, especially if he thought to meet his master on the way. This, however, offers us no occasion for fear; only it hints to us that we had better keep steadily on our way."

"You are right," answered the maiden. "We will allow no grass to grow under our feet."

The road laid close upon the bank of the river, and nearly all the time the bosom of the murmuring stream was in sight, reflecting, in dim flashes, and quaint lines, the bright stars that looked down from the cloudless sky. Conrad was not really uneasy; and yet, as the new feeling grew stronger and stronger within him, making the maiden more precious in his sight, his anxiety for her safety began to take form and substance. As he thought more upon the subject of the late conversation, the idea that Adolphe might meet the prince in the wood and thence turn his steps toward Rennes, became strongly impressed upon him. He reasoned thus to himself:

"The Prince would not be seen upon the road with the lady of Rennes; nor would he allow her to remain at the Castle of Saint Cyr without joining her. Very likely, when he knew that his base emissaries had seized upon her, and were bearing her away to the Norman frontier, he followed close upon their heels ; and if such should happen to be the case, Adolphe may meet him this very night. By my life the prince would not be long in seeking so lovely a prize !"

These thoughts caused him to put his horse into a faster pace, and for half an hour, over a level road, he rode on at a gallop. By and by they reached a point where the path turned away from the stream, winding up over a steep hill, and as the horses walked slowly up, side by side, Rosaline called her companion's attention to the scene. It was wild and romantic, and even Conrad forgot, for the while, the thoughts that had been busy within him. From the brow of the precipice they gazed down into the gloomy depth, where, far below them, made visible by the flashing reflection of the star-beams, rolled the narrow river, like some golden-scaled serpent, of huge proportions, winding its way through a sea of ink.

" O," murmured the maiden, " I should like to live among the mountains, as you do. I should like it better than the turmoil of the life that those lead who dwell in courts. Even in the darkest hours there is a calmness of grandeur that leads the soul up to Heaven, and fixes the mind upon holy thoughts. And then in the bright sunlight what joy and rapture to be free and happy, bound by no stern rules of fashion, and subject only to the laws of God and nature. How I would sing with the birds, and skip with the lambs. Would you wish to exchange your mountain home for a haunt in the city ?"

" Not unless some duty called me," replied Conrad, hardly knowing what he spoke. " It has been said," he added, in a slightly tremulous tone, " that home is where the heart is ; and where love aboundeth, there may the true heart find content. I have been very happy in my forest retreat during the years that have passed ; but who shall say that that happiness can continue. The human heart is a wayward thing. My heart may fix its deepest, strongest love upon something that does not belong to the forest ; and then my happiness among the mountains would be gone, for hope would be ever pointing in another way."

"A stout heart may win the object of its love," said Rosaline, in a low tone.

"Not if that object be entirely beyond its reach," returned the youth, regretfully. "The child may fall in love with the evening star, but the bright object will always have to be loved at a distance."

"But," pursued the maiden in a stronger tone, "the man of sense and judgment will not fall in love with that which is not possessed of a soul like his own. Love is not fixed to station or power. True love is like the blessed sunlight. It warms alike the hearts of the high and the low."

Conrad pressed his hand upon his bosom, and bowed his head. O, if he could have spoken all he felt, he could have told Rosaline of Rennes of one prize that would have made his forest home a paradise forever. But he dared not speak. And yet he dared to gaze upon the lovely being by his side, and feast his soul upon the newly born love.

At the foot of the hill they once more struck the river's bank, and the horses were put again into a gallop.

"How far now to Rennes ?" asked Rosaline.

"A good six leagues. We have been only an hour on the road since there were eight leagues before us."

"We shall reach the castle by midnight."

"If no accident happens."

And Rosaline repeated, as an echo :

"*If no accident happens.*"

CHAPTER VI.

AN ACCIDENT, AND ITS RESULT.

A low, boggy place, where a sluggish brook emptied into the river, over which was a bridge of logs, old, rotten, and moss-covered. The light jennet, with the lady upon its back, trotted smoothly over; but the heavier beast of Conrad's stopped, with a loud snort, and tried to avoid the direct way.

"Over—over, my pet," cried the youth, patting the animal upon the neck. "It is but a bridge;—the footing is good. Come—over we go."

The horse snorted, and snuffed, and still refused to go. Conrad coaxed and patted; but to no avail.

"This will never do," he said, clenching the rein with a firm hand, and driving the spurs deep into the flanks of the refractory beast. "You must go over. Now—up! up!"

The will of the master, thus made manifest, was all powerful, and the horse started forward. A few steps were taken—a slip—a plunge—and down through the rotten fabric went a fore-foot. Before Conrad could dismount the horse had struggled to free himself, and the result was, that the log gave way, pitching him forward, and throwing his rider out from the saddle. Our hero picked himself quickly up, without having received a bruise worth noticing, and hastened to the assistance of his horse; but he was too late.

"Is the animal badly hurt?" asked Rosaline.

"I fear so, lady."

"Can I help you? If I can, let me know it, for I am not afraid of work, even though there be danger in it."

"Remain in your saddle, dear lady. You cannot help me here. Look the other way. Turn your eyes."

"What have you done, Conrad?"

"I have done a work of mercy, lady Rosaline."

"But your sword is out. What is it?"

"Be not alarmed. It is a sad event, but it cannot be helped. O, a better blood now warms my blade than flowed from the veins of Goliath and Baptiste. I found both the forward legs of the noble beast broken, and with my own hand have I delivered him from his suffering."

At first Rosaline thought more of the melancholy accident to the horse than of the result to herself and companion; but when Conrad had joined her, and started up on foot by the side of her jennet, she remembered that the accident had a wider reach.

"Heavens!" she cried, "must you walk?"

"For the present I must; but I will walk fast. Our journey will not be so quickly performed as we had hoped; but if you reach your home in safety, we will not complain."

"But, good Conrad, can you not ride with me? I think my horse is——"

"Hush, lady. Your horse has work enough already. I am used to walking, and we will make better way than you think for."

"You may find a horse on the road," suggested Rosaline.

"Not until we reach Saint Mary; and that is four leagues distant. But do not let the mishap trouble you.

I will walk by your side, and should any good fortune turn up for us, we will be ready to seize it."

If this mode of proceeding had its disadvantage, it also had its advantage, for the travelers could now converse without difficulty. Rosaline had studied much; and it so happened that the course which she had pursued under the guidance of her various tutors, was, in many points, like that which Conrad had pursued. Her mind was clear and comprehensive; her perceptions keen; and her judgment good; and as the conversation turned upon themes familiar to both, the discussion became animated and interesting. They talked of art, of war, of the rise and fall of nations, and of the language of Spain and England and Germany; and it was evident as they proceeded, that Rosaline was surprised at the display of knowledge which marked her companion's speech. She listened to him attentively, and was, ere long, seeking information from him upon topics which her tutors had never explained.

Thus passed an hour, and Conrad was upon the point of asking some question touching the affairs of the royal court of Brittany, when his attention was arrested by a sudden movement of Rosaline's horse. The animal pricked up its ears, gave a quick, startled snuff, and seemed quite uneasy.

"He may see something in the wood," said Rosaline.

There were woods upon the left hand, while the river ran upon the right.

"He does not act as though he saw anything unusual," replied Conrad. "He either hears or smells something. Suppose we stop a moment and listen."

Rosaline drew in the rein, and Conrad bent his ear to the ground.

"I hear nothing," he said, after listening for a while.

" It must have been some strange scent that touched the animal's sense. We will move on again."

In a little while the wood was left behind, and the path lay along at the foot of a high bluff that flanked the river on that side. The road was wide enough, and plain, for the stream was now low, and the banks were broad, and had a gradual, easy slope.

" We were speaking," said Conrad, " of the court of Theobald. I have heard much of the old king, and I think I like him. I think he is a good man."

" He is a good man," returned Rosaline, emphatically; " but he has been a most unfortunate man; and he is now a most unhappy man. The prince, his son, shows no love for him, and brings him often to grief."

" You speak of Bertrand ?"

" Certainly. He is the only child the king ever had."

" He must be a monster !" said Conrad, smiting his hip with his clenched hand. " If he hath no love for his kind old father, he is most unnatural; and his treatment of thee proves him to be basely wicked. Alas ! what must be the fate of Brittany when he ascends the throne, and takes the sceptre !"

" I dread to think," returned Rosaline, shuddering. " His first acts may be of vengeance !"

" Not upon thee, sweet lady ! Not upon thee, if I have an arm to give thee succor."

" Ah," murmured the maiden, " when that time comes a home in the deep forest—"

Her speech was cut short by the movement of her horse, the old signs of uneasiness being repeated; and this time the snuffing was louder and more startling.

" I think my poor horse misses his mate," said Rosaline.

" It may be that; it may be something more," returned Conrad. " Stop a moment."

Again the lady drew in her rein ; and once more the youth bent his ear to the ground. He listened a few moments, and then started up.

" We are—"

" What ?"

Conrad had commenced to speak in a tone of excitement, but he calmed himself, and added :

" I think some one is on the road behind us."

" What is it !"

" I hear the tramp of horses in full speed."

" Do you think we can be followed ?"

Conrad was looking eagerly around, and seemed not to notice the question.

" Do not fear to tell me the truth, sir. O, I had rather know the worst at once, for then I may be preparing for the result."

" I did not hesitate because I feared to answer you, my lady ; but I was looking to see if there was any place where we might turn away from the road."

" Then you think we may be pursued by our enemies ?"

" The thing is possible, certainly. Master Adolphe may have turned about, and met the prince ; and if they have come together, and have concluded to follow us, they would be very likely to hit upòn the road to Rennes."

" Mercy !" gasped Rosaline.

" Keep up your heart, lady. All is not yet lost. In ths first place, it may not be the prince, at all. Let us not fear too much. If I could find a cover, I would draw aside, and allow the approaching horsemen to pass ; but I see no such opportunity here. Let us move on."

As we have before said, the road at this place lay between the river and a high bluff, and there was no possible way of turning out unless they crossed the stream. The face of the bluff was almost perpendicular, as though the water had cut its way through a long, high hill. Conrad turned to the river. It was dark and deep, and its current was swift.

"Can we not cross?" asked Rosaline.

"Not here," replied her companion. "The river has grown deeper, and the force of the tide is too strong."

They hurried on, but the prospect of escape did not brighten. The bluff upon the left seemed to grow higher and more frowning, while the river upon the right rushed on with increasing fury. The clatter of the coming horses could now be plainly heard, and it was evident that they were not a great way off. Conrad gazed around once more ; but he could see no way of avoiding the pursuers. Had he been alone, with a powerful horse, he might have tried the stream ; but he dared not venture the light-limbed jennet, with its precious burden, in such an ordeal.

Nearer and nearer came the pursuers, and finally the youth laid his hand upon the lady's rein.

"We had better stop here," he said. "We cannot avoid them."

"And what will you do?" asked Rosaline.

"I will remain between you and them, and ascertain what they want. They may not be enemies."

"But—if it should be the prince."

"Then I will ask him what he seeks."

"O ! you will not oppose Prince Bertrand. It would be madness ! It would be fatal ! You must not expose yourself to certain death !"

"Dear lady, be under no apprehensions on my account. Leave all to me, and trust me for the result. If it be the prince, and he forces you from my protection, you will at least believe that I did all I could for you."

"Yes—yes; but do not run into new danger. If it be my fate—"

"Hush, lady. They are close at hand. Leave all to me. Do you remain where you are, and hope for the best."

Conrad strode back over the road, and at a short distance he met an advancing horseman.

"Hold!" he cried, in a tone that at once brought the horse to a standstill, nearly throwing his rider over his head. "Who comes here?"

The man whom Conrad had hailed did not answer; but another quickly rode up, who proved to be master Adolphe.

"By Saint Michael!" cried the latter, catching a glimpse of the interloper by the dim starlight, "it is our mountaineer."

"What is all this?" asked a third horseman, riding up, and stopping by the side of Adolphe.

"We are ordered to halt, my lord."

"Halt! By whom?"

"By no less a personage than our mountain guide."

"What! Is it the Conrad you told me of?"

"The same, my lord."

"Ha! then the lady Rosaline cannot be far away."

"I think I see her now, your highness. If I mistake not, she sits yonder, upon her horse."

"Then, by the gods! she is safe! What, ho, meddler! Who are you?"

Conrad's sight was keen, and his eyes had become so used to the gloom that he could see quite distinctly. He could see plainly enough to tell that there were four men before him, all well mounted and well armed. One of them was, he felt sure, Prince Bertrand; one was his old traveling companion, Adolphe; and the others were evidently servants, who had accompanied the prince from Vannes. He could see that the prince was tall and broad-shouldered, though not of good shape. His neck was too short, and his shoulders too round; and our hero had little difficulty in imagining, from his ill-formed outline, that his face was harsh and unpleasant.

"Why don't you speak? Who are you?"

"I am an honest traveler on honest business," replied Conrad. "Who are you?"

"By the Shades of Pluto! I'll let you know who I am if you don't quickly take yourself out of my way!"

"Easy, sir. I have the road, and you will answer me before you pass."

"What, ho! Here—Adolphe—Poins—Tithon. Sweep that dog from my path!"

The three men thus addressed drew their swords and pressed their horses forward.

"Hold!" exclaimed Conrad, in a tone of such authority that the horses stopped. "Do not rush into needless trouble. If you wish to pass quietly on your way, I shall not interfere."

"Answer me," cried the prince, raising himself in his stirrups. "Is not that lady Rosaline yonder?"

"That lady, sir, is under my protection."

"It is the lady," spoke master Adolphe.

"Then seize upon her, and let her protection devolve upon me."

Adolphe again started forward; but Conrad caught his rein and stopped his horse. The man-at-arms, with an oath, raised his sword, intending, no doubt, to cleave the skull of the venturesome mountaineer.

Conrad thought very quickly. Instinctive reason told him that the trial had come, and that if he would defend the maiden he must overcome obstacles as they arose. His first decisive movement was a rapid and effective one. He held the horse by the left hand, standing by the animal's near fore foot, his right hand grasping the hilt of his drawn sword. When he saw Adolphe raise his weapon to strike, he simply drew back his right arm, and in an instant more he had driven his keen blade upward through the fellow's bosom.

"Down with him!" cried Bertrand. "Strike him down!"

"Holy Mother! I am a dead man!" gasped the unfortunate man-at-arms.

Poins and Pithon hurried forward just in season to see Adolphe tumble from his horse. Conrad saw them coming, and with a quick movement he gave the foremost horse a prick that made him rear upright into the air, throwing his rider backward upon the ground. The second horseman was crowding up, and before he could really determine what had happened, his horse had leaped upon one side, away from the approach of the mountaineer, bringing both his iron-clad forward feet down upon the prostrate form of the unhorsed rider. Thus was a second man disabled without the need of a sword-thrust.

"Poins! Poins!" shouted the prince.

"'Fore God!" exclaimed the other. "Poins is under my horse's feet! What ho! Hallo! Poins—are you hurt?"

But Poins did not answer; and the other, who must have been Tithon, sprang from his saddle, and bent over the form of his prostrate companion.

"Poins—Poins—are you badly hurt?"

The man groaned, but made no other answer.

"Mercy! The blood is running from his head; and I fear his skull is broken!"

"Never mind," said the prince, leaping from his saddle as he spoke; "let him be, and come with me."

Bertrand strode forward until he came close upon our hero, when he stopped.

"How now, thou snarling, snapping dog! Do you know whom you have met?"

"I should judge that I had met enemies," replied the youth, without show of trepidation.

The prince gnashed his teeth, and lifted the point of his sword; but he restrained himself a little longer.

"Know, then," he hoarsely cried, "that I am *Bertrand, Prince of Brittany!*"

Conrad had been reared amid mountain solitudes; and his adorations had only been given to the God of Heaven. The sound of earthly title did not strike upon his ear with much of awe-inspiring power; and the name which had just been so imposingly pronounced did not startle him at all. The name of Bertrand, Prince of Brittany, only called to his mind a cruel, unnatural child, and a heartless, wicked debauchee. He simply grasped his sword more firmly, and waited to hear what further the prince would say, but before Bertrand again spoke, his ear caught the sound of a low, quivering voice behind him; and upon turning his head, he beheld Rosaline approaching him on foot.

"O! Conrad—expose yourself no more. My fate is sealed. Let me not drag you down with me!"

The youth took one step back, and waved his hand towards the trembling maiden.

"One moment, Rosaline—lady—only one moment, Back to your horse. I must speak with this man."

CHAPTER VII.

THE CASTLE OF RENNES.

The prince seemed, for the moment, to be utterly confounded by the coolness of the man before him. He had looked to see the simple mountaineer shrink back in confusion at the sound of his name; but, for once in his life, he was destined to find that name wholly without power. He saw the lady Rosaline approach; he heard the mountaineer speak to her; and he saw her withdraw again. Then he stamped his foot with rage, and called out:

"Do you dare, dog, to raise your hand against your prince?"

"At this hour, in this place, and under such circumstances, I know no prince," replied Conrad. "Yet, sir, if you bear the name of prince—if you are the son of our king—I would spare you. You may turn about, and go in peace."

"'Sdeath! thy blood must run rank with insanity. I tell thee, I am the prince."

"Do you seek that lady?"

"Yes."

"For what?"

"To you it matters not why I seek her."

"I know why you seek her. You would most cruelly wrong her. You say you are the prince. Let me tell

you what I find you : I find you a base, bad man, seeking the destruction of the peace and joy of a weak
woman. That woman has sought my protection, and
she shall have it."

" Do you mean that you will oppose me ?"

" Aye."

" That you will dare to raise your hand against the
prince ?"

" To me you are not the prince. A true prince
would be ashamed of such service as you are now
engaged in."

" By the gods ! I am the prince ; and I must have
yonder lady !"

" Were you ten thousand times a prince, you should
not touch her in the presence of my living body !"

" Beware !"

" Hold, sir ! I mean what I say," cried Conrad, as
Bertrand made an aggressive movement. " If you force
me to it, I shall raise my arm against you. I swear it
by the God that made me !"

The bold prince shrank from before the fire of those
eyes, and turned to his attendant.

" Tithon !"

The man had been an astonished witness of the scene,
and as his master thus spoke, he stepped forward, with
his drawn sword in his hand.

" Tithon, cut down this dog from my path !"

The soldier advanced, and measured the mountaineer
with his eye, at the same time remarking, in a tone
which lacked something of assurance :

" You give me a tough job, my master."

" Then the more glory to you if you accomplish it."

Conrad's quick eye detected the meaning of the
prince. He thought to engage him with his man-at-
arms, and in the meantime slip by to the lady. But our

hero had not the least idea of allowing such a thing to be done. He moved back a pace, and caught the sword of the advancing soldier by a side parry—then he made one of his most effective assaults, before which his adversary was so completely at fault that he went down almost without an effort at defence—went down beyond the power of further help to his august master.

Bertrand had taken a step towards the lady; but Conrad was quickly before him.

"No more, sir!" our hero cried. "You and I are now alone in this lady's presence; and, if it please you, she shall decide whither she will go."

"No, by heaven!" returned the prince, furiously. "I am not in the habit of being thus driven. Stand aside!"

"Beware, Bertrand! Your title shall not overcome me."

"But my sword shall!" retorted the angry man. And as he spoke, he made a lunge at the mountaineer.

Conrad saw very quickly that he had nothing to fear from this assault. He parried two thrusts in succession, and then he caught the sword of his opponent by a sliding stroke along the blade, fastening his point beneath the other's guard. The question was now simply strength of wrist. The prince felt his danger, and bent his elbow down to hold his weapon; but he might as well have bent against a rock. As though making the movement for pastime, Conrad wrenched the opposing sword from its owner's grasp, flinging it high into the air; and in a few moments more a dull plash in the river told that the prince's blade was gone forever.

With a fierce oath, Bertrand sprang for the sword which Tithon had dropped; but he was not allowed to reach it; for Conrad, seeing and comprehending the movement, determined to put an end to the scene as quickly as possible. He leaped forward and grasped the prince by the shoulder, and drew him back upon the greensward.

"Bertrand, you have tried my patience to its utmost, and I will grant thee no more liberty to annoy me."

"Ha! would you kill me?"

"No. If I had meant to do that I should have run my sword through your body when I had you before at my mercy. I simply intend to bind you, and leave you here to keep company with your fallen companions."

Bertrand was young and powerful; but he had not the steel-like muscle of the mountaineer. He sought to free himself from the grasp that was upon him; but he was as a child in the hands of its master. Conrad bent him down, and having torn the rich sash from his loins, with it he bound its owner's arms behind his back. Then he went to where Tithon had fallen, and took off the soldier's belt. When he returned, the prince was almost upon his knees; but the work was easily finished; and in the end his royal highness lay upon the ground, bound hand and foot.

When this had been accomplished, the youth went to where the fellow lay who had been called Poins, and who had been crushed beneath the feet of Tithon's horse. He was yet insensible; and though the flesh had been terribly cut upon the side of the head, the bone did not appear to be broken.

"I think," said Conrad, approaching the prince, "that your man Poins will ere long recover his senses; and when he does he may come and set you free."

"Go—go," gasped Bertrand. "Don't stop to torture me with your voice. We shall meet again—be sure of that. O! when we do meet!"

"I think I can understand your feelings, sir," returned our hero, in a tone of provoking moderation; "but

I cannot believe that you will lay up any ill feeling against me. You will have time for reflection after I have left you, and you will not fail to see that you have been entirely in the wrong. And, furthermore, I am sure that you will acknowledge to yourself that I have simply done my duty. I pray you, sir, think of these things calmly."

Bertrand groaned, and gnashed his teeth in rage, but made no reply in words; and shortly afterwards Conrad rejoined the lady.

"Now, my dear lady, I will once more help you to your saddle; and then I will select me a horse, and bear you company to Rennes."

"O, Conrad, what have you done!" The tone was eager, and the small white hands were clasped in agony.

"Alas, lady," cried the youth, for the moment mistaking her meaning, "have I done wrong? Would you have preferred that the prince——"

"No, no, no," interrupted Rosalin. "I did not mean that. But what can now save you? You have made an enemy who will hunt you till he has destroyed you!"

"Then you would rather go with me to your home, than to have me leave you with the prince?"

"Yes—certainly. But——"

"There are no buts, lady. I promised that I would protect you, and I have thus far kept my word. If the prince shall seek my life for what I have done, I shall defend myself to the utmost. I this night found him acting the part of a villain, and I have treated him accordingly. If he shall, in the time to come, seek to act the part of an assassin, I shall not hesitate to meet him as such; and may the result be between me and my God."

"You are a good man!—a noble man!" exclaimed the

maiden, in the fulness of her heart ; "and may Heaven reward and protect you !"

"I thank thee, lady, for those words. They are a sufficient reward for all I have done. And now let us be on our way."

Conrad helped her to her seat, and then went and secured the horse which Tithon had ridden ; and when he had mounted, and tried the rein to assure himself that the beast was all right, he put himself by the side of his charge, and once more they started towards Rennes.

" Do you think," asked Conrad, as the horses came to a walk at the foot of a gentle hill, " that the prince will follow you to your father's castle ?"

" No," replied Rosaline. " He would not dare to do that. Such a movement would be an open act of hostility, and my father's retainers would not hesitate to resent it. Bertrand would not dare to bring on a direct rupture between himself and the powerful duke."

" But," said Conrad, " how could he have hoped to take you away as he did without bringing on a rupture between himself and your father ?"

" Perhaps he thought, when he had me in that dismal old ruin, that I would consent to be his wife. And, if such a result had failed, he probably meant to crush me to ruin, trusting that his instrumentality in my disappearance would not be discovered. I think it is plain enough. If they had succeeded in killing you, as was their plan, only the prince and his sworn tools would have known my whereabouts ; and my father might not have been able to trace my steps, nor to have fastened any crime upon the prince. It was the plot of a bold, bad man, who sets no bounds to his base passions, and who stops at nothing which can pander to them."

" Heaven bless the hour that led them to my mother's

cot for a guide !" ejaculated the youth, as he tightened his rein at the top of the hill.

Rosaline murmured a fervent amen, and added some further words, in a low, tremulous tone, which were swallowed up in the clatter of the horse's hoofs as they started once more into a gallop.

The hamlet of Saint Mary was passed at about three o'clock, and just as the first streaks of dawn were lighting the eastern horizon, they drew up before the stout castle of Rennes. The drawbridge was down, but the gates were closed, and the porter's lodge was dark. Conrad saw a horn hanging upon one of the posts, and taking it from its peg, he blew upon it a long, loud blast. In a little while a wicket was opened, and a man looked forth.

"Who seeks admittance to the castle at this hour ?" was the demand.

"The lady Rosaline," replied our heroine, urging her horse forward over the bridge.

In a moment more the sound of a bell broke upon the air, and presently afterwards the gates were thrown open and the riders entered.

The castle of Rennes was a grand old structure, commenced by a powerful baron- of Brittany in the sixth century, and finally completed by an ancestor of the present duke. It was strong enough to withstand the assault of a large army, and its garners could hold provisions enough to sustain its garrison a year. Its walls and towers were of gray stone, and from its highest turret the watchman had a view of all the surrounding country.

As Conrad and his companion entered the spacious court, they were met by half a dozen men at-arms, who had been called up by the striking of the bell. They recognized their young mistress, and two of them held her horse while two more approached to assist her from her saddle.

"Is your father with you, or near at hand?" asked one who seemed to have authority.

"No, good captain. I left him at Vannes. This gentleman has been my companion and protector on the road, and I recommend him to your most kind regards. His name is Conrad. And this," the maiden added, turning to our hero, "is Nicolas, the captain of our men-at-arms."

Conrad descended from his saddle, and extended his hand to the captain, who took it with a cordial grasp. There is a language in the grasping of hands; and both the youth and the sturdy captain felt the quiver of respect and esteem coursing along the nerves, from the fingers to the brain, and thence to the heart. Nicolas was a stout, frank-faced man of forty; and though, by the opening daylight, he could see that the new-comer was quite young, yet he saw something more in that bold, manly face, which engaged his admiration.

"You are welcome, sir, to the castle, so far as I have the right to speak," he said; "and be sure that the recommendation of our mistress will open all hearts to you."

Conrad expressed his thanks, and was upon the point of turning to his horse when Rosaline addressed him :

"Good sir, let my people look to your horse, while you come with me to my father's dwelling. I think we both need rest."

The captain led the way across the court to the house. of the lord, while the men-at-arms led away the horses. When they reached the hall they found others of the servants up, who wondered much upon beholding their young mistress arrive at such an hour, and with only a stranger for her guard and companion.

" Where is the duke ?" asked old Rachel, the house-keeper.

" I left him at Vannes."

" But why did you come off alone, and in such a strange manner ?"

" Good Rachel, I am tired and hungry ; and this gentleman is the same. Let us have something to eat now, and at some other time you may ask me what you please."

The maiden spoke smilingly, and the old housekeeper took no offence, but hurried away to prepare food for the hungry ones.

" You will rest awhile beneath our roof," said Rosaline, turning to her companion.

" Yes, lady," he replied. " I will take such rest as will befit me for my return to my home."

" You must wait until my father comes."

" Do not ask me to stay beyond the hour of noon. I would like to see your father ; but I must return to my mother. She will be uneasy."

" As you will, kind sir. Only, if you hurry away thus, I shall claim a promise that you will at some time come again."

" If I make no promise, I shall break none," said Conrad, with a smile ; " so, to be on the sure side of truth, we had better leave the affairs of the future to themselves. Still,"—and his voice suddenly quivered and grew softer as he continued—" I should like to come again. I should feel sad if I thought I were never more to look upon the sweet face of the lady of Rennes."

Rosaline gazed down upon the pavement for a moment, while the rich color of warming blood mounted to her cheeks and temples. Then she raised her eyes, and put forth both her hands ; and, while a warm smile lighted up her beautiful face, she said :

"It must not be so. We have not thus been brought together, to be sundered forevermore. I claim it from you as a duty that we meet again."

Conrad could not resist the impulse. He held both the lady's hands, and one of them he raised to his lips, saying, as he imprinted a kiss upon it:

"Your command is to me a law. If I live I will visit this castle again."

Rosaline thanked him with a grateful look, and shortly afterwards led the way to a small drawing-room near the dining-hall, where refreshments had been served.

Half an hour afterwards Conrad had been conducted to a spacious chamber, where, without much hesitation, he threw his weary limbs upon the bed that had been prepared for him. Sleep came quickly to his relief; and though the scenes of the night had been gloomy and sad enough, yet his dreams were pleasant, and full of promise.

CHAPTER VIII.

CASIMIR.

The sun had been some two hours up from its bed when a party of four horsemen came dashing up to the castle gates from the southward. They were covered with dust, and the horses were well nigh worn down. He who rode in advance was a man of five-and-forty; hale and noble looking; of medium height, and well-knit frame; and whose garb bespoke him to be one in authority and high in rank. In fact, he was Casimir, Duke of Rennes, a nobleman beloved by his friends, and honored and feared by his enemies. At the present time his brow was dark, and the expression of his face denoted the deepest anxiety. As he entered the court he sprang from his saddle, and addressed the first person who presented himself, which happened to be the old porter.

"Good Lancelot, I have ridden fast and far. Have you heard anything from the lady Rosaline?"

"Why, bless you, my master, are you anxious on her account?"

"Aye—that I am. Has anything been heard of her?"

"The lady Rosaline is safe and sound, my lord."

"Safe, say you?" cried the duke, starting forward, and grasping the old man by the arm. "Is my daughter in the castle?"

"She is, my lord; and looking as well as I ever saw her, save the shade of fatigue that marked her pretty face."

Casimir pressed his hand upon his brow, and drew a long breath, seeming thus to gain much relief.

"Thank God, my child is safe!"

"How, my lord—has there been any danger?"

"There has been much alarm, good Lancelot. But tell me—when did she arrive?"

"This morning, just as the day was breaking."

"Did she come alone?"

"No. She was accompanied by a young man, named Conrad. They two came alone."

"Who was this man?"

"I don't know, my lord. I only know that he is the fairest youth that my eyes ever rested upon; and, if I have not lost my faculty of reading men's faces, he is as brave and true as he is handsome."

At this juncture the captain of the men-at-arms came up to welcome his lord, and of him the duke sought further information concerning the coming of his daughter ; but Nicolas could tell no more than the old porter had told. He only knew that Rosaline and her companion had arrived just as the day was breaking ; and that they had ridden all night ; and that they were now resting within the domicile of the castle.

"But this youth," said the duke—"did you learn nothing of him ?"

"Nothing, my lord. His face betokeneth nobility ; but his garb was humble ; and I noticed stains of blood upon his stockings, and upon the skirts of his doublet. He bore a brave, manly look, and the grasp of his hand was warm and vigorous, as though not ashamed of anything it had done."

"Then it could not have been the prince," said Casimir, in a tone of relief.

"What prince ?"

"I know of but one who bears that title in Brittany."

"If you speak of the prince Bertrand, my lord, I should say that this youth was about as unlike the prince as it is possible for man to be. This Conrad is handsome and brave ; and one loves him from instinct."

"You do not flatter the prince, captain."

"Pardon me, my lord. I meant no disrespect to his royal highness."

"You are pardoned," said the duke, with a smile. But in a moment more the smile had faded away, and a cloud came in its place.

"This is most wonderful," he muttered to himself, as he moved towards the domicile. "Who can this youth be ? Surely there is none in Vannes can answer the description. But I shall not be long in ignorance ; and, in the meantime, let me thank God that my sweet child is safe."

He entered the dwelling of the castle, and in the hall was met by Rachel, who informed him that Rosaline still slept. Anxious as he was to see her, he would not have her disturbed then. He called for refreshment, and when he had eaten he retired to his own chamber, where he threw himself into an easy chair, and soon fell asleep. He was weary, for he, too, had ridden all night.

Rosaline, almost entirely recovered from her fatigue, awoke towards noon; and having prepared a simple toilette, she descended to the hall, where she met a servant who informed her of her father's arrival. She had just turned to seek him, when he descended the broad stairs. She flew to his arms with a quick cry of joy, and if the duke had held any doubts or suspicions, they were all banished before the light of that joyful smile.

"My blessed child, Heaven be praised for this!" he ejaculated, winding his arms about her, and pressing her to his bosom. Then he held her off and gazed eagerly into her face.

"You are safe and well, my precious one. You are not harmed?"

"No, my father—O, no. Though harm hath gathered about me like deepest night, yet am I once more with thee as safe as when you saw me last."

Several of the servants had entered the hall, and the duke, not caring to question his daughter in their hearing, took her by the hand, and led her away to his own private apartment.

"Now, Rosaline," he said, when he had closed the door and taken a seat, "you must relieve my anxious thoughts. O, how I have suffered! I have searched for you throughout Vannes; and from Vannes to this place, a distance of thirty leagues, I have ridden in eight hours. But let me hear what has happened."

"Have you not suspected who caused my disappearance from Vannes ?" asked Rosaline.

"Yes," replied the duke. "At first I suspected prince Bertrand."

"And have you had occasion to rid yourself of that suspicion ?"

"Not entirely , though I must admit that he has the benefit of much doubt. Early on the morning after your disappearance I sought the prince, believing that he knew something of what had happened. He denied all knowledge, seeming to be utterly astonished ; and declared that he would take two of his attendants, and set off at once after you, which he did."

"O !" groaned Rosaline, "the prince is a villain of the blackest dye. But listen, and I will tell you all."

And then the maiden commenced, and told to her father the whole of her adventure, from the time of her seizure in the garden by the prince's servants, to her arrival at the castle. It was a long story, for she omitted nothing, even repeating all the conversation of the villains which she had overheard, and detailing, with wonderful minuteness, the speech and the movements of her deliverer. When she spoke of the prince she shuddered, and her lips turned pale ; but when Conrad was her theme the rich color mounted to her face, and her eyes grew soft and moist with grateful warmth.

"My child," said Casimir, after the story was concluded, "do you tell me that this youth performed these prodigies with his own arm ?"

"Yes, my father, even as I have related it."

"This is a most marvelous story,". said the duke, after a considerable pause. "I am not astonished at the wickedness of the prince ; but I wonder much at his bold audacity. And yet I can see how, in the blindness of his passion, he hoped to escape immediate detection."

And then Casimir questioned his child anew, upon each important particular, until he had heard the whole story over again.

"One thing is evident," he said, after he had heard for the second time the story of Conrad's feats: "This youth has deceived you."

"Deceived me?" repeated Rosaline, with an uneasy gesture. "O, no, no—you do not know him. There is no deception in his nature. He is the very soul of truth and honor. You will say so when you see him."

"You speak from a sense of gratitude, my child; but I do not blame you. If, however, you will look at the matter with unprejudiced judgment, you will see that he cannot have told you the truth. According to his account, he is a simple mountaineer, who had never seen service before; and he would have you believe that his conflict with Baptiste was the first mortal combat in which he was ever engaged. Now just look at it. Baptiste was noted as one of the best swordsmen in Brittany. He had slain at least a dozen men in duels; while the giant, Goliath, was held to be invincible. And then I know that prince Bertrand is a most accomplished cavalier. In fact, he has been pronounced a perfect master of the sword. And yet you tell me that this Conrad slew Baptiste and Goliath in fair and open combat, and that he held the prince as he would have held a child."

"Yes, my father."

"Then it is apparent enough that the youth is some bold adventurer, who has made war his profession—some follower of needy princes, ready to sell his services to the highest bidder."

A flush of indignation mantled the cheeks and the

brow of the maiden; but before she could make any response, some one knocked upon the door.

A servant entered, and announced that the gentleman who had come with the lady Rosaline was about to depart.

"Not until I have seen him," cried the duke, starting to his feet. "Let him be who or what he may, I owe him a heavy debt. Bring him to me. Tell him that I wish to speak with him."

The servant withdrew, and Casimir then turned to his daughter.

"You may leave me, Rosaline; but fear not that I shall demean myself unseemly before your protector. I am grateful to him, as he shall see."

The maiden arose and left the apartment without speaking; and ere long afterwards Conrad was ushered into the duke's presence.

Casimir arose, and took a step forward, and there stopped. He gazed into the face of the young man before him, while Conrad, with equal interest, gazed upon him. The nobleman felt his doubts melting away beneath the light of that frank, open face; and his suspicions began to take wings before that upright, manly form.

"Gentle sir," he finally said, extending his hand, "you surely did not intend to leave the castle without seeing the father of the lady to whom you had rendered so much service."

"I knew not, my lord, that you were astir," replied Conrad, taking the hand which had been extended to him. "I heard that you had returned; and I supposed that you were still resting."

"But you could have called for me."

"Ah," said the youth, with a light smile, and with a

gentle shake of the head, "that would have looked as though I held you in my debt."

"And am I not in your debt?"

"Not at all, my lord."

"Not for the life and honor of my child?"

"No ; for I am already more than repaid. I would not sell the knowledge of the deed I have done for a mountain of gold."

"And did you not dare to receive my gratitude ?"

"Why should I seek that which I knew I already possessed. When I had reached my mountain home should I not have held the happy conviction that the Duke of Rennes was grateful even to blessing me in his prayers ?"

"Aye, surely," replied Casimir, shaking the youth's hand warmly. "You are right in that, at least. And now that you are here, I trust that you will grant me a few moments of your time."

"I am entirely at your service, sir," said Conrad, taking the seat which his host proffered. "I have a mother, and a kind old tutor, waiting for me among the mountains ; and my only need of haste is, to relieve their anxiety."

"You made them no promises when you would return ?"

"No."

"Then they will not be over-anxious. My daughter has told me the story of her adventures ; but there are some things I would like to hear from your own lips."

The youth promised that he would answer to the best of his ability ; and thereupon his host drew from him almost a repetition of the story which Rosaline had told. When Conrad spoke of his own deeds he was modest and calm, seeking to glide over them with as little show of pride as possible. He could not hide all

his pride, however; though what did appear was of the
noblest kind. He explained the motives which had
actuated him in his disposition of the villains; not only
had he the desire of saving the lady from their foul
grasp, but they had made him an unconscious party to
the crime; and hence he had felt that the vindication
of his own honor and integrity demanded that he
should undo, if possible, the base work which had been
furthered under his guidance.

"You say your home is in the mountains, with your
mother and your old tutor?"

"Yes, my lord."

"And have you never served under arms?"

"Never, sir. In that respect you have already heard
the simple truth."

"Has your home always been in the mountain cot?"

"Ever since I can remember."

The duke had no more thought of doubting Conrad's
word. As he gazed into the handsome, beaming face,
and listened to the bold, musical tones of the unhesitat-
ing voice, he felt that deceit could have no home there.
In short, his confidence in the youth's truth and honor
was firm and abiding. And, more than that, he felt a
deep respect for the noble character which had been
thus presented to him.

And there was something more. Since Conrad had
begun to speak, the duke had watched him narrowly,
reading every line of his countenance, and noting its
minutest changes. He was sure he saw familiar shadows
in that face.

"Were you born amid the mountains?" asked Casimir,
after a pause.

"I think not, sir; though I must have been a mere
infant when my mother took me there."

"What is your mother's name?"

" Marguerite."

" And what is the name of the old tutor of whom you have spoken ?"

" Francesco."

The duke repeated the latter name to himself several times.

" You are sure that Marguerite is your mother ?" he said, after studying awhile.

" Why do you ask that ?" returned Conrad, eagerly.

" I have a reason for asking it."

" Indeed, my lord, I know not how to answer you. By every tie of love and gratitude, Marguerite is my mother ; but I have lately had reason to think that I am but an adopted child. And yet I have never asked her the question. Several times the words have been upon my lips ; but, as though some subtle sympathy told her my intent, she has avoided them. My instinct tells me that the subject would pain her, and I have spared her."

" Have you ever asked Francesco about it ?"

" Yes, sir ; and he pretends that he knows nothing. His replies, though seemingly explicit, have given me more food for doubt than anything else."

" Have you any other friend than those you have mentioned ?"

" O, yes, sir. All the shepherds, and peasants, and hunters of the Nord are my friends."

" I mean, is there any other who has seemed to take an interest in your education ?"

" Only one, sir—Dagobert, the good old Abbot of Saint Aubin."

" Ah," cried Casimir, with a perceptible start, " is he your friend ?"

" Yes, sir."

"He is a good old man. I have seen him. I know him well."

As the duke thus spoke, he arose and took several turns up and down the apartment. He gazed sharply at Conrad's profile each time he passed him, seeming all the while busy with perplexing thought. Finally he stopped and laid his hand upon the youth's shoulder :

"You left the prince bound hand and foot?"

"Yes, my lord—almost six leagues from here."

"And you do not know that his companion could live?"

"I was not sure."

"Then let me ask a favor of you. Will you go with me to the place?"

"With pleasure."

"Enough. We will be off at once. We may find the prince still helpless."

Conrad followed the duke down into the court, and very soon two horses were ready for them ; and having mounted, they rode away at a gallop. In less than an hour and a half they reached the spot where the affray had taken place, having spoken but very little on the way. They found the dead bodies of Adolphe and Tithon ; but the prince and Poins were gone.

"It is as I had thought," said Conrad. "The man-at-arms was not dangerously hurt. He must have revived, and set his master at liberty."

"It must have been so," returned the duke. "And so, all we have now to do is to retrace our steps."

"Must we leave these corses here?"

"Not for long. I will send some of my people from the hamlet of Saint Mary to bury them. You will return with me to Rennes."

"Is there need of it, my lord?"

"Most certainly there is. You need refreshment ;

and, moreover, you had better go away with your own horse."

Casimir made the last remark with a smile; and Conrad, with an answering smile, returned:

"The horse which bore me to your castle is a borrowed one."

"But," retorted the duke, "you had earned a right to his use."

"That may be, my lord."

"Then come and get him. But, my dear friend, that is not all. I must send some of my people to Vannes; so, if you come with me, you shall have company for the most of your journey."

Conrad had no further objection to make; so he turned back with the duke towards Rennes.

CHAPTER IX.

A NEED OF HELP AT THE COT.

It was quite late in the afternoon when the duke and his companion arrived at the castle; and when they had eaten dinner, the sun had well nigh reached the tops of the western hills. Of course Conrad could not think of starting for home before another morning.

"You had better remain here to-night," said Casimir; "and early on the morrow you shall have company. Your mother will not worry."

"If she does," replied the youth, "she will feel the more joy when she meets me. But under the circumstances, I think I had better stop."

So the matter was arranged; and while the duke went

to attend to some business affairs, Conrad walked out into the court, where he met the captain of the men-at-arms, who received him cordially, and with much respect. Our hero was at first much surprised at the manifest deference of the officer's manner ; for the captain of the men-at-arms was the highest officer of the household, standing next to the duke in authority. But the matter was soon explained. They had walked a short distance, and had spoken upon a few unimportant topics, when Nicolas said :

"My dear Conrad, is it true what I have heard touching your encounter with the people of the prince ?"

"That depends upon what you have heard," replied the youth, with a smile.

"I have heard most marvelous things," continued the captain. "Lancelot told me ; and Rachel told Lancelot ; and Rachel says that the lady Rosaline told her. It is said that you overcame Baptiste and Goliath."

"That is true."

"In open combat ?"

"Yes."

Nicolas gazed upon the young mountaineer in surprise.

"How was it ?" he at length asked. "I wish much to hear the story."

"I know not that I ought to tell it all," said Conrad, hesitatingly ; "but, as you have already heard so much, and as you are an officer in the interest of the duke, I may, without impropriety, give you the chief items."

"It would please me much, good sir, indeed it would."

Conrad saw, from the captain's manner, that he was passionately fond of adventure, and when he came to relate the story with the warmth and appreciation of so much sympathy to help him, he gave new spirit to his words, and fairly fought the battles over again.

"By Saint Michael!" cried Nicolas, after the story was completed, and after he had asked numerous questions, "you must not refuse me a favor I have to ask. I am an able soldier, and for fully twenty years I have been under arms. I have a pair of fencing swords, and I must test the quality of your prowess. I look not to overcome the victor of Baptiste and Goliath, but I look for the sport."

"Indeed, captain, I shall not refuse you; for I am as fond of the exercise as you can possibly be. I love it. I never feel so gloriously the full measure of my spirits as when my old Francisco holds me a difficult bout."

"Then come. Let us to the sport before the daylight is gone."

The captain led the way to the guard-room, which was large and high, where he soon produced the swords of which he had spoken. They were of ordinary size, with straight blades of the finest temper, the edges round, and the points blunt; and by the time the combatants had taken their positions, at least a score of men-at-arms were present to witness the sport.

Conrad's first guard was a subject of admiration to all the beholders. "What ease and grace!" remarked one. "Look at the swelling of that chest!" said another. "See the bend of the arm, and the play of the cords in that wrist!" added a third. "Aye," chimed in a fourth, "and mark the flashing of those eyes! By heaven, they snap like sparks of fire!"

The play commenced, and Conrad very soon found that his opponent was not only a master of the art, but also that he had been trained very nearly in the same school as himself. In the size of the men there was but little difference. Nicolas was a trifle the stoutest, while Conrad was, perhaps, an inch the tallest. For some minutes the swords flashed and clashed, moving in light circles and at various angles.

"Ah—be careful!" whispered Conrad, so low that only his opponent heard him. "If you venture that again you will lose your sword."

"No, no," replied Nicolas, with a confident smile. "My wrist is too quick and strong for that."

It was a favorite feint of the captain's—a succession of brilliant side plays, with a lunge at the throat. He tried it again. Conrad allowed the feints to pass with little effort to meet them, for his eye told him their aim; but when the thrust came he had gathered all his energy. He raised his hand to his chin, at the same time leaping quickly back, and caught the opposing point beneath his guard. Then, as quick as lightning, he twirled his sword with a rotary motion, completely winding it about the blade of his antagonist; and in a moment more the captain's weapon was clanging upon the pavement at the opposite side of the room.

"That was a splendid lunge of yours," said Conrad, with honest appreciation; "but you see I understand it."

"Aye, and you understand its master, too," cried Nicolas. "By heaven! I must improve my sword-play."

"My old tutor is a perfect master," remarked Conrad, "and I do really wish you could visit me at my mountain cot, and see him handle his sword. He is three-score-and-five, and his hair is gray, but his eye is still as keen as fire, and his wrist is as subtle as a bow of steel."

"Let me promise myself that pleasure," said the cap-

tain warmly. " If I live, and the duke will spare me, I
will pay you a friendly visit."

" Good !" exclaimed Conrad, extending his hand. " I
shall look for you ; and you may be assured that your
welcome will be warm and heartfelt."

It was too late to try another pass, or Nicolas would,
for his own benefit, have asked for further play. As it
was, however, he felt a deeper friendship than before
for the young mountaineer, his late discomfiture not
worrying him in the least. He was a brave man, confident of his own prowess, and he regarded the man who
had proved to be his superior as worthy of respect and
esteem, and this return he frankly and freely gave.

" Well and nobly done !" pronounced a deep voice,
near the door, as the sword of the captain fell upon
the pavement ; and those present gave way instinctively
for the new-comer.

In the meantime the duke had written a letter, and
then turned to speak with his daughter, who had been
for some minutes standing by his side.

" Well, father," she said, as he turned a questioning
look upon her, " you have seen the young mountaineer, and conversed with him. What do you think
of him ?"

" I will be frank with you, my child. I think my suspicions were groundless. Conrad is a brave young
man, and his speech is true. We must give him some
fitting reward."

" How ? What reward can you give for such services
as he has performed ?"

" O, that is simple enough," replied the duke, with a
smile. " The lad is poor, and will be benefited by some
gift—perhaps of money."

" In mercy's name—no ! no !" cried Rosaline, catching
her father's arm. " Don't offer insult."

" Insult, my child ?   Would it be insult to offer money
to a poor man who had honorably earned it ?"

" *Earned it !*" echoed the maiden, gazing vacantly
into her father's face.   " Has he worked like a laborer
for hire ?   *Earned it !*   Can such deeds as his be done for
the money which the lord pays to his servant ?" '

" But, Rosaline,"—the duke spoke in a low, calm tone,
and with a keen, searching glance—" does not the work
merit a reward ?"

She made no reply.

" Would you turn such a friend away without recompense ?"

" No—no—certainly not."

" Then what recompense would you give ?"

The girl sank into a chair, partly to collect her
thoughts, and partly that she might, for the moment,
hide her face.   By and by she answered :

" I know his proud, noble feelings ; and I know what
reward will please him best.   Let him bear away a
pledge of friendship and esteem from the Duke of
Rennes, and he will be satisfied."

" Would it not please him to add a like pledge from
the lady of Rennes ?"

" If he has not that pledge already, I fear no words of
mine could make the possession more complete."

" Have you given such a pledge ?"

Rosaline met the inquiring look and there was a
strange flutter in her heart.   She was too honorable,
too truthful, and had too much love and respect for her
father, to dissemble or prevaricate.   She knew his meaning, and would not stoop to a profession of ignorance.
She rested her brow upon her hand, not to reflect upon
an answer, but to call to mind what had passed between
her and her preserver.   At length she arose, and rested
her hand upon her father's shoulder.

" I cannot now remember what words of gratitude I have spoken to Conrad ; but I know that I have spoken enough ; and I doubt not that I have betrayed more than I have spoken. But, sir, no words have passed from my lips that the daughter of a duke should not have uttered ; nor has Conrad lisped even a syllable which the poorest peasant in the realm might not with propriety have spoken to a queen."

Casimir took his daughter's hand, and thanked her for her frankness. He knew that she meant to tell him the whole truth, and yet his quick eye had discovered more than she had spoken—perhaps more than she herself knew. He had seen the youth, and conversed with him, and he knew something of the influence which such a nature must necessarily wield over the feelings and emotions of a gentle, confiding, pure-hearted girl, especially under the powerful help of such circumstances as had attended the companionship of Conrad and Rosaline. He reflected awhile, still holding his daughter's hand, and finally said :

" You are right, Rosaline. I will not offer him money. I will give him my friendship."

The quick light of joy which shone upon the maiden's face was answer enough ; and when she was gone, the duke said to himself :

" The palace will burn as quickly as the hut, if the fiery torch be applied. All hearts are fashioned after one eternal model, and the lines of rank and station cannot circumscribe their mysterious beatings !"

Then he arose, and went down into the court, and arrived at the door of the guard room just in season to witness the closing scene of the play between his captain and Conrad.

" Well and nobly done !" he said, advancing into the

centre of the room. " I think you find a strong arm in this young man, my captain."

" The strongest I ever met," replied Nicolas. " It is strong and quick, and guided by a judgment as cool and unerring as mortal judgment can be."

The duke saluted Conrad kindly, and then walked away with Nicolas, whom he had called to see on business.

Conrad hoped he might see Rosaline before he retired to rest, as he wished to know if she had come forth from the late severe ordeal without serious shock to her system. He did not acknowledge to himself that he wished to see her for anything more. He might have asked her father how it was with her ; or he might have asked some of the servants ; but he dared not. He dared not trust himself to exhibit his feelings before them. Surely there must have been some deep emotions stirring within him ; and, more still, he must have had knowledge of them.

He retired to his couch at an early hour, and as he laid his head upon his pillow he acknowledged to himself, for the first time in spoken words, that which his heart could no longer keep secret from his understanding.

" And this it is to love !" he murmured, with his hands clasped over his heart. " O, that the sweet angel were but some mountain maid, that I might woo and win her !"

Then he remembered what the maiden had said about a strong heart's winning the object of its love. He called to mind every look and tone ; and he almost made himself believe that she had shown to him something more than the mere return of gratitude. He might have gone on thence and built a fair palace of love in skies of the future ; but the form of the proud duke arose darkly before him, shutting out the entrancing vision.

At an early hour our hero was aroused from his slumbers by the sound of the herald's trumpet, and springing quickly from his bed, he was soon dressed and ready for breakfast. He found Nicolas, with half a dozen stout men-at-arms, at the table, and, as he took a seat with them, he learned that they were to be his companions as far as Mauron. They were going to Vannes. The meal was disposed of with much social chat, and, as they arose from the table, the captain announced that the horses were ready and that they were soon to be off.

In the hall Conrad met the duke and Rosaline. Surely the maiden did not suffer from the effects of the trial through which fate had led her. Her eyes were beaming brightly, and her cheeks were suffused with a warm glow. As she met the look of the youth, she left her father's side and took a step toward him, at the same time extending her hand. The words of greeting which she spoke were not so deep in their meaning as was the quick light of the eye and the wreathing of the happy smile that grew to life upon her beautiful features.

"Good Conrad," spoke the duke, quickly taking his daughter's place, "it is beyond the power of language to tell you how much I owe you for what you have done; but your own heart will tell you how deeply I must appreciate your services. You will take with you the lasting friendship of myself and my daughter; and in the future I may have opportunity to give you some more substantial token of my esteem. In the meantime, be never backward in calling upon the Duke of Rennes for any assistance you may need. Adieu for the present."

Conrad took the duke's hand and thanked him for his kindness. Then he turned and bowed to Rosaline, and very shortly afterward he was in his saddle.

It was a bright, pleasant morning, and the horses were eager and strong. The distance to Mauron was ten leagues, which place was reached in season to give the beasts an hour's rest before dinner. At this point Conrad was to separate from his companions.

" Remember," said our hero, addressing the captain, as they came out from the inn, " you have promised to come and see me in my mountain home."

" Aye," returned Nicolas ; " and to see that rare old tutor of yours. I shall be there, never fear. And in the meantime, let me advise you to look out for yourself. You have enemies."

" I am aware of that, good Nicolas ; but I have no present fear."

" Ah," pursued the captain, shaking his head, " there is no telling how the wicked prince may strike. But I may learn something of his movements while I am in Vannes ; and, on my return, I may call upon you. At all events, if I learn anything which your safety requires you should know, I will not fail to see you ; for such was the order I received from the duke."

" You will meet with a warm welcome—you and your companions," said Conrad.

And with this they parted, Nicolas and his followers keeping the road to Vannes, while Conrad turned to the north towards the mountains.

The distance was an easy afternoon's ride, and our hero did not hurry. As he rode on alone his thoughts were busy with the scenes and incidents of the past few days ; and when he talked with himself, which he did much of the time, the fair lady of Rennes was his theme. As he entered the deep forest, other thoughts forced themselves upon him—thoughts which he at first attempted to put lightly away, but which came at each succeeding visit with new power. They were thoughts of the powerful enemy he had made; and by the time he had reached the entrance to the vale where his cot stood he had admitted to himself the necessity of care and caution.

The sun had already touched the tops of the mountains, and the vale was in deep shadow, when he arrived at the opening of the cleared space; and he was not a little astonished upon beholding half a dozen horses hitched to the trees close at hand. A few steps further on, and he saw the cot. And another scene met his gaze. A gray-haired old man and a woman were being dragged along from the cot by a number of armed men. The woman was his mother; and he could hear her cry for mercy! The man was Francisco, and he was bound with his hands behind him.

For an instant Conrad grew sick and dizzy with the sight; but it was only the sudden hush which precedes the bursting forth of the hurricane.

CHAPTER X.

A NEW TROOP.

Prince Bertrand did not lie long bound as his captor had left him. Master Poins had not been quite so senseless as he had appeared. He had, in reality, recovered his senses in season to see his master disarmed and bound; but a regard for his own safety had suggested to him the propriety of remaining quiet until the dreadful mountaineer had gone. As soon as Conrad had disappeared he rose to his feet, and approached the spot where the prince lay; and when the illustrious prisoner had been released from his bonds, his first effort of returning power was to curse his attendant. Poins bore it with becoming fortitude, outwardly begging for mercy, but inwardly thanking his stars that the sword of the mountaineer had spared him to be the recipient of the prince's curses.

After a while, however, Bertrand had cursed enough, and his next idea was concerning the man who had so humbled him. He would have followed him if he had dared; but his cooler judgment told him that his purpose of vengeance would best be served by proceeding cautiously.

" Of one thing," said he to his companion, " I am certain : This fellow is no common mountaineer."

" Who is he ?" asked Poins, with honest simplicity.

" That is what I am determined to find out. But we can learn nothing here. I know where the rascal lives ; and Adolphe informed me that an old man and woman were left in charge of the premises. Of this couple I will gain the information I seek. Come—let us be moving. Does your head pain you much ?"

Poins groaned terribly, for he was just beginning to realize how badly his head was bruised. Returning sense brought with it the power to feel pain. He went down to the river and bathed the wounds, and when he had bound a scarf about his head, he mounted a horse, and set off by the side of his master. After a smart ride of three hours they reached the town of Montfort, where they rested until nine o'clock of the following forenoon. Then they set forth again, and towards noon they met a party of six armed men, well mounted, and wearing the badges of the prince's followers.

"Ha!—Bernardo—is this you?" cried Bertrand, as he recognized the leader of the party.

"Yes, my lord."

"And whither go you?"

"Did you not bid me follow you, by this road, to the confines of Normandy?"

"Ah, yes—I remember. By Saint Michael! this is most fortunate." Then, turning to Poins, he added:

"You and I will be saved some trouble. I will have that old man and woman brought to me at my castle of Montevere; and, on the whole, I think the plan will be a good one. They had better not be at home when Master Conrad returns, for I have no great desire that the fellow's story should be told to too many."

"But he will tell his story at Rennes," suggested Poins.

"Of course he will; but I apprehend that the duke's people will not be in a hurry to circulate it. Nevertheless, I will break up this nest; and I'll have master Conrad under my thumb; and, as a commencement, I'll secure these two old ones who have charge of his family secrets. He a mountaineer! The thing is preposterous. He is something more than he appears; and what he is I am determined to know."

"Have you orders for us, my lord?" asked Bernardo, as the prince turned towards him again.

"Yes,—and important ones, too. In the forest to the northwest, there is a cot; and in that cot there are an old man and an old woman. I want them brought to me at my castle of Montevere. The place is not more than eight or nine leagues away, and you can easily reach it, and secure the prize, and join me at Montevere by midnight. I shall then have further work for you."

"In what direction lies the next movement?"

"In the same. After you have brought away this old man and woman, you will return and wait for a young villain who will be likely to wander back there in a day or two. This youngster's name is Conrad; and if you find it necessary to inquire for the cot, you will ask for the residence of Conrad."

"I think I can find the place," said Bernardo.

"You cannot help it. But I part with you not quite yet. Face about your troop, and follow me."

It was a custom of the prince's, when abroad on his excursions, to have small parties of his best men-at-arms scouring through the country upon the roads he was likely to travel ; for he often found use for them. And these soldiers were ready and anxious to serve him. They never asked themselves what was right, or what was wrong, so long as the prince had ordered it. This was not because they loved the prince ; but it was very evident that the prince of to-day was soon to be king ; and then those who had served him faithfully would stand in the way of reward. So Bertrand had plenty of willing tools, for he held high office in the army, and half the soldiers were at his command.

At the distance of two leagues the party reached a small river, where the prince pulled up and addressed his officer :

"Here, Bernardo, we separate. You will follow this stream towards the north, for I am very sure that these waters roll through the vale in which Conrad's hut stands. I do not think you can miss the way."

"There is no danger of that, my master."

"Then you understand what you are to do ?"

"I am to bring an old man and woman to you, at the castle of Montevere."

"Exactly."

"But had I better not know the names of these people?"

"Aye—I forgot that. Let's see: their names are—"
Poins came to his assistance.

"The old man's name is Francisco, and the old woman's is Marguerite."

"Those are the names," added the prince; "and now to your work."

"One word," said Bernardo; "am I to treat them as friends?"

The prince was still smarting under the memory of the treatment he had received at the hands of Conrad, and the spirit of vengeance extended even to those who had reared the daring youth.

"No!" he thundered, bringing his clenched fist down upon the pommel of his saddle. "They are the nurses of vipers! You would not be unnecessarily severe to a dog; but you would not allow a dog to snarl and bite."

"I understand," returned Bernardo; "and your commands shall be obeyed."

The prince and Poins forded the stream, and kept on to the westward, while the six men-at-arms turned to the northward.

Bernardo kept on at a good pace for an hour or more, when he arrived at a point where two streams came together, and where there appeared to be two well-trodden paths. He forded the stream to the right, and followed the other. At the end of another hour he concluded that he ought to be somewhere very near to the place he sought. In a little while he came to an open space, where he met a boy, with a bow in his hand, a quiver of arrows at his back, and a brace of hares over his shoulder.

"Hark'e boy! Do you know where a youth named Conrad, lives?"

"Yes, sir,—I know where he lives when he is at home."

The little fellow had a keen eye, and he surveyed the armed party very narrowly.

"Where is his cot?"

"Not on this road, sir."

"Ha,—have we come out of our way?"

"That depends upon which point you started from."

"We came from the south."

"Up the river?"

"Yes."

"Didn't you find two roads below here?"

"Where the two streams came together?"

"Yes, sir."

"Yes."

"Well, sir,—you took the wrong road. Your quickest way to reach the cot is to go back and commence over again."

"But there must be some way to cut off such a tramp."

"Not unless your horses can climb over perpendicular walls of rock, and pick their way through woods where a fox would lose himself."

Bernardo uttered a round oath, and then ordered his men to turn.

"Don't you mean to pay me anything for my information?" asked the boy.

"Not for such information as that," growled the officer ; and, without further remark, he turned his horse and galloped off, followed by his companions.

The boy watched the troop until they were out of sight, and then went on his way, muttering to himself and shaking his head. In less than half an hour he was at the cot in the vale, where he found old Francisco just coming out, on his way to the cave.

"Ah, Simon—is this you?"

"Yes, good father."

"You are on the wrong track for home."

"Not so far on the wrong track as are some others I wot of."

"But it is late for you to be wandering, Simon. Your mother will be watching for you."

"I came, father, to ask your pardon for a falsehood I have been telling. Listen: Not far from here, and not more than half an hour ago, I met six armed men. They were villainous-looking fellows, whose dark eyes flashed mischief; and I know that they belonged to the roving band that I have heard you speak of—the band that goes about when the wicked prince has bad work to do. The leader of these men asked me if I knew where Conrad lived; he wanted to find the cot. I didn't like the looks of the men; and I didn't like the tones of the leader's voice; and I set them on the wrong track."

"Why did you do that, my son?"

"Simply that I might come and inform you of what was going on. I suppose they will find you; but you will have had warning, and may be prepared."

"And for what do you imagine I can be prepared?"

"Indeed, good father, I cannot tell. Perhaps I did very wrong."

"No, no, Simon. I thank you for your thoughtfulness; and though your effort may prove of no advantage to me, yet I appreciate your kind intention."

Francisco walked some distance with the boy toward his home, questioning him, as he went, touching the interview with the armed men. Simon had but little to tell in addition to what he had already related. The old man thanked him once more, and assured him that

he had done nothing wrong ; after which he left the
lad to pursue his way alone.

" I will say nothing of this to Marguerite," said Francisco to himself. " There may be nothing out of the
way. This may be a portion of the party that Conrad
went to guide into Mayenne."

The old man was not given to useless surmising, nor
to groundless fears ; and he very soon resolved that he
would wait until the men-at-arms themselves made
their appearance.

The evening passed away ; the night came and went ;
and another day drew near to its close.

" It could have been nothing very important that
those men wanted."

The hermit had scarcely murmured these words
when he beheld six men approaching from the wood.
They were soldiers, and the old man quickly discovered,
by their uniforms, that they belonged to the private
corps of the prince. Marguerite, who had been all day
long on the watch for Conrad, heard the tramp of heavy
feet, and came out from the cot just as the men arrived.

" Is this the place where a youth named Conrad
lives ?' asked Bernardo.

" This is the place," replied Francisco, regarding his
interlocutor narrowly, and then sweeping his eye over
the others.

" Is your name Francisco ? "

" It is."

" And is this woman's name Marguerite ?"

" It is." The old compaigner was a rare hand at
reading human faces, and he was not many seconds in
making up his mind that six wretches stood before
him. Their characters were, to him, plainly written in
their looks. They were bold men ; but not brave men.
They were stubborn, wilful men : but not sternly

honest. They were soldiers, and might as well have worn the garb of brigands.

"Francisco and Marguerite, you must go with us."

"Ha!" The old man started. "Whither go we?"

"You shall find out when you get there."

"I do not comprehend you, sir. If you wish us to accompany you, you must be more explicit."

"We'll be explicit when the time comes; but for the present we have had just about as much perplexity as we can bear. We've been hunting for you since yesterday noon; and I verily believe that just four-and-twenty hours ago we were within less than half-a-league of here."

"You must have taken a roundabout way, then."

"Aye—we did. A young imp, in the shape of a boy, set us on the wrong track. But we've found you at length, and you will make haste to go with us."

"You will tell me what this means before we go."

"No,—I haven't time."

"Are we to be prisoners?"

"That is as you please to take it."

"By what authority do you come hither upon such an errand?"

"No matter. Are you ready to go with us?"

Francisco's blood began to boil. What could be the meaning of all this?

"Look ye," he cried, starting back and drawing himself defiantly up, "I know that you are servants of Prince Bertrand. Has the prince sent you upon this errand?"

"We came not here to be questioned," replied Bernardo, angrily. "By the gods! we have had trouble enough in finding you, and we don't choose to have more trouble in accomplishing our purpose, now that you are found. If you have horses at hand you may ride ; otherwise we must provide some other way."

At this juncture Marguerite sank upon her knees.

" In mercy's name, gentlemen, drag me not from my home !" she cried, raising her clasped hands toward the soldiers. " What have I done ? Why would you take me away ?"

" Stop the witch's mouth !" cried one of the heaviest of the ruffians, with a brutal oath. " 'Fore God, we'll be on the road the whole of another night."

" Lay not a hand upon her !" exclaimed the old man, as one of the soldiers started towards the kneeling woman. He had his heavy staff in his hand, and as he spoke he raised it above his head.

" By Saint Michael !" growled Bernardo, " the old dog means to bite ! We must make quick work of this."

Five of them sprang upon Francisco, wrenching the staff from his grasp and bearing him to the ground. They leaped for him while he was looking towards the woman, or they might have had more trouble ; and, even as it was, they found some difficulty in binding him. But the work was at length accomplished ; and, as the old man was lifted to his feet and led away, two of the ruffians seized upon the woman and dragged her on after her companion.

CHAPTER XI.

Conrad approached the scene of this outrage at a gallop, and as his eye caught the uniforms of the ruffians, he recognized them as belonging to the same tribe of villains as had belonged those who had already crossed his path. And more than this, the thought flashed upon him that they had come directly from the prince ; he was sure that such was the case—as sure as he could be of anything of which his senses had not taken direct cognizance.

" Hold there !" he shouted, reining in his horse close upon the leader of the gang. " What foul doing is this ?"

The voice was one of authority and power, and the men stopped and looked up ; but when they saw the humble garb of the speaker they started to move on again.

" Don't stop," said Bernardo. " I will look to this young gentleman."

Conrad leaped from his horse, and sprang to Francisco's side. His first impulse, as his feet touched the ground, had been to draw his sword ; but another thought came in its place. Before those who led the prisoner could devine what was meant, the youth had drawn his dagger, and cut the cord that bound the old

man's arms. It was but the work of an instant, performed as quickly as it had been conceived ; and before
the soldiers could discover what had been done, Conrad
had leaped back and drawn his sword.

" Rash boy, what would you do ?" cried Bernardo.

" Thus will I do !" spoke the youth, cleaving the skull
of the man who held Francisco's right arm.

As the fellow dropped senseless and powerless, Conrad
passed a quick word into the old tutor's ear :

" The sword ! The sword !"

Francisco needed not a second hint. He shook off
the grasp of the ruffian from his left arm, and, with a
movement as nimble and brisk as sprightliest youth,
he grasped the sword of the fallen man, and darted to
the side of his friend and pupil.

" Look ye," exclaimed Conrad. " Hold ! One
word !"

Bernardo had started towards him, but at that motion
he stopped—stopped in spite of himself. He was like a
man suddenly brought from pitchy darkness into the
full glare of day. The movements of the new-comer
had flashed upon him so like a lightning-bolt that his
mind was for a moment unseated. Hence he stopped
the more readily at the word of command ; and his
companions gathered about him, one only remaining a
few paces away in charge of Marguerite.

" You are servants of the prince Bertrand, and have
been sent by that person to carry off these old people,"
continued our hero, as the men-at-arms came to a standstill.

" Very well," replied Bernardo. " Suppose it is so ?"

" I know it is so."

" And I can tell you one thing more, my youthful cutthroat : You will go with them."

"Aye," cried Conrad, "I mean to do that very thing; but, mark me, we go not with you."

By this time the officer had fully recovered himself, and raised his sword for work.

"Do not hesitate," whispered Conrad, into Francisco's ear. "I know these fellows. I have a wonderful thing to tell you. We must cut them down!"

The old man needed no further inducement. His blood was up, and the fire of other days carried strength and will to his arm.

"Surrender!" ordered Bernardo. "We would not take your lives."

"Then go, and leave us in peace," replied Conrad.

The officer laughed.

"We are not boys," he said.

"Nor are you men," was Conrad's quick retort. "You are villains and cowards, or you would not be thus dragging away two gray-haired old people as though they were dogs!"

"That word seals your doom!"

So spoke Bernardo, with all the confidence of a master; and as the words passed his lips, he sprang forward. He had not prepared for conflict, for he thought he had only an inexperienced youth to deal with. He beheld a form of power and beauty, but he did not think of there being anything more. He struck at Conrad's sword, as though he would simply knock it down; and that stroke was his last. His own weapon was caught, as though in a whirlwind, and in a moment more he was borne back with the blade of his opponent through his neck.

"Strike! strike!" cried Conrad, as he shook the leader of the gang from his sword. "I know these men. We must conquer them or die!"

Francisco was once more a soldier; and the master

who taught Conrad how to use the sword, now gave proof that he could work as well as play. The men-at-arms were bunglers, at best; and in this sort of combat they were decidedly the weaker party. Conrad moved to and fro with the rapidity of thought, keeping his enemies all the time before him; and that gray-haired old man, who, but a short time since, was being dragged helpless away, now fought like a hero in his prime. At one time Conrad was opposed to two of the rascals, while a third attacked Francisco. This latter ruffian was by far the best swordsman of his party, and he had some wit, too. He fought entirely upon the defensive, moving backward in a circle, and never offering to make a lunge nor to strike a blow. By and by he had contrived to work around to the rear of the youth, and then his object became apparent. With a tiger-like bound he left the old man, and sprang upon Conrad's back.

Francisco saw the movement at its start, and cried out to his pupil. Conrad heard the cry in season to swing around, thereby avoiding a thrust which had been aimed at his side. In another moment master and pupil were together, and two of the enemy went down beneath their trenchant blades.

Five of the ruffians lay stretched upon the greensward, and the sixth threw down his sword, and begged for mercy.

"Hold!" exclaimed Francisco.

"Fear not," replied Conrad, lowering his point. "I strike not an unarmed man."

The battle was over, and while Conrad led his mother back to the cot, Francisco took the only living one of the enemy in charge. When the youth returned, the prisoner was sharply questioned, and he told his story honestly.

"You met the prince not far from Montfort, you say?" remarked Conrad, interrogatively.

"Yes, sir.   We met him and Poins."

"Yesterday noon?"

"Just before noon, I think."

"And but for the mistake of the boy, you would have taken this old man and woman away yesterday?"

"Yes, sir."

"To the castle of Montevere, I think you said!"

"Yes."

"And the prince is waiting there for you?'

"We were to meet him there."

"That is enough.   You need have no fear.   We shall not harm you; but for the present we mean to keep you safely under our care."

The prisoner had a slight wound upon the shoulder, and when this had been dressed, he was bound, hand and foot, and carried to one of the outbuildings, where he was left to his own reflections.

When Conrad and Francisco returned to the cot the shades of night had gathered over the vale, and Marguerite, who had been in no way harmed, soon brought in a lighted candle.   The good dame had not been bodily injured, but she was nevertheless weak from excitement and fear, though she breathed easier when she found that her friends were safe.

"Now, my son," said the old man, as soon as they were seated, "I am anxious to hear the meaning of all this; for I know that you have a story to tell."

"Aye, father—I have a story; and a wondrous one it is, too."

And thereupon the youth went on and related all his adventures, from the time of starting off with Baptiste and Adolphe, up to his arrival at the cot an hour before. Marguerite sat, pale and trembling, with her hands folded in her lap; while Francisco seemed more inclined to admiration and astonishment; rather dwelling, during the recital, upon the brilliancy of his pupil's deeds, than upon the danger incurred. But when the story had been concluded, and the old man had had time for reflection, a cloud came upon his brow, and a look of trouble settled upon his face.

"Merciful Heavens!" gasped Marguerite, "what shall we do! O, the boy must not be taken from us!"

"My mother," said Conrad, "you fear something more than mere danger to my person."

"I fear everything!" cried the woman, wringing her hands in agony.

"Hush, good sister," interposed the hermit. "We may avoid the danger you fear."

"But how shall we avoid it? The boy will be dragged forth, and——"

"Stop, Marguerite. Say no more."

Conrad understood too much of this.

"Look ye," he said, addressing Francisco! "There was one thing of which I did not tell you. The Duke of Rennes, when he had taken a fair view of my face, seemed struck by something which he saw there; and he asked me if I was sure that Marguerite was my mother."

Marguerite uttered a low, quick cry of alarm, and Francisco shrugged his shoulders.

"And furthermore," pursued Conrad, "he seemed to remember you, good Francisco. In short, there was something in my appearance which seemed to perplex him; and I am sure that his questions and behavior did much perplex *me*."

"Indeed, Conrad," replied the old man, earnestly and solemnly, "I cannot tell you what the duke may have suspected. For the present let us attend to other things.

We have enough to think of without dragging up matters of mystery. Is it not plain to you that we are all three in danger?"

"Certainly, father. I cannot hope that the wicked prince will allow us to dwell here in peace."

"Most assuredly he will not ; and our only plan of safety is to get away from here as soon as possible. Bertrand has too many tools at his command for us to brave him. I am in favor of going this very night. It seems that these soldiers were sent upon us yesterday ; and had they met with no trouble they would have delivered us up to their master many hours ago. Should more men-at-arms be sent this way, the prince will learn that he has new cause of vengeance against us."

"Yes, yes," cried Marguerite, "we must leave this place to-night."

"And whither will you go?" asked Conrad.

"To the Abbey of Saint Aubin," answered Francisco. "Dagobert will give us safe shelter."

Our hero thought as did the others. There could be no further safety for them at the cot, and the sooner they got away the better.

"The night is likely to prove fair," he said ; "and we may reach Rennes before morning. Aye—we can rest there some hours before day, if we let our horses go at their own speed. I suppose you intend to go by the way of Rennes?"

"That is the best road, certainly."

Marguerite needed no inducing. She had resolved that she would remain in the vale no longer, if she could get away ; and the Abbey of Saint Aubin was the only place to which she thought of fleeing. So the arrangements were quickly made ; and within an hour after they had entered the cot, Conrad and Francisco went out to prepare the horses. When they were ready to set forth, the prisoner was brought out, and his bonds taken off ; and then the hermit asked him whither he intended to go.

"Can I have my horse?" the man asked.

"Certainly."

"Then I shall make the best of my way into Normandy. I have friends there."

"Do you mean to leave the prince?"

"Aye, I might as well take my own life, as to return to the prince with the answer I should be forced to carry."

Francisco believed that the fellow spoke the truth, and he was suffered to depart.

After this the old man and his pupil went out to the scene of the conflict, and dragged the five dead bodies down to the river, and then returned and assisted Marguerite to her saddle. They had little property of value to leave behind them, and as little to burden themselves with on their journey.

"Alas !" said the good woman, as they rode forth from the vale, "I fear that we shall never see this quiet retreat again ; and something whispers to me that our period of repose is at an end."

"Courage, Marguerite. The good abbot can give us shelter for the present ; and, if the need shall come, we can leave Brittany."

"You heard what Conrad said touching the duke's questions?"

"Yes."

Marguerite looked to see that the youth was beyond hearing, and then she proceeded.

"It is possible that Casimir already suspects."

"How can he suspect?"

"Is not the boy's face a tell tale? Look at him and

remember how the duke met him—met him flushed with the pride of victory and with the fire of the warrior in his eye. Remember—the duke knew his father—"

"Aye," said Francisco, thoughtfully; "the duke was one of his father's nearest friends."

"Certainly," responded Marguerite; "and I think the duke hath eyes. Think of it."

"You may be right, my sister," returned Francisco. "It may be that Casimir has some inkling of the truth."

"And if he has an inkling, may not others have the same? I tell thee, Francisco, we must flee from Brittany. Remember our promise."

"I do not forget it."

"You cannot forget it."

At this point in the conversation the road became wider, and Conrad fell back to Francisco's side, shortly after which the pace was increased to a gallop.

At midnight they reached Montfort, but made no stop. At a short distance beyond Montfort Conrad discovered that his horse began to grow lame. He stopped and examined the animal's feet; but could find no outward sign of trouble. An hour passed, and the lameness was too palpable to be mistaken. The right fore foot seemed to be weak, as though the ankle were sprained.

"I am sorry for the poor horse," said our hero, as Marguerite began to worry; "but I think he will carry me safely to Rennes."

"He is very lame," returned the dame, with much concern. She regarded accidents, in the pursuit of important purposes, as sure precursers of evil, and on the present occasion she was very anxious.

"We have not much further to go, good mother—not

more than two leagues, at the outside. The beast will carry me through."

They were at the top of a hill, and when about half way down, the horse stumbled, and came nigh pitching upon his knees. Conrad drew the rein with a jerk, and, without thinking, gave a vigorous plunge with the spur. The beast leaped up, and dashed down the hill at the top of his speed. It was a rocky, uneven place; and when the horse next stumbled, which he did while under full headway, he went over upon his shoulder, throwing his rider off among the rocks by the roadside. Francisco hurried to the spot, where he found the horse dead, and Conrad insensible. The beast's neck was broken; and at first the fear fell like a thunderbolt upon the old man that his pupil was lost to him forever.

Marguerite was soon upon her knees by the side of the fallen youth; and as she raised his head upon her lap, she discovered that blood was running down his face. A cry of alarm escaped her.

"Merciful Heaven! is this to be the last of the house!"

The agony of the woman caused Francisco to be more cool; and he suggested that they should find out as quickly as possible the nature of the injuries which their charge had received.

There was one wound upon the side of the head, from which the blood was flowing freely; but they could find no other hurt. This was bound up with a napkin and a scarf; and shortly afterwards Conrad opened his eyes, and spoke; but not with reason. He seemed to fancy that he was in the hands of Goliath and Baptiste, and he called the name of Rosaline. A little while he ran on thus, and then became again unconscious.

"We must take him to the nearest inn," said Marguerite.

" We will take him to the Castle of Rennes," returned
Francisco.

" But—the duke—"

" Stop, good Marguerite. If the boy is to be long
prostrated, he must be where his enemies cannot trouble
him. If we take him to an inn, or to the cot of a peasant, the followers of the prince may find him ; but if we
take him to the castle, no danger from that source can
reach him."

Marguerite saw and understood the force of her companion's reasoning, and she was content to admit that
the plan was proper.

So they placed Conrad upon the back of a horse, in
as easy a position as possible, while Francisco walked
by his side, carefully guarding against further accident.

------◆------

CHAPTER XII.

NEED OF COURAGE.

When the Duke of Rennes was informed that Conrad
du Nord had been brought to the court of the castle,
wounded and insensible, he made as much haste to have
the youth attended to as he would have made had the
king been brought to his gates in like condition. It
was early in the morning ; but most of the inmates of
the castle were stirring ; and the youth was borne to a
well-appointed chamber, where a physician belonging
to the household was soon in attendance. Marguerite
would not leave her charge until she knew the worst ;
so she remained by the bed, and helped the leech. The
blood was washed from the head and face ; and it was

finally decided that the only serious injury was the wound already attended to. There were several bruises upon the back and left shoulder ; but of a light character. After this conclusion had been arrived at, restoratives were applied, and at length the patient opened his eyes.

The physician apprehended no great danger. He thought the youth would soon recover ; but, for the present, to avoid fever, he recommended that as few should remain in the room as possible. So all went out save the doctor and Marguerite, some of the servants waiting near at hand to answer in case their services should be required.

The duke called Francisco to his own apartment, where he asked for an explanation of what he had seen. The old man commenced at the beginning, telling of the coming of the six men-at-arms to the cot ; of the arrest of himself and Marguerite ; of the timely arrival of Conrad ; and of the battle, and its results, closing with an account of the accident by the road-side.

During the recital the duke watched the narrator very narrowly, seeming to study every change of his countenance.

"I think you were wise in leaving the cot," he said; "and it is fortunate that you have reached my castle. Had you been forced to seek shelter for the youth at any other place, there would have been danger. The truth is, my good sir, the prince is carrying a high, bold hand in Brittany. He is not only powerful with his own immediate followers, but he is gradually bending the retainers of the king to his purposes."

"I know that such is the case, my lord," returned Francisco, with a sad shake of the head ; "and I only wonder that the king does not interpose his royal hand."

"Ah, Theobald is old."

"Not so old as I am by more than five years," cried the hermit; "and my arm is as strong, my eye as piercing, and my head as clear as when I served—"

"Served where?" asked the duke, as the old man hesitated.

"In the army, my lord."

"What army?"

"I know of but one army."

"But there are many departments to that army, my good Francisco. I think you served in the household of the Duke Charles."

"Yes, my lord."

The old man seemed troubled as he replied, but Casimir passed lightly on, and relieved him from his disquietude.

"I can easily see how you have retained your faculties, father;—I can see that you have lived a life of sobriety and temperance, and that your passions have been kept under control; but it has not been so with the king. He never was a strong man. His brother Charles would have made a better king."

"Much better," responded Francisco, reverentially.

"As it is," pursued the duke, "we must make the best of it. The prince has power, and for the present our young friend must be kept out of his way. I am glad Conrad is here. He has rendered me a most important service, and I cannot do too much for him. I trust this present injury may not prove serious."

Francisco hoped so, with all his heart.

"You were going to Saint Aubin, I think you said?" remarked Casimir.

"Yes, my lord. The abbot is a friend of mine."

"Very well—this accident need not prevent you from pursuing your journey, if you are desirous of doing so."

"I am very desirous. I wish to see Dagobert."

At this juncture a servant came and announced that breakfast was ready, and the duke invited the old man to go down with him.

After breakfast the physician pronounced his patient out of danger ; and before noon the youth was in perfect possession of his senses.

The lady Rosaline had been very anxious—so anxious that she had not dared to question her father—and when she heard the report of the physician she became bright and hopeful. At length she contrived to obtain an interview with Marguerite, from whom she gained the same story which Francisco had told to the duke ; and when she had heard it, Conrad stood higher, if possible, in her esteem, than before.

On the following morning the physician announced that his patient was not entirely out of danger, but that, with care, he would soon be well again. Francisco and Marguerite were consulting upon the course they had better pursue. The dame was very anxious to see the old abbot, and it was rather necessary that her companion should accompany her. The duke overheard them, and took the liberty to join them.

"If it is your wish to proceed to Saint Aubin," he said, "you need not wait here on Conrad's account. I will be responsible for his safe-keeping. He shall have the best of nursing, and in every respect he shall find himself at home."

"It is important that we should see the abbot," returned Francisco ; "and if the boy can be cared for without us, I think we had better go."

"It is not far from here ?" said Marguerite, interrogatively.

"Not over eight leagues," replied the duke. "You may easily take dinner at the abbey."

The good dame reflected awhile, and finally concluded that she would go. As her decision was all that was waited for, there was no further question ; and preparations were at once made. Marguerite went in to see Conrad ; and when she had told him where she was going, she assured him that she should not remain long away from him.

"I might do my business with the abbot, and return in a day or two," she said ; "but there is no need of such an arrangement. It is better that you should come to us at Saint Aubin as soon as you are able. Will you do so ?"

Conrad promised that he would.

"Then," pursued the dame, "I shall try and rest easy. I am sure that the duke will take good care of you while you are here ; and he will also see you safely to the abbey."

"You may rest assured upon these two points," spoke a voice from the other side of the room. It was the duke who had entered. He had not seen the youth since the previous evening, and he had come to inquire, personally, after the patient's health, and also to offer the hospitality of the castle. He sat down by the bedside, and while he conversed with Conrad he scanned those features carefully over again. He was thoughtful not to weary the invalid with too much conversation, and when he had said what he had to say, he arose and withdrew. In the hall he met Francisco.

The horses were ready caparisoned in the court, and the old hermit was in a hurry to depart. When he saw the duke coming, he acted as though he would avoid him ; but the thing was not possible. Casimir hailed him, and asked him to follow him to his library.

"I wish to speak with you a moment, good Francisco."

The old man bowed his head, and followed, but with a seemingly reluctant step. He felt sure that he was to be questioned upon some topic of which he would rather not speak. When they had reached the library the duke closed the door, and motioned his guest to a seat.

"Francisco," Casimir commenced, in an earnest, direct manner, "I have called you hither to ask you a few questions upon a very important matter; and I hope you will find it in your pleasure to answer me."

"Allow me to hope, my lord, that you will ask nothing which I cannot answer," replied Francisco.

"We shall see. In the first place, however, let me assure you that I will ask nothing which there can be any harm in answering."

"Of which, my lord, you must allow me to be the judge."

"Certainly. And now, to commence: I speak of Conrad. He has been brought up from infancy by Marguerite, and you have been his tutor?"

"Yes."

"But you are not his father?"

"No."

"Is Marguerite his mother?"

"Ah, my lord,—you are forcing me to hesitate."

"Not at all, good Francisco. Your answer already given is sufficient. Marguerite is not his mother."

"My lord," plead the old man, with a look of earnest, prayerful appeal, "do not question me further. I am bound by an oath. Have mercy."

"You need not break your oath, Francisco, for you can give me some satisfaction without doing so. I know that Conrad is not the son of Marguerite; I know that he is not the son of any living parent; and I furthermore know that both you and she were once in the service—"

"My lord, you must not approach me thus. You might as well put questions direct, as drive me into unanswerable corners."

"Another answer," said the duke, with a smile. "I tell you my trusty friend, to me the whole story is written on the youth's face."

Francisco gave a start, but made no reply.

"Now," pursued Casimir, after a short pause, "I must put a question direct. Why was the life of that child concealed, and the falsehood of his death published?"

The old man steadied himself, with his hands upon his knees, and gazed down upon the floor.

"You may answer me the question, Francisco."

"I will answer it, my lord ; but you must look to see your next question treated in a different manner. The child was hidden away to save its life?"

"How ? To save its life?"

"Yes."

"Surely, it's life was not threatened."

"I can tell you nothing of that. All I can say is, its mother feared for it. What she may have seen in the future I cannot say."

"It is enough," said Casimir, rising from his seat, and starting across the room. "The mother may have been wise. At all events she acted after the promptings of her own heart ; and I think her love for the child led her to do as she did. Dagobert knows of this ?"

"Yes, my lord."

"Thank you, Francisco. I will detain you no longer."

"But, my lord duke—I must ask you to be—"

"Pooh ! Have no fear on my account. I tell you,

the boy has not a better friend on earth than I will prove myself."

There was something in the duke's manner which Francisco did not like ; but he had no opportunity to offer further remonstrance ; for Casimir had opened the door, and passed out into the hall.

The horses were ready in the court, and a dozen of the duke's men-at-arms had been detailed to accompany the travelers on their way. Marguerite was waiting ; and now that she was ready for the start, she was anxious to be on the way. The old hermit attempted twice to speak with his host upon the subject of the secret of which they had been conversing ; but he did not gain the opportunity.

"Have no fear, good Francisco," said the duke, after the old man had gained his saddle. "All is safe with me. The boy could not be in better hands."

"I must trust you, my lord; and I shall try to put away all uneasiness. You have a sacred charge.; for you have promised to be a friend to him who has been indeed a friend to you."

A final word of parting was spoken, and Francisco and Marguerite rode out from the court, accompanied by the friendly guard which their host had seen fit to give them. Casimir watched them until they had passed beyond the walls, and then he returned to his library, where he spent a full hour in deep thought, sometimes sitting, sometimes standing, sometimes walking to and fro, and all the while talking with himself.

"Let things take their own course," he finally said, sinking into a chair and gazing into the vacancy before him. "Thus far I have had no hand in the mysterious workings ; and I will stand aloof and see what the result shall be."

He still gazed into the vacant space, as though his imagination were drawing pictures there, and framing marvelous structures for some future time.

Conrad improved wonderfully. The wound upon the head was not at all serious, and the perfect freedom of his system from all impurity gave him safe conduct from fever. At the end of the second day he was allowed to dress himself; and on the morning of the third day the physician permitted him to walk in the garden.

"Whither now, my child?" asked the duke, as he met Rosaline in the hall.

She trembled, and cast her eyes upon the pavement.

"You do not answer me," pursued Casimir; but his tone was low and kind.

"Dear father," the maiden at length replied, "I trust that I am doing nothing wrong. Conrad is in the garden. I have not seen him, to inquire after his health, since his mother went away."

"And you are now on your way to offer him your greetings?"

"Yes—if you do not forbid it."

"No, no, my child; I have no disposition to lay such an injunction upon you. We owe the youth too much. Your life and your sacred honor he hath saved to us. I do not fear to trust him; and surely I should have no fears of trusting you. Go to him; and if your presence can cheer him, he may the sooner recover."

Rosaline sped away, and found Conrad walking beneath the shadowy arms of the great chestnut trees. She stopped when she came near unto him; but he, seeing her smile of greeting, quickly advanced to meet her. He was too glad to see her—too happy in the bright presence—to hesitate; and she, when the rich

voice of her brave preserver sounded again upon her
ear, put away all false reserve, and met him as a sister
might have met a brother.

As brother and sister they conversed during the
bright hours of that forenoon. On the following day,
however, somewhat of the brotherly and sisterly freedom was lacking. And on the day following that, they
seemed to have lost all their lightness and joy.

It was towards the close of a warm, beautiful day,
and the lengthening shadows were gratefully cooling
the verdant spots where the rays of the sun had been
pouring down with unwonted heat. Conrad and Rosaline were sitting in the chestnut grove, both silent and
thoughtful.

"You are not able to go yet," said the maiden, in
answer to a remark which her companion had made
some time before.

"I am better able to go than I am to stay." He
gazed into her beautiful face a few moments, and then
he added : "I am not used to falsehood, nor to deception of any kind. I will speak the truth, trusting that
it will not offend you. Were I of gentle blood—were I
of a family that held rank somewhere near your own—
I would stay in Rennes yet awhile longer." He would
have turned away and concealed his face, for he knew
that his lips quivered, and that his eye was tearful ; but
the immediate answer of his companion prevented.

"Conrad," she said, with noble frankness, at the same
time laying her hand upon his arm, "I am no more
used to deception than are you. I have no right to bid
you remain, if you have made up your mind to leave
us ; but there is one who has that right."

"Rosaline——"

"My father has that right."

The blood mounted to the youth's temples, and his whole frame trembled.

" Your father ?" he repeated.

" My father !" she answered, in tones of strange melody.

" In mercy's name, do not misunderstand me, lady !"

" I am sure that I do not."

" But—if your father should bid me stay ?"

" I should be happy."

" Rosaline !—O, this is too bright ! Should I stay longer here, I could never leave, but—"

The fair girl looked up into his face, and whispered : " Speak on."

" I could never leave, but with the prize my heart would win ! Do not blame me for speaking thus."

" Courage, Conrad. I know your heart, for I am not blind. Your arm failed not before the prince ; and you need not tremble before the duke." She placed her hand upon his open palm, and as he closed his grasp upon the precious offering, he knew that the love of the noble girl was his.

But he dared to say no more. It was but a promise from Rosaline that she would wait for her father's decision He must see the duke ere the prize could be secured.

Courage {

So whispered Conrad to himself ; and yet he trembled with more than mortal fear. He could have met a score of Brittany's bravest warriors in battle array with more hopeful courage than came to sustain him as he approached the proud duke with that momentous question upon his trembling lips.

CHAPTER XIII.

THE DUKE SPEAKS PLAINLY.

It was late in the evening when the duke retired to
his library, and thither Conrad followed him. Casimir
greeted his young guest cordially, and pointed him to a
seat. The host was calm and patient, while the visitor
was nervous and uneasy. When our hero found himself seated in the presence of the Lord of Rennes, with
that strange business upon his hands, he would have
given much to have been lifted by some kind power
from the chamber, and set down in the court, where the
fresh air might have fanned his flushed brow. What
hope had he of success? What hope had he that his
petition would be received even respectfully? What
right had he, a poor mountaineer, nameless and home-
less, to lift his eyes to the lady of Rennes? What right
had he to approach her with love? The more he
thought of it, the more perplexed did he become ; and
the longer he sat there, the more apparent became his
trouble.

The duke saw very plainly that the young man
needed help, and he kindly offered relief.

"My dear Conrad, you have something to say to me."

The young man started, as if from a troublous dream.

"Surely, you should not hesitate to trust me. I owe
you too much."

" No, no, my lord ; you do not owe me that which can warrant the liberty I have thought of taking."

"You will allow me to be the judge."

The duke smiled as he spoke, and Conrad felt more courage.

" I know, my lord, that I have no right to approach you as I have thought to do ; but I throw myself upon your mercy. I do not claim that the service I have rendered entitles me to much consideration ; and yet I must plead that service in extenuation of the liberty I am about to take. If you turn me away with a refusal, which you have a perfect right to do, you will, in consideration of said service, pardon me at the same time."

" My brave boy," said Casimir, with warm frankness, "you are pardoned beforehand. Now speak."

Conrad had need of all his strength, and before he opened his lips with speech, he sought to control his scattering senses.

" My lord duke," he commenced, in a low, breathless tone, but gaining strength as he proceeded, "circumstances over which I had no control brought me into companionship with your daughter ; and I think I may say that the circumstance of my service to her was also independent of my own will. Yet I saved her from a terrible fate ; and, as was natural, she leaned upon me for support. What could I do ? I gazed into her soft, bright eyes, and listened to the sweet music of her voice. I felt my heart throb, and my blood warm with strange emotion. Pardon me if I speak plainly. I felt this, and I knew that it was love. My reason told me that such love would be hopeless, and I determined to stifle it. I came with the lady to your castle ; and I went away without daring to lift my hopes to the object upon which my heart had fixed its first strong love. I went away, thinking that I might see Rosaline again, and yet

half resolved that I would not. Once more blind circumstance brought me hither, and once more I found
myself in her company. And, sir—believe if you can—
the secret of my love was dragged forth without any
direct intent on my part. But the story was told—the
lady knew that I loved her ; and the blessed belief was
given me that my love was returned. Now, sir, you
know all. You can speak the word which shall send
me away with the dawn of another day, or——"

"Or I can bid you stay at the castle awhile longer,
you would say ?"

" Yes, my lord."

The duke did not seem at all surprised at what he had
heard. He listened as he would have listened to the
details of an ordinary business transaction.

"Conrad," he said, "you have been frank, and I will
be the same. I do not now tell you that you may hope
for the hand of my daughter ; nor do I refuse. I must
have time for the answer ; and during that time there
may be much to be accomplished. In the first place, I
could never consent to bestow my child upon one without name or station."

Conrad's countenance fell, and his lip trembled.

" Then, sir," he said, " the answer is already given."

" Not so, my boy. Give me your attention a few
moments, and assist me to discuss a very important
matter. Marguerite is not your mother."

Our hero was all attention in a moment.

" I have conversed with Francisco, and of so much I
have assured myself. But I could learn no more from
his lips. He is under an oath to keep his secret."

" To keep the secret of my parentage ?" cried Conrad,
starting up from his chair.

" Easy, my boy. Sit down, and listen to me. You

must not blame Francisco. You have more occasion to
bless him."

"Aye—so I have," murmured the youth, sinking back
into his seat. "But why, if they have known my
parentage, should they have kept the secret from me?"

"That," replied the duke, with a smile, "is more than
we can determine; for neither Francisco nor Marguerite is here to answer. We must confine ourselves
to that which is within our reach. You have already
placed yourself in a position of anxiety; and if I add
thereto, it is because I hope the end may be a pleasant
one. I can tell you what I know—or, at least what I
have the best reason for believing. Your parents both
died when you were an infant. Your father was slain
in battle, and your mother lived not long after she
learned of his death. Now it may be that your father
was of gentle blood. I think it more than probable;
and if such should prove to have been the case, and
your identity can be established, I should not hesitate
to bestow upon you the hand of my child."

Conrad gazed upon his host in speechless suspense.
He had never before thought of such a parentage, and
yet the prospect did not strike him with much surprise.
It seemed as though the words of the duke had
awakened a slumbering instinct of nobility in his soul,
which, with its first dawn of life, overleaped the barrier
of impossibility.

"Tell me, my boy; suppose I could establish the
fact that your parents were both of noble blood, would
you openly claim the station thus offered?"

"Do you ask me such a question, my lord?" The
flash of the eye; the compression of the finely curved
lips; the mantling flush upon the broad, full brow, and
the swelling of the deep chest, were more emphatic than
were his words.

" You would claim your station, Conrad ?"

" Aye, sir." The thought thus engendered within him gave a new tone to his handsome face. " If such blood flows in my veins, I owe it to the memory of my parents that I should have place in Brittany. Good mercy ! what a field is opened before me. What shall the end be !"

" I trust that it will be well. At all events, my boy, it cannot be worse than it is."

" Ah, my lord, you forget that the pain of the fall is according to the height attained."

" Upon my soul, Conrad, I do not think there is danger of a fall. If I had thought so, I should not have led you thus far. I have no disposition to trifle with such feelings as yours."

" My lord duke, you must have learned something concerning my parentage."

" What I have told you."

" But have you learned nothing more ?"

Casimir saw the young man's drift.

" You must not question me too closely, Conrad ; for I do not wish to lead you beyond what is substantial. I have not learned from Francisco the names of your parents ; and if I have a suspicion, it is one which I had better not speak at present."

" Let me seek Francisco and Marguerite at once," said our hero.

" Not yet," replied the duke. " If you will leave the matter in my hands, I will sift it to the bottom ; and I make no hesitation in assuring you that the truth cannot be kept from me. I know where to look, and I know whom to question. In fact, I have a good clue to the whole labyrinth. Will you leave it with me ?"

" Of course, sir, I cannot refuse."

" Certainly you cannot. And now, let me answer

your first question ; or, rather, let me make an addition to the answer I have already given you. I have told you that I neither consented nor refused. And—"

" There is no need," interrupted Conrad, " I know what you would say. If it is proved that I am of gentle blood, and my identity can be established, I may sue for Rosaline's hand. But if—"

" Stop, my boy ; you have gone far enough. If your nobility by birth is proved, you may ask Rosaline to be your wife. If your name must remain forever as it is— if we gain nothing in our search—you must not sue for my child's hand without my permission. Let it rest there."

" It shall be so, my lord."

Conrad arose, and moved towards the door ; but his step was reluctant ; and finally he stopped and turned.

" My lord, you must allow me to ask you one more question. When will you commence your investigation ?"

" As soon as possible, my son. I shall make my arrangements to-morrow."

With this our hero bowed and withdrew.

" By heavens !" cried the duke, when he was alone, " I cannot be mistaken in this. Pshaw ! is it not as plain as the sun at noonday ! If my cousin were back upon the earth, and should present me the boy as his son, my convictions could not be stronger ! I can solve the problem, and I will do it."

In the meantime Conrad repaired to his own apartment, where he spent a full hour in perplexing study and reflection ; and even after he pressed his pillow, sleep was for a long time kept at bay by the wonderful fancies that haunted his imagination.

The following morning was the sixth since the departure of Francisco and Marguerite, and when Conrad arose, and descended to the court, he felt as strong and well as he ever felt in his life. In a little while the duke joined him, with a greeting such as a father might have given to a son.

" My dear boy, you are looking as well as ever."

" Aye, my lord ; and I feel as well."

" I am going to Saint Aubin to-morrow."

" To see Francisco and Marguerite ?" said Conrad, with sudden interest.

" Not exactly. I shall probably see them ; but my especial business is to see the old abbot. You can go with me, or you can remain here."

" I shall do just as you wish, my lord."

" Then we will decide during the day. Something may transpire to assist us in our determination."

And something did transpire, though not such a thing as the duke had counted upon.

Towards noon Conrad met Rosaline in the garden. She gave him her hand with a smile, and he raised it to his lips. She spoke first of the conference which he had held with her father.

" And does the thought please you, Rosaline ?" he asked, still holding her hand, and gazing down into her face.

" O, how can it be otherwise ?" she replied, in earnest, tender tones.

" But, dearest, we must not hope too much. Has your father told you all ?"

" I think he has."

" Then you know that my fate hangs upon a brittle thread. Last night the star of promise shone brightly; but at times, since then, it has beamed more dimly. You know that I love you—that I hold you precious above all other earthly things. And I believe that your heart—"

"Is all your own," said the beautiful girl, resting her head upon his shoulder.

"And yet," cried Conrad, winding his arm about her, and pressing her to his bosom, "our fate hangs upon something in the future which is fearfully uncertain. Though I clasp you now to my throbbing bosom, and tell you of my love, the time may not be far distant when such will not be my right—when the blessed privilege will be denied to me."

"No, no,—O, no!" cried Rosaline, starting from his shoulder, and gazing again into his face. "That cannot be. My father will not be cruel. He hopes that he may find in you the son of a noble house. But if— if—"

"If he does not find that," interrupted Conrad, "he will turn from me, and lead you away with him."

"No, no, Conrad—I do not think so. O, I know he will not do that. If such had been his intention he would not have allowed us to cherish such hopes as he knows must now fill our souls. If he even finds that you have an honorable name—"

"An *honorable* name!" repeated Conrad.

"Yes—if he finds no more than that, he will surely allow us to live and love."

Conrad started as though an asp had stung him; and his thoughts found words before he was aware what he said.

"And if he finds it otherwise? Why was my name hidden? Why was my birth thrown into the gloom? Why did my mother send me away, and bind my guardian by an oath to keep the thing a secret forever? Heavens! What if there should be found a stain upon the name I am entitled to bear! What if my mother hid me away from the world in mercy! What if—"

"Hush!" cried Rosaline, clinging to his arm, and

trembling like an aspen. "Do not think of such things."

"How can I help thinking of them ? O, Rosaline, in this hour, when I realize how much of joy and promise depends upon the result of the coming investigation, and how much of mortal woe may follow thereafter, my fear finds an enemy in every corner, and I almost shrink from the ordeal."

"Do you shrink when you think what may be gained ?"

"No, loved one ; 'tis when I think what I may lose !"

"My heart's best love you already have," said the maiden, reaching her arm about his neck; "and no power on earth can take it from you. I know you only as the Conrad who saved me from ruin ; and in the time to come I will know you only as the brave man whom I fondly and truly love. Let come what will, my heart cannot be turned from you."

"Blessed one !"

They were startled by the clatter of horses' hoofs upon the bridge, and shortly afterwards they saw a troop of armed men ride into the court.

"Who can they be ?" queried our hero. "I think I have never seen those uniforms before."

"I know them," replied Rosaline. "They are of the royal guards."

"Are they the king's troops ?"

"Yes—members of his own guard. And they must have come lately from Vannes."

"They must be upon some important mission," suggested our hero.

Rosaline had no doubt of it.

"For," pursued the mountaineer, "the royal guard do not go abroad except on business for the king."

"I think it is so. Ah—see. My father goes forth to meet them. We shall soon know what they want."

Something like a shudder passed through Conrad's frame ; for, with the coming of the royal guard came, to him, a presentiment of evil !

CHAPTER XIV.

SIR PHILIP DE SAVENAY.

The duke had been informed of the approach of the coming troop, and he reached the court in season to welcome the leader as was befitting one in his station.

Sir Philip de Savenay was the leader in question, and he was followed by twenty stout guardsmen, all well armed and mounted. Sir Philip was an old soldier, whose gray hair and grizzled moustache showed the bleaching of time and exposure ; and, as captain of the Royal Guard, he was the most important military officer in the kingdom. He possessed a powerful frame, and his sword was one of the best in Brittany.

"My good Sir Philip," said the duke, as the captain dismounted, "you visit me with a gallant array of the royal force."

"Yes," replied de Savenay, with a smile ; "the king likes that his captain should have good company."

"Do you go beyond Rennes ?"

"I cannot tell, my lord. I am on business for the king, and I must travel until I find that of which I am in search."

"And you have stopped here to rest. Good, my dear

Sir Philip. The dinner hour is close at hand, and you and your men are most welcome."

"Not entirely for rest have we stopped at your castle, my lord," said Sir Philip, with a slight show of uneasiness. "The fact is, I have been sent to arrest a man whom the king desires much to see."

"Ah,—and did you think to find him here?"

"I was directed to inquire here, my lord."

"Who is the man thus noticed by his majesty?"

"He is named Conrad—by some called Conrad du Nord."

The duke changed color, and his fingers worked nervously in the folds of his doublet.

"Are you sent to arrest this man as a prisoner?"

"Yes."

"By order of the king?"

"Yes. I received the order from the king's own mouth."

"Do you know why he is arrested?"

"By my life, I think there is reason enough if one half the complaints against him are true."

"Who has made these complaints?"

"Prince Bertrand."

"Upon my soul," cried Casimir, with extreme bitterness, "the prince is an oracle. Of course he is not to be disbelieved."

"You will remember, my lord duke," said de Savenay, proudly, "that I come not from the prince. I do not serve him."

"Pardon me, Sir Philip. In expressing my opinion of the son of our unfortunate king, I meant no reflection upon the character of your present service. Conrad du Nord is my friend, and he is even now—— Ah—here he is, within sound of our voices."

The young man would have drawn near ; but the duke motioned for him to remain where he was.

"By Saint Michael !" exclaimed de Savenay, after he had viewed our hero, "he is a most proper appearing youth. He does not look like a cutthroat."

"Like a cutthroat, de Savenay ? What mean you ?"

" I think the prince accuses him of some foul butcheries. It is said that he killed Goliath, and Baptiste, and Adolphe."

" So he did," returned the duke.

" That could not have been done in any fair manner."

" It was done fairly, Sir Philip. And, furthermore, I am able to inform you that Conrad was the party attacked. You look astonished. So I was astonished when I first heard the story ; but when I came to know the youth, my astonishment was changed to admiration. I saw him disarm my captain with perfect ease."

" Did he disarm Nicolas ?"

" Yes, readily."

" I am filled with wonder, my lord. The story of such exploits must be interesting."

" After dinner, Sir Philip, you shall hear it."

" Pardon me, my lord duke. My orders are explicit, and I must obey them. I must arrest the young man."

" You would not arrest him against my will ?"

De Savenay started and looked into the duke's face.

" Surely, my lord, you would not oppose the royal order."

" Not exactly, Sir Philip. I have a better plan for all concerned. I will accompany you to Vannes, and Conrad du Nord shall go with me. I will myself present him to the king."

De Savenay reflected a few moments, and then replied :

"If such is your decision, made upon your own responsibility, I have nothing further to say."

"Such is my decision; and I take the responsibility."

"And now, my lord duke, there is one thing more: There are two old people—a man and a woman—who have lived with this youth——"

"Were you ordered to arrest them?"

"Not exactly to arrest them; but I was ordered to find out where they were."

"Did the king so order?"

"No," replied the captain, biting his moustache. "The prince gave me that bit of duty."

"Let me advise you, my dear Sir Philip, to give the prince's orders the go-by. He has nothing to do with the captain of the royal guard."

"But," said de Savenay, with a dubious shrug of his shoulders, "ere long the prince will be king; the royal guard will be his guard; and he will then have the power to punish——"

"Hold, Sir Philip!" cried the duke, striking his clenched hand upon his bosom. "You forget the blood that runs in the veins of our nobles. When Bertrand is king, he will conduct himself as becomes a king, or his crown may tumble from his head? By the eternal throne of heaven! if he——"

"My lord——"

"Don't interrupt me, Sir Philip. I know what I say, and I am responsible for it. And, furthermore, the time may not be far distant when I will speak these very words to Bertrand himself. Do you think the King of Brittany would dare to make war upon the Duke of Rennes? I swear to you, the deed would break the sceptre and shatter the throne to atoms? My cousin of Anjou would like to see some such work."

De Savenay bent his head, and scraped the pavement with his foot.

"My lord," he finally said, in a careful tone, "you can speak your thoughts, for one third of the realm is under your command; but I must be more circumspect. The prince gave me no direct order. He simply bade me, if I found the old people of whom we have spoken, to——"

"To what, Sir Philip? You need not hesitate to speak plainly before me."

"To send some of my men with them to the castle of Montevere."

The duke bit his lips and shook his head.

"Francisco and Marguerite are not here; nor are they near here. When the king wants them I will give them up. Is that satisfactory?"

"If the old people are not with Master Conrad," replied de Savenay, "I shall not trouble myself to find them, as I have no orders from the king concerning them; but touching the youth——"

"I will present him to the king myself," said the duke. "And now let us adjourn to the castle, where we can rest while we talk."

The old knight was conducted to a comfortable apartment, where some rare old wine was placed at his disposal; while his followers were taken care of in the quarters of the castle guard. After this the duke sought Conrad, whom he found in the great hall.

The young man had heard most of the conversation between Sir Philip and his host, so there was nothing to be explained to him concerning the captain's business.

"Of course," he said, "the prince has lodged a complaint against me, and the king wishes to examine into the matter for himself."

" I am not very sure that such was the plan," returned
Casimir, shaking his head. " The prince entered a
complaint, and the king sent to have you arrested ; but
I doubt if it was intended that the king should hear
your defence. It would be a very easy matter for Bertrand to take possession of you as soon as you were
delivered up by the captain. But, my dear boy, the
villain shall be circumvented. I will deliver you up
with my own hands ; and I will retain you in custody."

" I see," said Conrad, bowing his head as he reflected.
" If I could have been taken to Vannes by Sir Philip, I
should have been thrown into prison, and thus fallen
directly into the prince's power."

" Exactly."

" But you can keep me from prison ?"

" Yes. I shall become responsible to the king for
your safe keeping ; and I may keep you where I please
so that I am able to produce you when he calls. Of
course, the prince will be enraged, and he will employ
every means in his power to get his hands upon you ;
and we shall have to be very careful, and keep a constant guard ; but of all this we can converse after we
get there. And now come with me and see the captain.
He is a good man, and you will lose nothing by gaining
his friendship."

They entered the apartment where Sir Philip sat,
and the duke introduced his youthful friend to the old
soldier. Conrad, when he came near to the stern-vis-
aged man, and gained a full view of the battle-scarred
face, conceived a deep reverence for him. He loved
that kind of men, for of such was his old tutor ; and he
believed that such men were inclined to be true and
honest. De Savenay must have read the youth's
thoughts, for he smiled, and the grasp of his hand was
warm and friendly.

" Sir Philip," said the duke, after they had seated themselves, " you are a knight, and you wear the cross of Saint Maurice ; and as a soldier you are my equal in rank and privilege. Holding you in this light, I am about to tell you a story which I meant to tell only to the king ; and when you have heard it you will know why I choose to go with you to Vannes."

And thereupon Casimir related to the captain all the circumstances connected with the abduction of Rosaline, and her subsequent rescue by Conrad. He told it all just as it had happened, plainly setting forth all the villainy of the prince, and generously recounting the brave and brilliant deeds of the young mountaineer.

" And now, my good Sir Philip, what think you ?"

Sir Philip did not at first know what to think. He was not much astonished at the bold wickedness of Bertrand ; but the deeds of Conrad filled him with wonder.

" Do you blame me that I hesitated at first to deliver this young man up as you at first demanded ?" asked the duke.

" By my faith, no," cried the old captain, smiting his fist upon his thigh. " I swear to you, by the cross I wear, I would not take him to Vannes without you !"

" Right, my good Sir Philip," echoed Casimir. " I shall not only go with him to Vannes, but I will care for him after he is there. If the prince thinks to gain anything by this movement, he is mistaken."

" But," said de Savenay turning to Conrad, " I do not understand how you have contrived to make such proficiency in the use of arms."

" In the first place, Sir Philip," replied our hero, modestly, " I have had one of the best tutors that the country could afford. I have loved the exercise ; and I have followed it up in practice without tiring. And, furthermore, Heaven has blessed me with a goodly share of strength and——"

"And true courage," added de Savenay, as the speaker hesitated. "But I should have thought that your old tutor would have grown tired of the exercise, if you did not."

"No, sir. He was a man of your own stamp. He loved the play, and his arm knew no weariness."

"Aye," interrupted the duke; "and I'll wager my best lance that you remember him well, Sir Philip. His name is Francisco."

"I remember one of that name," said the captain; "and he was my friend. We fought side by side in the battle where Duke Charles was slain. I can call to mind no other."

"There would be no need of it if you could," replied the duke, smiling. "Conrad's tutor was in the service of Charles, and was, for some years, his chosen henchman."

"And is this the old man I was instructed to convey to the Castle of Montevere?"

"The very same."

"Then, by my knighthood! let the prince beware!" Sir Philip started to his feet, and smote his hands together. "I tell you, my lord duke, I am with you, heart and soul. Be it mine to help you in the protection of those who may need our services!"

He extended his hand, and Casimir grasped it quickly and warmly.

"My dear Sir Philip, I accept the pledge; and in return I give you my assurance that I will stand by you if you are brought to trouble. But I do not apprehend any trouble. I think I shall very easily bring the king to the work of justice, so far, at least, as our friends are concerned."

Dinner was announced, and when the meal had béen eaten, the duke commenced to make preparations for his departure. Conrad was forced to accept a suit of clothes such as a gentleman might wear at court. The small clothes were of tan-colored silk ; the rest of scarlet, faced with white ; with a doublet of fine blue velvet trimmed with silver. His cap was of the same material as his doublet, looped upon the left side with a gold button, and bearing an ostrich feather. His heavy leathern belt was replaced by a scarf of silk and silver webbing, to which his trusty sword was suspended. In this guise he presented himself in the hall, and when Sir Philip saw him, he started as though he had met a long lost friend.

" Mercy !" he cried.

" What is it ?" asked the duke, drawing the captain away to the door.

" Have you marked that man's face, my lord ?"

" Surely I have. He has been here several days."

" But—see—"

" Hush ! There is no need of attracting his attention."

" But," pursued de Savenoy, in a lower tone, " I have seen him before. He is no mountaineer. This garb brings forth his true character."

" Ah,—and who is he ?"

The captain bent his head with hard thought.

" I cannot now call him to mind. But—I cannot be mistaken. Have I not seen him before ?"

" I cannot tell as to that."

" In mercy's name, my lord, do not trifle with me. Surely I cannot be a dupe to blind fancy. Who is he ?"

" Never mind now, Sir Philip. If you watch the youth, do not let him know it ; and.if you read anything definite in his face, come and inform me."

The captain was not at all satisfied with this ; but, as his host was otherwise engaged, he asked no more questions.

Rosaline was filled with alarm when she learned that Sir Philip had come to arrest her lover ; but when her father had explained the matter, she became more calm. She met Conrad in one of the ante-rooms ; and when she saw how bright and hopeful he looked, she put away her fears. At first she did not notice the change in his costume, for it improved him not a whit in her eyes.; though, when she did discover it, she was glad that her father had been so thoughtful.

"If you remain long in Vannes, I may join you there," she said, as they walked towards the door ; " but I hope it may not be so. I would rather you should come back here."

" Let it be as it may," returned Conrad, " I hope we shall not be long separated. Join your prayers with mine, dearest, and Heaven may be merciful to us. Ah, here comes your father. I must bid you adieu."

He pressed his lips upon her pure white brow ; then murmured a blessing ; and as she responded with words of prayer and promise, the duke joined them.

" Courage, my children," he said. " I have seen very dark clouds in my day ; but I have never yet seen any that the sun could not dissipate."

Thus speaking, he kissed his daughter, and then led Conrad out into the court, where the horses were in waiting.

It was a stout troop that rode forth from the old castle, for the duke took a score of his own men-at-arms to bear him company.

At the end of an hour Sir Philip touched the duke upon the arm.

" My lord, I have read that face !"

" Ah !"

" Yes,—I am sure of it."

" And you know the youth ?"

" Nay ; but I know whose features he bears. By heaven ! the counterpart is exact. It is—"

" Hush ! Give it not to other ears."

The old soldier whispered the name, with his lips close to the duke's cheek.

Casimir smiled and nodded.

" Am I not right ?"

" Time will tell."

" But, my lord—"

" Easy, Sir Philip. I can tell you nothing more. In the time to come we may find a key to the mystery."

The old knight resumed his place at the head of his troop, ever and anon turning a furtive glance upon Conrad du Nord, and then shaking his head with an expression of sore perplexity.

CHAPTER XV.

THEOBALD.

Theobald, king of Brittany, was in the chamber where he gave audience to his own immediate officers. He was sixty years of age, and looked to be ten years older. His tall form was bent, and his limbs trembled when he walked. The majesty of his manhood was gone, and much trouble had worn his disposition down to fretfulness and ill-temper. One thing could not fail to arrest the attention of the careful beholder of that royal face. The marks of doubt and fear were stamped thereon too plainly to be mistaken. And what had the king to fear ?

"Ponce," he said, turning to the page who attended him, "I hear footsteps."

"Yes, sire. I think it is the prince."

"Look and see."

The boy went to a small window that commanded a view of the corridor, and reported that it was the prince.

"You may leave me, Ponce ; but come back when the prince is gone."

The page withdrew, and shortly afterwards the prince entered, looking more sinister than usual. He cast a quick glance at the king, and his gray eye brightened with snake-like lustre when he noticed how those aged limbs quaked and shook.

"Good morning, my royal father," said Bertrand, bowing very low, and pressing his hand upon his bosom. "I am glad to see you looking so well."

"Do I look well, my son ?"

"Indeed you do."

"Then I look better than I feel."

"How do you feel ?"

"I am weak and faint, and my eye grows dim."

"Can you not see plainly ?"

"Yes—yes—I can see well enough ; but the light pains me."

"Pshaw! You are imaginative, father. You are as strong as you were ten years ago, if you would only think so. Why, you are only sixty. You have a full score of years yet in store for you. Look at Sir Philip de Savenay. He is five years older than you are ; and I doubt if there is a man in the realm who could even now stand before his stout arm."

"Ah—speaking of Sir Philip," said the king, "puts me

in mind of the mission upon which we sent him. Has he returned yet ?"

"Not yet; but I think he will be here before noon. And, my father, if you are not feeling very well, and would avoid unnecessary labor, I will attend to his report."

"If it is a capital case, my son, the king ought to give it his attention."

"But we need not make a capital case of it at present. I will commit the prisoner, and then he can await your pleasure."

"My son," said Theobald, with painful hesitation, "if such a thing is to be done, it must not be known. It is the duty of the king to attend to such matters."

"Not always, sire," replied Bertrand, readily. "The king may be seriously indisposed; and if such be the case, you would not have the wheels of government stop."

"No, my son; but, in such a case, important matters could be postponed."

"That is just it, father. In this case we simply postpone the final trial; and, since you are particular, I will tell you my object. I fear that there may be some deeply-laid conspiracy among those mountaineers, and I am determined, if possible, to search it out. To this end I would have the arrest of this Conrad kept as quiet as possible. If I can have charge of him, I will use him very carefully; and if there be any conspiracy, I will sift it to the bottom."

"Let it be as you will, Bertrand. Only you must be judicious. We cannot afford to transgress the laws of the realm."

A bitter answer was upon the lips of the prince, but he restrained himself, and smilingly promised his father that all should go well. Then he took a bit of parchment from his pocket, and laid it upon the table before the king.

"If you will sign that, sire, the whole business will be properly arranged. I will take the prisoner, and use him for the good of the crown."

"What is it?" asked Theobald, drawing the parchment towards him.

"It is a simple order to your captain, instructing him to deliver his prisoner into my hands."

"Is there more than one?" asked the king, running his eye over the order.

"More than one what?"

"More than one prisoner."

"Why do you ask that?"

"Because I see that you have written it *prisoners*."

"Have I? O, a mere slip of the pen. But it makes no difference. I did not notice it before."

The king, thinking nothing more of what might be a harmless mistake, took a pen, and, with a hand painfully tremulous, signed the order. The prince took it as soon as the royal name had been attached, and put it away in his pocket; and shortly afterwards he left the chamber.

When his son had gone, the king called his page and directed that his breakfast should be brought in. The meal was simple, consisting of bread and goat's milk, and a couple of eggs. When it had been placed before him he sent his page away again, and then went to one of the ante-rooms, and called to a small dog that lay sleeping upon a mat in the sunlight. The animal leaped quickly up at his master's call, and came frisking and jumping about him with evident delight.

"Ah, my poor Fides, you are at least my friend," said Theobald, patting the dog upon the head. "You I can trust; and yet to what a base use I am forced to put you. Ah—this is but a poor life, after all!"

As the king spoke, he broke his bread into small pieces, mixing different parts of the loaf together, a portion of which he put into a silver basin, and poured some of the milk upon it; and this mess he placed upon the floor for his dog to eat. Thus had the animal eaten for a long time, and when his meal was offered, he made quick work in disposing of it. After the dog had devoured the bread and milk he spent nearly half-an-hour at play, and at the end of that time the king sat down to his breakfast, being satisfied that the food which harmed not his dog would work no harm to him. As for the eggs, he found the shells perfect, and the contents fresh; and he eat them, as was his wont, beaten up in his milk.

" We are safe for this time," he said, allowing the dog to leap up into his lap, and lick the crumbs from the table. "Alas! what a life is this? O, my poor Fides, did people know what use I made of you, they would not envy me the crown that galls my brow. But I cannot bear it much longer. Once I prayed to God that he would give me an heir to my throne—I spent a whole year in earnest prayer. O, my sainted wife, as you look down from the dim world of spirits, can you not pity the poor wretch you left behind? Would to heaven the boy had died instead—"

He was startled from his reverie by the sound of footsteps in the corridor, and hastily arising from the table, he put the dog back into the ante-room, and closed the door.

When the prince left the royal presence he went down into the court-yard of the palace, where some of his followers were in attendance. Poins was there, and upon him he called.

" Poins, do you know the way to the top of yonder tower ?"

" Yes, my lord."

" From the top of that tower you can look out upon the Redon road. Sir Philip, when he returns, will come that way. I would have early notice of his approach. Do you understand me ?"

" Yes."

" You will find me here when you have a report to make. Away, and keep your eyes open."

The sun was but little past the meridian when Poins came down from the tower with the intelligence that the captain of the royal guard was approaching the city.

" Has he the prisoner with him ?" asked the prince.

" I could not tell," replied the man-at-arms. " I plainly saw Sir Philip, riding at the head of the troop, but a cloud of dust obscured much of the rest."

" He must have found him, or he would not have come back so soon. We will go out. Let my men be called."

In a little while, at the head of a dozen men, the prince rode forth from the palace yard, and just in the outskirts of the town he met Sir Philip de Savenay riding some distance in advance of his troop.

" Ah, my dear de Savenay, well met !" cried Bertrand, as the captain approached him. " Is the prisoner safe ?"

" Yes, my lord."

" Good ! You will have no further trouble with him."

" He has been no trouble to me, I assure you."

" I suppose not. The royal guard is not a thing to be openly resisted. But I will relieve you, my good Sir Philip."

" How ?"

" I will take the prisoner into my own hands."

" I do not understand you."

" The young mountaineer is with you ?"

" Yes."

" Then I will take him."

" But I must report to the king."

" There is no need of that.   Here is an order for you."

De Savenay took the parchment, and when he had read it, he said :

" I have no power to answer that order, my lord. Conrad du Nord is not my prisoner."

" How ? Did you not tell me that you had him safely ?"

" I told you that he was safe ; but he is not under my charge. Casimir of Rennes— Ah, here comes the duke himself."

" How now," demanded the duke, riding up to the spot. " Ah, my lord, is this you ?"

" Aye," cried the prince ; " and I think we are well met. Sir Philip informs me that you have charge of a certain youth named Conrad."

" Such is the case," replied the duke.

" Then you will read this order, sir."

" This order is not addressed to me," said Casimir, after he had read it.

" But you see the purport of it. The prisoner is to be delivered up to me."

" My dear prince," returned the duke, with a calm pride, " I have nothing to do with orders addressed to the king's officers. I am on my way now to see the king, and if he has orders for me, he will deliver them."

" Beware, my lord duke ! I am not to be trifled with. You see and understand the royal will. I demand of you the prisoner !"

The duke's lip quivered, and his hand involuntarily dropped towards the pommel of his sword ; but with a mighty effort he restrained himself, and made a motion to turn his horse.

"Ha !" exclaimed Bertrand, growing red with passion, "will you not answer me ?"

"Not now—not here. I have nothing to do with you."

"By the gods !" retorted the prince, gnashing his teeth, "answer me, or I'll strike you where you sit !"

So foolish a speech, instead of increasing the duke's anger, filled him with disgust. He raised himself in his stirrups, and bent upon the plotting prince a look of supreme contempt.

"Young man," he said, in a tone so low that only Sir Philip heard him beside, "the king of Brittany dare not insult the Duke of Rennes ! Then let the prince be careful !"

As he spoke he drew his rein, and moved away. The prince drew his sword half out from its scabbard, and would have dashed after him had not the captain interfered.

"Hold, your highness ! You know not what you do."

"Back, Sir Philip. By the eternal gods ! I'll not be put upon by him ! Back, I say !"

"Nay, my lord, I cannot permit it."

"Do you dare to oppose me ?"

"I dare to do my duty ; and when you find time to reflect you will not blame me."

At this juncture Poins made bold to pluck his master by the sleeve.

"My lord," whispered the faithful follower, "you will spoil all. The duke is not the man to meet thus. Take your own time and trust to fortune."

Bertrand, with the first effort of reason, saw that he.

was injuring his own cause ; and, though the alternative was, to him, a most painful and humiliating one, he summoned strength enough to overcome the outward passion. He struggled a few moments, like one who chokes, and then turned to the old knight with a smile upon his face ; but it was a wicked, fiendish smile.

"Sir Philip, you recall me to your senses. I will suffer the affront for the present. Heaven knows I have no disposition to interfere with the affairs of the king's officers."

And with this he rode away, followed by his men-at-arms.

After the prince had gone, the captain fell back and spoke with the duke.

"My lord," he said, "we must beware of Prince Bertrand. Tartarian fires are burning in his bosom, and fiendish schemes are forming in his brain. He has gone away from us now ; but he has only withdrawn, as the tiger does, for a more deadly attack. I know him well."

"You do not know him better than I do, Sir Philip. But I think we may prove a match for him. You will not shrink from your duty through fear of his vengeance ?"

"No—never."

"And how is it with these men who accompany you ?"

"I cannot answer for all of them, my lord. Most of them are stern and true ; but there may be one or two who would serve the prince."

"I had supposed as much. But, never mind. I fear not the result. Let us hurry on, for I would reach the king before yonder villain gains too much of his ear."

The troop started into a brisk gallop, and ere long had halted within the court of the royal palace. The duke saw the followers of the prince just dismounting ; but the prince himself was not with them.

" Sir Philip," said Casimir, " we must lose no time. Do you lead the way, and I will follow. Come—the mission is yours, and the king must be looking for you."

De Savenay waited not for a second bidding. He gave a few directions to his men, and then turned towards the palace. The duke drew the arm of Conrad through his own, and followed. The captain of the royal guard was the highest officer of the household, and no one dared to stop him. He made his way to his own private closet, which was close by the king's chamber, where he found two of his subordinate officers on duty, of whom he inquired if any one had lately passed into the royal apartment.

One of them replied that the prince had just gone in.

" Then," said Sir Philip, turning to the duke, " we had better leave Conrad here for the present."

Casimir saw the propriety of the arrangement, and at once consented to it.

" Gentlemen," he said, addressing the officers on duty, both of whom were well known to him, " this young man is my friend. I leave him in your care uñtil I return."

They greeted our hero warmly, and promised to look to his comfort.

Then Sir Philip passed on to the king's chamber, followed by the duke. They found the prince there, and he had already entered a complaint ; for the monarch, as soon as he saw his captain, cried out :

" Ah, Sir Philip, how is this ? Do you trample upon my authority ?"

" Not I, sire. Why do you ask that ?"

Theobald was about to answer, when he caught sight of the duke.

" How ! Is this my cousin of Rennes ?"

" Yes, sire," replied Casimir, advancing and saluting the king respectfully.

" And to what kind stroke of fortune do I owe this visit ?"

" I will inform you in good season, sire.   I think your captain has some report to make."

" Aye, Sir Philip," cried the king ; " how is it ?   Did you refuse to deliver up your prisoner according to my order ?"

" No, sire.   I had no prisoner in my possession."

" How ?   Have you not brought that bold mountaineer ?"

" Not I, sire.   My lord the duke hath brought him ; and he alone is responsible."

" Sire," spoke Casimir, as the king turned towards him, " for reasons which I trust I can make good to your majesty, I have brought Conrad du Nord under my own guardianship.   But I must crave a private audience."

The prince stamped his foot and bit his lip.   He was angry ; and, had he given way to his passion, he would have stormed most furiously ; but he did not do it. With just such another effort as he had made only a short time before, he swallowed his wrath, and hid his clutching fingers within the folds of his doublet.   He knew that in an audience with the king, the duke and the captain both had precedence of himself.

" My father," he said, with that same fiendish smile lurking about the corners of his mouth, " since our cousin of Rennes desires audience, I will withdraw." And without daring to trust himself with further speech, he turned and strode from the apartment.

" By heaven !" whispered Sir Philip, into the duke's ear, " the prince needs looking after.   As true as you live, there is some deadly mischief working in his brain !"

" We will take care of him, never fear."

"Ah, my lord, you don't know him if you do not fear him. I tell you he goes forth upon some fatal work. If you would save your friend, you must watch the prince !"

CHAPTER XVI.

THE PRINCE GETS READY FOR WORK.

Prince Bertrand did not stop on his way from the royal chamber. He supposed that Conrad du Nord might be in the palace—perhaps near to the king—but he cared not to see him then. He had another plan in his mind. In the court he found Poins, whom he called apart from the rest of his followers.

"Did Thamar accompany Sir Philip to Rennes ?" asked the prince.

"He did," replied Poins.

"I think Thamar is devoted to me."

"You may depend upon him, my lord ; I will stake my life."

"I am going to my own apartment. Send Thamar to me. Convey the order to him privately, and bid him make no demonstration of his coming."

Thamar was a stout, dark-visaged guardsman, who had been recently promoted to the royal corps upon the recommendation of the prince ; and when he received the message which Poins brought, he hastened to obey. He found Bertrand alone, in a closet adjacent to the bed-chamber ; and it was easy to see, from his manner, that he was anxious to please the heir to the throne of Brittany.

"You have ridden far, and you may be seated," said

Bertrand, after the usual salutations had been exchanged.

This was an honor, and the guardsman seemed well pleased with it.

"Now, master Thamar, I wish you to give me your attention." The prince could assume a tone of exceeding frankness when he chose, and in such a tone he now spoke. "It must be evident that ere many years—perhaps ere many months—I shall be king of Brittany; and I am even now estimating the characters of those who may be called to serve me in the best offices. When I recommended you to the station you now occupy, I believed that you would honor the office; and, I am free to confess, I had another object in view: I desired that you should become acquainted with the routine of the business of the royal guard. Sir Philip de Savenay is getting old; and, when he gives up the command, I would have good and efficient men from among whom to select his successor."

Thamar understood this, and his face glowed with ambitious hope. He was a brave soldier, and had made his mark on more than one battlefield; and he did not think it a great stretch of imagination to fancy himself qualified to fill the office in question.

"My lord," he said, "I already owe you much. You have but to command me."

"I think you are honest."

"Try me. If I fail you, my life is at your disposal."

Bertrand smiled as he replied:

"Your life is too valuable to be thrown carelessly away; so, I pray you, don't fail me. The time will come when I may place my correcting hand upon the most powerful noble in the realm; but at present I am forced to use caution and circumspection. I have enemies, my good man, and some of them are high in power. They are jealous and uneasy. They see me approaching the throne, and they fear for their safety in the future ; and all plots aimed against me will involve my friends in the evil result. But my triumph is as certain as is the coming of another sun ; and the only anxiety I have is to punish the evil doers. You have been to Rennes with Sir Philip ?"

" I have, my lord."

" You know why the captain was sent ?"

" Yes."

" Were you within earshot when Sir Philip made known his business to the duke ?"

" I was."

" Tell me what you heard."

Thamar repeated the conversation which had taken place between the duke and Sir Philip.

" Two things are evident," remarked Bertrand, after the guardsman had concluded : " Casimir has conceived a friendship for this bold mountaineer ; and he also knows where those two old people are, and means to protect them."

" I should think so," replied Thamar.

" Perhaps you think something more," suggested the prince, as he noticed a peculiar expression upon the man's face, as though he had some opinions which he found it difficult to contain.

" I do think something more, my lord ; but, after all, I may be telling you nothing. Perhaps you know more than I do."

" Explain yourself, Thamar."

" Does your highness know anything of this mountaineer beyond what appears upon the surface of affairs ?"

" I only suspect," replied Bertrand, starting with sudden interest. " I suspect—aye, I know, that he cannot be the simple recluse he professes to be. But I know nothing. What do you know?"

"I cannot say that I know anything, my lord; though I think I have reason to suspect much. If you will listen to me, I will give you the result of my observations."

"In the first place," said the guardsman, laying his hands together, and speaking very carefully, "when I had heard of the exploits of this Conrad, I made up my mind that he was no ordinary man; or, at all events, that he was not a simple mountaineer. This conviction led me to examine him very closely when I saw him, and also to observe very narrowly all that transpired in relation to him. I gained a position near to the captain, and was able to hear much that was evidently not meant to be heard. Why was the proud duke so tender of the youth? Why did he allow him to walk in the garden with his daughter?"

"How?" cried the prince. "Allow him wandering alone with the Lady Rosaline?"

"Yes, my lord. I saw it with my own eyes. As we rode into the court, this Conrad and the Lady Rosaline were coming up from the garden."

"By the mass, this is friendship with a vengeance! And I have no doubt that the lady seemed pleased with the company."

"They were like two fondling doves, my lord."

Bertrand ground his teeth, and stamped his foot till the floor shook.

"Go on—go on," he said, as soon as he could control himself. "By the eternal gods! if I do not bring this plotting interloper down! But go on."

"Why was the proud duke so tender of the youth? Why did he allow him to walk in the garden with his daughter? I asked myself these questions, my lord, and I wanted an answer to them. It was not mere curiosity on my part. Far from it. Had I been alone in the matter, these things would not have led unto a bit of extra exertion. But I wished to serve my prince. I knew that Conrad du Nord was your enemy, and I meant, if possible, to know who and what he was. So I watched. I knew that the old hermit, Francisco, and the woman Marguerite, were not man and wife; and I judged that the youth was not their son. This brought me to the idea that there might be some mystery about his birth. Would the proud duke of Rennes suffer his only child to associate on terms of close intimacy with a man of low birth, especially when that man was young, brave, and handsome? It did not seem reasonable, and I continued to watch. By and by the young man came forth, clad in silk and velvet, and his presence was noble and commanding. I saw that Sir Philip watched him narrowly, and I soon made up my mind that the old captain suspected as much as I did, if not more. We had been on the road an hour or so, and I was riding close by Sir Philip's side. Ever and anon he would turn and study Conrad's features, and then mutter to himself. By and by his countenance suddenly brightened, and I heard these words drop from his lips—'*By heaven, I know him now!*" and when he had thus exclaimed, he rode back and spoke with the duke. He said, '*My lord, I have read that face.*' Casimir uttered an exclamation of surprise. Then the captain added: '*Yes, I am sure of it.* '*And you know the youth?*' said the duke. Sir Philip answered: '*Nay; but I know whose features he bears. By heaven! the counterpart is exact.*' And then he was going on to speak the name, when the duke stopped him, and bade him not to give the secret to other ears. I could hear no more distinctly, though I was able to understand that Casimer assented to the captain's statement, but refused to give him further information. After this I saw much to confirm me in the belief that Conrad du Nord was of illustrious birth ; that the duke knew all about it ; and that Sir Philip had discovered just enough to fill him with amazement.

Bertrand moved not until the guardsman had ceased speaking, and then he leaped from his chair and started across the room. His hands were clutched ; his head bent ; and his whole frame convulsed. At length he stopped, and gazed into his informant's face.

" Thamar, have you told me all that you know ?"

" I think I have, my lord."

" You are a keen observer."

" I think I can read what is before me," said Thamar, modestly.

" Aye," added the prince ; " and you can do more. If I am not mistaken, you are the man I need to help me. Adolphe and Goliath are both gone. Adolphe was a faithful friend ; and if you will take his place, I shall not fear to trust you."

" Shall I leave the royal guard, my lord ?"

" No. It will be better that you should remain there. If you have a mind to devote all your energies to my interests, that position will afford you numerous advantages."

" I am of your opinion ; and you may trust me fully. You have but to make known your wishes, and I will obey, if it is within my power."

" I shall trust you, Thamar ; and if you continue to serve me as you have begun, your reward shall be such as a noble might crave. I have one thing further to ask you : Did you learn where that old man and woman were ?"

" No, my lord."

" Or did you hear anything that might lead you to mistrust where they were ?"

" No. I only made up my mind that the duke knew all about them."

"Very well. You may go to your troop, and keep your eyes and ears open ; and be ready to answer any signal I may send. If I want you I shall send Poins ; so you will know what is wanted if you see him coming. Of course I need not caution you against speaking of the things about which we have been conversing."

" My lord, save in your presence, or at your order, I know nothing at all of the things whereof we have spoken."

"Good ! That will do. I thank you now, Thamar ; and for the future you may count upon something more."

The guardsman left the room ; and when he was gone, the prince sank into a chair, and rested his brow upon his hands. He remained thus for some time, and then arose, and commenced to pace the floor.

"If I can only find out the duke's full force," he soliloquized, " I can meet him on even ground. But he must work smartly if he thinks to carry his point. He is my enemy, and will most assuredly tell to my father the sad story of my running away with his daughter. Bah ! what of that ! My poor old father will chide me, and there will be an end of that matter, so far as the king is concerned. But Casimir will remain my enemy ; and I may count upon the hand of the Lady Rosaline as lost to me. But this new lover. By the mass, I must look into that secret. I think I owe him something ! He kills my best men ; he robs me of my sweet prize ; he draws his sword even against myself ; he puts his steel through Bernardo's body ; he bears away his old guardians in safety ; and now he comes to court under the friendship of the powerful duke. By the gods! I must conquer him, or my self-respect is gone forever."

He sat down again, and after studying awhile, he slowly and thoughtfully said to himself, with his hands laid calculatingly together :

" I will not hurry to make any open demonstration against him. If it comes handy, he shall have a sword through his heart. But I will fathom his secret if I can. I will know who and what he is. 'Sblood! I am forced to own to myself that I fear the young rascal. He has the ring of danger in him. Already I have too many enemies in Brittany ; and, if I would ever sit safely upon the throne, I must not have any more."

When he had thus spoken, he called in an attendant, whom he sent in quest of Poins. The man-at-arms soon presented himself.

" Poins, do you know where the cell of Father Jerome is ?"

" Do you mean the old monk, my lord ?"

" Yes."

" I can find him."

" I must see him this very night. He is my confessor, Poins ; and I have something of the greatest weight upon my mind which I desire that he should know. Tell him to come to me ; or, if that may not be, to send word where I may find him. I would see him as soon after dark as possible."

" I will tell him, my lord."

" Do so ; and bring me his answer."

Shortly after Poins left, a messenger came from the king, requesting the attendance of the prince in the royal chamber.

Bertrand had expected this ; and he was prepared. He found his father alone, with a look of trouble upon his face.

" My son, what is this I hear?"

" If I am to judge from the cloud upon your brow, my noble father, I should say that you had heard something that moved you unpleasantly."

" Aye, Bertrand—it is indeed so. What have you been doing?"

" First, my father, tell me what has been said against me."

Casimer had told to Theobald the story of the wrong which had been done to his daughter; and of the parts which the prince and the young mountaineer had played in the affair; and this story the king now repeated to his son. The prince heard him quietly to the end, without apparent emotion of any kind, and then said:

" The duke has told you very near the truth, sire; though the impression left upon your mind is any-thing but fair. I did cause the Lady Rosaline to be carried away. But why? I meant to make her my wife. Had not you supposed that I was to have her hand?"

" Yes, my son."

" Aye—and upon that event I had fixed my brightest hopes of life. But, sire, when I came to ask her plainly for her answer, she refused me. I knew that she was not herself. Was I to submit to such treatment? Was the house of Rennes to spit upon the son of the king? But, father, you waste your feelings in holding the impressions which the duke has given you; he has not departed much from the truth; but he has not told you all. Where is Conrad du Nord?"

" He is with the duke?"

" Has he left the city?"

" No. He remains to answer any further summons I may make."

"Very well. Now listen to me, my father. Suppose I should tell you that this same Conrad du Nord was the accepted lover of the duke's daughter?"

"How!" exclaimed the king with a start.

"I wonder not that you are surprised, sire; but such is the case. And let me tell you something more: This Conrad du Nord is an unknown, nameless adventurer. The duke has picked him up, and means to marry him to his daughter. Have you seen the youth?"

"No—not yet," replied the king.

"If you do see him, you will behold a young man of bold, commanding presence, such as nature gives to those who are her favorites. With such a tool Casimir thinks to work some mischief. Suppose his cousin of Anjou should join him in some plot against the throne!"

"But—John of Anjou is my friend."

"Aye—but not mine. I tell you, my father, there is something deep in all this."

The poor old king trembled from head to foot. He forgot entirely the business upon which he had called his son, this new whisper having filled his soul with alarm. Bertrand knew his weaknesses, and knew just how to play upon them.

"I do not think Casimir would plot against me."

"Not if the plotting could place his blood upon the throne?"

"My son!"

"Courage, sire. Leave this in my hands. I was just commencing the work of investigation when your messenger found me. I may be in error. I hope I am. But I will not be long in error. Will you give me three days in which to sift this matter?"

The king was weak, and the prince was strong; and

the quaking old monarch was easily persuaded to give up to his son.

"Until you hear from me again upon this matter," suggested Bertrand, "you had better not suffer the duke to approach you. However, in this you will act your own pleasure. I have only to ask emphatically that you will be careful how you trust him."

"I shall not see him," replied Theobald, with a shiver. "If he can do me wrong, I do not wish to see him ; and if he is truly my friend, he will forgive me when he knows all. I shall not see him until I hear from you again."

Bertrand went away with a look of triumph upon his face.

By and by the page brought up bread and goat's milk for supper. The king called his dog, and fed him ; and when, at the end of half an hour, the animal skipped as gaily as ever, the poor old man sat down to his frugal repast !

CHAPTER XVII.

WEAVING THE NET.

It was nearly dark when the prince returned to his own apartments, and he found Poins there waiting for him, with the information that Father Jerome would come to the palace at nine o'clock. Bertrand eat his supper, and then went out and gave some directions to his men-at-arms. At the appointed hour the monk arrived.

Jerome was a member of the order of St. Benedict ; a man somewhere near seventy years of age ; of medium

height, and tending to corpulency. It is not certain
that all the old monks of that period were corpulent;
nor can we swear that Father Jerome was a free liver;
but we must put him down as we find him,—and we
find him blessed with a marked rotundity of body. The
superabundance of flesh may have been begotten of
the most simple and austere diet; and, for ought we
know to the contrary, wine may have been a stranger
to his lips until this present evening; but it was to be
a stranger no longer; for one of the first offerings of
the prince's hospitality was wine, and Father Jerome
drank a full measure of it—drank it as though he was
used to it. The monk had a small, dark, keen eye; a
nose rather broad; a large mouth, with lips thicker
than a sculptor would put upon the face of a hero; and
when he drank his wine he smacked his lips, and winked
his bright little eye.

"Father Jerome," said the prince, "I know you
thoroughly."

The Benedictine sipped from his second measure of
wine, and winked again.

"I suppose you think you know me?" pursued Bertrand.

"Thou art Bertrand, the son of Theobald," answered
the monk, with mock gravity.

"And do you not believe that I shall be king of
Brittany?"

"Aye—verily I do."

"The chances are, good father, that I shall be king;
and when I am king, I mean to hold the sceptre in my
own hand."

"You will have that right, my son."

"And be sure I shall exercise it."

"You would not be king if you did not."

"You are right."

The prince arose and went to the door, and when he came back he said :

" I know you, Father Jerome ; and I am going to be perfectly frank with you. I want you to help me ; and in return, whenever you wish it, I will help you."

" That's frank and fair, my son," returned the monk.

" Perhaps," pursued the prince, who felt sure that he knew his man, " there may be something even now in view that you would like. If you help me, I shall pay you ; and, if we can agree upon the terms, the price might be as well fixed now as at any time. I can tell you exactly what I wish you to do for me. Can you do the same ?"

The Bendictine smiled, and winked, and rubbed his hands.

" There is one thing I should like very much," he said.

" What is it ?"

" I should like to be Abbot of Saint Aubin."

" Father Jerome, help me in my present need, and when I am king you shall be Abbot of Saint Aubin."

" Do you promise that ?" cried the monk, with a start of glad surprise.

" I do, upon my knightly word."

" My lord, I will help you if I can. We understand each other."

There was no mistaking the meaning of the Benedictine. He wished to be Abbot of Saint Aubin ; and to reach that position he would do anything which the prince would dare to plan.

" What am I to do ?" he asked, after the prince had gone once more to the door and returned.

" I will tell you in as direct a manner as possible," said Bertrand, drawing his chair up in front of his visitor. " Have you yet heard of the young mountaineer called Conrad du Nord ?"

" No, my son."

" Then I must tell you of him. He has been reared in the Nord Mountains, by an old woman named Marguerite, who has passed for his mother. Close by their cot, in a mountain cave, has lived an old man of the name of Francisco, who has passed for a hermit, and who has been the youth's tutor. This Francisco, it now seems, was once a soldier, and he has made his pupil one of the best swordsmen in Brittany. Circumstances which I need not now stop to relate, have brought this youth across my path, and it is not impossible that he may become dangerous to me. The same circumstances which brought him across my path introduced him to the Duke of Rennes ; and the duke has conceived a wonderful friendship for him. There is some mystery about this Conrad's parentage ; and I think the duke has some clue. In fact, I know it must be so. Casimir has been heard to speak words which directly proved it. And, furthermore, he has allowed the adventurer to make love to his daughter."

" Are you sure of all that you have told me ?" asked Jerome.

" Yes, father."

" Even to the love affair between this youth and the Lady Rosaline ?"

" Yes."

" How old is this Conrad du Nord ?"

" I should think not far from my own age ; younger, if anything."

" Has any one else seen him, besides the duke, to be struck by his appearance ?"

" Yes. Sir Philip de Savenay."

" And what has Sir Philip discovered ?"

"He has discovered that the youth's features are remarkably like those of some friend whom he knew years ago."

" How looks the hero ?"

"He is tall and well-formed ; with mighty power of limb ; he has light hair, and large, lustrous eyes ; and his presence is bold and commanding."

" Can you tell me anything more ?"

" I can think of nothing."

" Where is the youth now ?"

" In Vannes. The duke has brought him hither."

The monk was deeply interested. He closed his eyes and pressed his fingers upon his brow.

" My son," he at length said, " I think you have hit upon some one who can help you. Somewhere over a score of years ago—I cannot now tell exactly the time —a child disappeared from Vannes. The circumstances which you have related would seem exactly to apply to the child I speak of. If I am right, the duke must be acting very strangely—he must be laboring under an error."

" What is it ?" asked Bertrand, eagerly. " What was this child ?"

The monk seemed not to notice the question. He remained some time in deep thought, and then said, as though he had not been disturbed :

" I do not think I am mistaken. But I must see this woman—this Marguerite—of whom you have spoken. Where is she ?"

" I cannot tell you. I think, however, that she is somewhere near Rennes."

" What makes you think so ?"

" Both she and the old hermit went to Rennes with their protegé ; the youth remained and they went on."

The monk nodded his head half a dozen times, and finally said :

"I can tell you where to look for them. They are at the Abbey of Saint Aubin. My word for it, you will find the woman there, if you do not find the man. Old Dagobert, the abbot, is her uncle. Bring her to me, and I think the mystery may be readily solved."

"But, good father, you have not told me what you have discovered. I am all anxiety. Who was the child you speak of?"

The Benedictine shook his head.

"My son, you must not press me too closely. The secret of that child's life is, for the present, under the key of my religious oath. Let Marguerite be summoned ; and, if it is proved that this child and Conrad du Nord are one and the same person ; and if it be also proved that the child has grown up to be the enemy of our prince, then I will let out the secret and save you."

"Save me ?"

"Aye—or serve you, as you please ; for, if it be as I think it is, your enemy is rushing on to his own destruction. One word of mine will blast him forever."

"Are you speaking truly?" demanded the prince, grasping the monk's arm.

"My words are words of solemn truth," replied Jerome, earnestly.

"And could this fellow wield any power in Brittany if he gained the station to which he was born?"

"Not alone. Designing men might make a tool of him—that is all."

"It is as I thought."

"But," pursued the monk, "if you are judicious, you have nothing to fear. Bring the old woman, Marguerite, as soon as you can."

"How is it with the man—Francisco?"

"I would rather trust the woman. She will not lie. The man is an old soldier, and he might trifle with us. Bring the woman alone if you can."

The Benedictine had arisen to go, but Bertrand stopped him.

"There is one thing, good father, I wish to understand more fully. You are not sure that the child of whom you speak—"

"I am not sure that the child lives," answered Jerome, without waiting for the conclusion of the question.

"And if this mountaineer should not prove to be the same—"

"My learning who he is might not help you."

"One thing further : If Conrad du Nord is not that child, can there be any possible danger to me through him ?"

"Yes," replied the monk, emphatically. "He may prove to be a most powerful enemy. It is not impossible that the duke may hold a suspicion of some truth which I cannot reach. If such should prove to be the case, you may have something to contend with ; and I may never gain the mitre and crozier of Saint Aubin. But bring the woman. Let us question her first."

"Holy father—"

"No more, my son. I know what you would ask ; and I will answer you without putting you to the trouble of framing speech. The path is before you ; a tree has blown across the way. We will remove the obstacle if we can. Should it prove too heavy for that, you must cut your way through it !"

"Thank you, father."

"You are not indebted to me yet. Wait. When you have found the woman send for me."

The monk drank another measure of wine, and then departed ; and as he went out, Poins came in.

" Poins," cried the prince, " who of all my followers is best fitted to take Adolphe's place ?"

" I should say, my lord, that you have a man in your employ who is better than Adolphe ever was. I mean Marius."

" By my life, I believe you are right. Why have I never thought of him before? Send him to me at once."

Poins went out, and ere long afterwards Marius presented himself. He was a middle-aged man ; of medium size, with a mild expression upon his well-cut features, and very quiet and modest in deportment. If Bertrand had not seen this man strike down strong foemen in battle, he would have been inclined to doubt his energy.

" Marius, have you heard the story of Conrad du Nord ?"

" I have, my lord, in part."

" Have you heard mention made of Marguerite and Francisco ?"

" Do you mean the two old people whom Bernardo was sent to apprehend ?"

" The same."

" I have heard of them."

" Do you know where the Abbey of Saint Aubin is ?"

" I know it very well, my lord. I was reared between Saint Aubin and Rennes."

" Good ! Now mark me : I think Francisco and Marguerite are at the abbey. I want to see Marguerite in this very room as quickly as possible."

" And Francisco ?"

" I want nothing to do with him at present. The woman must be brought alone, and privately."

" My lord, if she is at the abbey, and is well, I will bring her to you."

" When can you do it ?"

" The distance to Saint Aubin is a good thirty leagues," said Marius, calculatingly. "I can change horses at least five times. Ten hours will take me there, with something to spare. If I start soon I can reach the abbey early on the morrow. A few hours rest, and I shall be ready for work. Of course we must return more slowly, if we have the woman ; but I think I may safely promise to be here sometime during the day after to-morrow."

" How many men do you want ?"

" Not more than three."

" Will you select them ?"

" Yes."

" Then go and do so ; and while the horses are being prepared, do you come back here. I would speak with you again."

In less than half an hour Marius came back, and reported that he was ready to set out. The prince gave him more particular instructions, and finally dismissed him upon his mission.

" Now, Poins, I have one more arrangement to make. I want half a dozen of the most daring and stout-armed of my retainers. I want men who fear nothing, and who would march through fire for a fitting object. Can you bring me such ?"

" I think I can."

" Go and find them, and bring them back with you; and, as you go out, send Thamar to me."

The factotum left the room, and shortly afterwards Thamar entered.

" My good Thamar, what have you discovered new ?"

" Nothing, my lord ; only I am more than ever convinced that what I have told you is true."

" Where is Conrad du Nord ?"

" He is with the duke, at his residence by the sea-shore."

" Then they mean to reside there while they stop in Vannes ?"

" It is probable."

Thamar was dismissed with thanks, and with instructions to keep his watch.

In half an hour Poins returned, followed by six stout, dark-featured fellows, who, from their uniforms, appeared to be men-at-arms of the prince's legion. They bowed respectfully, and then stood back, with their left hands resting upon the pommels of their swords, as though they were ready for anything. Bertrand gazed at them, and the significant nod of his head seemed to indicate that he was satisfied.

" These are all true men, my lord," said Poins.

" Who speaks for them ?" asked the prince.

" I can do so," replied one of the number, stepping forward a pace. " Whatever I promise, my lord, you may consider as promised by the six."

" I think your name is Pluton ?"

" It is, my lord."

" Do you know the young man called Conrad du Nord ?"

" I saw him, this afternoon, go away with Casimir of Rennes."

" The very same.   He is in my way."

Pluton dropped his hand upon his sword-hilt, and bowed.

" The fellow must not be assassinated outright," pursued the prince. " There must be some shadow of provocation.   I would give a hundred crowns for a hole through his body, provided that hole was sufficient to let his life out."

" I understand you, my lord."

"But, remember,—it must look like a quarrel."

"It shall be so. And if the duke discovers us——"

"You had better leave no track for discoverers. However, if you do as I have said, and complaint is entered against you, I will stand between you and harm."

"I merely asked the question, my lord, in order that my companions might not think me forgetful ; but I do not intend that the work shall be unnecessarily exposed. We will report in due time."

When these workmen had gone, the prince retired to his bed-chamber, feeling that he had accomplished enough for one day.

———————•———————

CHAPTER XVIII.

HOW PLUTON SUCCEEDED.

A warm, pleasant afternoon. Casimir of Rennes and Conrad were walking upon the sea-shore.

"Patience, my dear boy. I am sure that all will come out well. If I were not confident, I should not hold out the light as I do. Rosaline will come to-morrow ; and I think that by the day after we shall be ready to proceed with our investigation."

"I try to be patient," replied Conrad ; "and I try to bear up hopefully. Still, I am as one groping in the dark."

"Not exactly in the dark?"

"Then it is worse, my lord."

"How can that be ?"

"If I am not like one in the dark, I am like one in a

place of uncertain light. Ah, if the bubble should burst—if the flash should fade away—the gloom of my life would be cold and cheerless. I should then wish that I had never seen the face of the angel !"

"Hush, my boy. There is no need of such reflections."

"How can I avoid them ? There are a thousand chances against me. My hopes all hang upon the possibility that my birth may be proved to have been a noble one. Should that fail——"

"Should that fail, my son, I will still bid you hope. What more can you ask ?"

"I would ask this," cried Conrad, energetically : "I would ask that Rosaline shall decide my fate. Dare you promise me that ?"

The duke hesitated ; but at length he said:

"I am almost tempted to give you the promise. However, let us wait until Rosaline comes. I will speak with her. As God lives, I mean to bless you if I can ; and if I hesitate about making such a promise, it is because I have not the right to do it."

At this juncture a servant approached, and informed the duke that he was wanted at the house. A messenger from Rennes had arrived.

"Come," said Casimir, laying his hand upon the youth's arm, "let us go and hear the news from the castle. Cheer up, and look forward with courage."

"I will follow you, my lord."

"You had better not wander here alone."

"I will not remain long behind you. Let me reflect a little."

The duke went away with his servant, and Conrad remained upon the sea-shore. He did not mean to stop long. He meant to follow slowly back, that he might have an opportunity of communing with his own thoughts. But when once engaged with the reflections that came crowding upon him, he forgot the house, and wandered away, with his head bowed, and his arms folded upon his breast.

"Would to heaven that I could see the end of this!' he murmured, as he slowly wended his way among the rocks. "All may be as bright as the duke foretells; but the decrees of fate are not in his hands. He knows not what may transpire to shake the fabric upon which my hopes are founded. O, my God, I have a fear which I shrink from whispering, even to myself. If my birth was honorable, why was it hidden so darkly? If I had been the child of the poorest peasants in the realm, so that I had been honorably begotten, there would have been no need of such mystery. O! if such a bolt should come crashing upon me, I shall curse the hour that opened my senses to life! Do not tell me that such thought is foolish; for, by the angel of fate, my mind runs legitimately thither. And, if the dark hand of an old shame is laid upon me, how shall Rosaline regard me? Ah, my lord duke, I can understand why you hesitate in your promise. You can see that the bursting of the thunderbolt is not impossible!"

Conrad had reached an open space close by the water's edge, where the sand lay hard and smooth, when he was interrupted in his reflections by the appearance of a stout man-at-arms, who seemed to have come from behind some of the neighboring rocks. Our hero would have turned and retraced his steps, but the stranger stopped him.

"How now, my young man. Don't fly away from me."

Conrad could not determine whether the fellow was insolent, or whether he was simply bold and frank.

"I am not flying, sir," he said, casting a searching glance over the soldier.

"You have been enjoying very excellent company."

"Ah—do you think so?"

"I merely judge from the earnest manner in which you were conversing. Zounds! I expected, when I heard your voice, to find a small party of very excited men."

Conrad colored and bit his lip. He did not like the manner of the fellow. There was something grossly familiar and bantering in his look and tone.

"He takes me for some favored friend of the duke's," he said to himself, "and he is jealous of what he considers my good fortune." Then he said aloud:

"You will excuse me, sir, I am in haste."

"Hold, one moment, if you please. Do not give a friend the cold shoulder in that fashion. Mercy! One would think you proud if he did not know the stock you came of."

Conrad's face flushed.

"What mean you, sir? Would you insult me?"

"Good mercy, no. I pray you, young sir, don't think of such a thing. Ha, ha—an insult is a dangerous thing. In the section I came from an insult is the signal for sword-drawing; and surely I should be a brute to urge you to draw your sword against an old soldier like myself. What a ridiculous thing it would be."

"It might be a very foolish thing," said our hero, entirely unable to comprehend what the fellow was driving at.

"So it would," retorted the man-at-arms, with a coarse laugh. "I should be directly accused of murder."

"I thought the laws of Brittany were not so strict as that."

" O, bless you—they are very strict about killing
unoffending citizens."

" I do not discover your point, sir."

" Don't you ? I think it is plain enough."

" Perhaps you will enlighten me."

" With pleasure. If I have a battle with a man of my
own station, his life is mine if he voluntarily places it
at the point of my sword. But if I draw my sword
upon a child, or against one who is wholly unable to
defend himself, then the law will not hold me guiltless.
Do you understand ?"

" I understand that you are trifling."

" How ?"

"I think you are trifling with me. If you are not, I
will thank you to leave me to myself."

" Mercy ! Cannot one claim a passing word of good
cheer without giving offence ? Look to it, my fair
young master, or I may think that you mean to insult
me."

" If you pass on, I shall surely not insult you !"

" And if I stay—would you dare to insult me then ?"

Conrad turned, and would have walked away ; but
the interloper stepped quickly forward, and laid his
hand upon his arm.

" Perhaps you mean this for an insult."

" What ?"

" This cool turning away from me without answering
my question."

" 'Sblood !" cried our hero, shaking the hand from
his arm, and looking into the fellow's face, " you are
approaching dangerously near to me. Who are you ?
I never saw you before, and I care not to see you again.
I select my own companions, and admit whom I please
to my counsel. Leave me."

" Bah ! you are hot-headed, my boy.   I shall have to give you a lesson in manners."

" Beware that I do not give you a lesson of a sterner character," said Conrad, shutting his teeth tightly together.

" Aha—are you there ?   Do you mean that you would cross swords with me ?"

There could be no more doubt touching the fellow's character and intentions.   His uniform was of the prince's legion ; and he looked fit for plottings and killings.

" Look ye," said Conrad, speaking almost in a whisper, " if you seek a quarrel with me, you are in dangerous business.   You find me alone, and engaged with my own thoughts.   Let me pass on, and all may be well.   I would have no further words with you."

" But I would have further words with you !" exclaimed the ruffian, again seizing the youth by the arm, and twirling him around.   " By Saint Michael ! I am not to be insulted thus, even though you be a favorite of some proud noble !   We'll see if your sword is as nimble as your tongue.   If you are not a coward, defend yourself !"

The young mountaineer made no effort to contain himself further.   He drew his sword, and placed himself on his guard.   The man-at-arms' object was now very evident ; for the ready manner in which he made the attack showed that such had been his plan from the first.   Conrad saw it all, and he was convinced that the prince was at the bottom of the scheme.

" Remember," said the assailant, as he threw his left hand behind him, " this is no child's play.   The sand at our feet is thirsty for blood."

" Be it so," responded Conrad.

The swords were crossed ; and for some moments the

parries were simply of preparation. Directly, however, the soldier made a furious lunge, and the combatants fairly changed places.

" 'Sdeath ! your sword is a stout one."

" It is sharp, too," returned Conrad, coolly and significantly.

" Mine is not blunt," said the man-at arms, as he made two or three rapid passes. But he very soon lost his confident air, and the look of easy assurance which had rested upon his face gave place to an expression of earnest concern. He found the point of the opposing sword very difficult to meet, and its gyrations and thrusts were becoming painfully perplexing. He tried all his feints, and they failed. Then he tried the strength of his opponent's wrist ; and that trial was his last. His sword became hopelessly entangled, and he cried out for help. He did not ask for mercy at the hands of his antagonist ; but he called for help, as though he had friends at hand. But he had delayed too long to save himself. The point of his sword was borne down till it touched the sand; and before he could recover it he was pierced to the heart.

But what had that cry for help meant ? As soon as Conrad had shaken the sinking ruffian from his sword, he started back and looked around him ; and he saw, coming up from behind a pile of great rocks, five armed men, clad in garbs like that worn by him who now lay bleeding upon the sand.

" How now, assassin !" exclaimed their leader, rushing forward with his sword drawn. " By the gods ! you shall pay for this !"

Conrad understood the whole plot, as though it had been told to him by the man who had framed it. He knew that these were emissaries of the prince, and that his life was wanted. Against those five stout men-at-arms he could not hope successfully to contend ; but he was determined to sell his life as dearly as possible.

Close behind him were two huge rocks, with a space between them sufficient for his standing. This position he gained as quickly as possible, and then turned upon the approaching foe.

" Hold, sirs !" he cried, planting himself firmly on his guard. " You have no cause for warring against me."

" Say ye so ?" returned the leader of the gang, who was none other than Pluton. " Have you not slain our comrade ?"

" Down with him !" yelled a powerful fellow, who stood by Pluton's side. " By Saint Paul ! he cannot break down my blade. Let me get at him !"

The leader moved a step away, and allowed the eager man to rush on. It was plainly seen that but one man could engage the youth at the same time, and Pluton seemed willing that his stout follower should make the attempt.

Conrad was not at all moved by the coming of this dashing, daring fellow. The rascal was huge of frame, and must have possessed immense strength ; but he came with too much confidence, as though simple brute force was to accomplish his purpose. He entered the pass between the two rocks ; and, with a roar of vengeance, not unlike the bellowing of a bull, he raised his sword and aimed a furious blow at the youth's head. Conrad smiled as he saw the direction of the ponderous blade ; for, upon the first instant, he knew that the giant was at his mercy. A very slight movement on his part turned the furiously driven point against the rock ; and from that moment he led the attack. The ruffian was startled ; then bewildered ; and then blinded ; but before he could withdraw from the trap into which he had so eagerly plunged, the trenchant blade of the mountaineer had cut the thread of his life, and he fell backward at the entrance of the passage.

Pluton by this time discovered that the man whom the prince so much feared was not an enemy to be despised by anybody ; and before he permitted another attack, he stopped to make a better plan.

"We have him now," he cried, moving back a pace, and pointing to an open way towards the shore. "Pierre and Ludovic, do you go round there, and attack the rascal in the rear. By the mass ! we have him now in his own trap."

Conrad was startled when he heard this ; for surely his fate was sealed if the murderous plan should be carried out. Against enemies on both hands, in such a place as that, it would be impossible to contend. He was upon the point of rushing out to attack the two in front before the others could get around to the rear of the rocks, when a new party appeared upon the scene.

"Halloa !" cried a voice. "What is all this ?"

Pluton turned and beheld the captain of the ducal guard at the head of a dozen men. He recognized the rich uniform in a moment, and he knew that his own safety would be jeoparded if he stopped for further explanation. So he gave the word to his companion, and ran with all possible speed down by the shore; where the other two of his men had just disappeared ; and in a very few moments they were all out of sight, among the rocks.

Nicolas, for he it was, advanced to meet our hero, who very quickly explained what had transpired.

"Never mind," said the captain, as the idea of pursuing the rascals presented itself. "Let them go. We know from whom they came ; and we shall know better how to manage for the future. The duke was right in sending me down here."

"Did he send you?"

"Yes, I met him at the garden gate. He was going in, and I was going out. He said he had left you alone down by the sea, and told me to come down and keep you company. And, by my life, I think I arrived just in season. The murderous rascals had planned a sure thing."

"I don't know," said Conrad, smiling.

"How? Do you imagine you could have withstood such odds?. Think of it: While those in front held your point, those in the rear would simply have run their sword straight through your body."

"Ah, my good captain, I should not have given them that opportunity. When I saw those two who were to have attacked me in the rear disappear, I had but one chance left, so far as my own endeavors were concerned; and that chance I was about to try when you appeared. I meant to rush out upon the two who remained in front, and press them with all my might, hoping to overcome them before the others could come to their assistance. However, I am very thankful that you saved me from the ordeal, for I might have failed."

"By the Holy Cross!" cried Nicolas, smiting his breast, "I almost wish I had left you to the work; for, upon my soul, I think you would have conquered them."

"It is better as it is," said Conrad. "I have shed blood enough."

"By Saint Michael! if the prince follows you much more, his prided legion will be materially thinned. But come—let us go to the house. We will send down some of the servants to take care of these dead men."

"There has been an arrival from Rennes?" remarked our hero, as they walked along. He intended to have spoken very unconcernedly; but there was a strange flutter in his voice.

"Yes, replied Nicolas ; " an advance courier from the train of the Lady Rosaline."

"Ah ; is she on her way to this place ?"

"Yes. She has hurried, it seems. She was lonesome at the castle, after her father had gone—very lonesome."

The captain looked into Conrad's face as he spoke, and then added :

"She will be here this evening—at least two days earlier than we had calculated upon."

The stout officer would have spoken further, but his companion had · become suddenly thoughtful and abstracted, and he chose not to disturb the current of his reflections.

CHAPTER XIX.

THE PROSCRIBED.

The Abbey of Saint Aubin was one of the oldest Benedictine institutions of Brittany ; and Dagobert, the abbot, was one of the oldest of the Church magnates. He had been present at the crowning of three kings, and was likely to be present at the crowning of the fourth. He was a man of robust frame ; blessed with a calm, healthy temperament ; and all his instincts and impulses were on the side of Right. The result of this was, that throughout the whole realm he was regarded as an oracle of truth and wisdom ; and the nobility respected him, while the common people loved and reverenced him. He had seen the lights and shadows of more than ninety years ; and though his hair was white as snow, and his brow deeply furrowed, yet his form was erect and his eye was clear. He bore the mitre and the crozier, and wielded the spiritual sceptre over all that part of the kingdom east of the Ille and Villaine.

Dagobert sat beneath one of the trees in the court of the abbey, and with him were Francisco and Marguerite. They had been conversing some time, and that the subject was of interest and importance was evident from the earnestness of their tones and gestures.

"It is best that the boy should leave the kingdom," said the abbot, in answer to a remark which Marguerite had made. "We will do our duty if we can. It is not for us to inquire what might be the result of making known his true name and station. It might open a pleasant way to him ; and it might doom him to disaster and violent death. Thus far in life he has been peaceful and happy enough ; and if his peace is to continue, we must send him away."

"Whither shall we send him ?" asked Francisco.

"Ah," replied Dagobert, shaking his head, " if he had come up as we had hoped, that question could have been easily answered. If he had taken to the Church, I could have opened the way to his speedy advancement. But I do not blame you, Francisco. The lion cannot be bent to the plow ; nor can an old soldier be expected to forget the lessons of his youth. If there is any blame, it must rest upon me. However, I think the boy's safety may be easily provided for. I shall go to Vannes within a few days, and I will make some arrangement for sending him away. How would you like a house in Burgundy, my sister ? That is far enough away from Brittany ; and I have friends there to whom I can recommend you."

The woman cared not whither she went, so that Conrad would be safe. She had given a promise to the boy's mother; and she wished to keep it if she could.

"Then let it rest as it is until we see Conrad."

Thus speaking the abbot arose, and walked with Francisco to the abbey, while Marguerite remained seated beneath the tree.

"I am not easy." said the dame to herself, after she was left alone. "They do not feel as anxious as I feel. The boy must not be discovered. I promised his mother; and I will keep the promise if I can. No good can come of his remaining in Brittany."

She was soliloquizing thus when she was interrupted by the approach of an old woman, who walked with a staff.

"A blessing upon thee, my sister," said the newcomer.

Marguerite returned the salutation, and asked the stranger if she would sit down and rest herself.

"No; I am not in need of rest. I am in search of a woman named Marguerite."

"I am Marguerite."

"I have a message from Rennes."

"I am expecting a message from that very place."

"This message is from a youth named Conrad."

"Good!" cried the dame, eagerly. "It is for me the message is intended."

"Do you know a woman named Rachel?"

"Yes. She is housekeeper at the castle."

"The very same. It is Rachel who has brought the message, and she is close at hand to deliver it. Shall I bring her hither?"

"Where is she?"

"She stopped at the little cot by the lodge."

"I will go and see her."

The messenger turned to retrace her steps, and Marguerite followed her. They passed out at the gate, and not far away they found the cot, which they entered. The outer door was closed, and when Marguerite looked to see Rachel, she saw, instead, an armed man. Those who usually inhabited the cot were not there. The person who had conducted her from the abbey grounds had disappeared, walking out with a firm, heavy tread.

"My good woman," said the man, "my name is Marius, and I have come to Saint Aubin on purpose to see you. You have not the least cause for alarm."

"But where is Rachel?"

"Who is Rachel?"

"The old housekeeper of the castle."

"O,—that was a little pleasantry on the part of one of my men. Ha, ha,—the rascal makes a capital old woman when he tries. But, dear Marguerite, this is all done for a most excellent purpose. You are wanted in Vannes. Now don't start, nor be frightened; and don't attempt to make any disturbance, for it cannot benefit you. The people who inhabit this cot I have sent away for a season; so we have the place all to ourselves."

"But are you from Conrad?"

"Just the same. You will see Conrad when we reach the end of our journey. But we won't stop to converse here."

Marguerite was frightened, and on the first opportunity she sprang towards the door; but she found it fastened. Then she turned and sank down upon her knees.

"Don't pray to me, my good woman. If all the priests in Brittany were on their knees, as you are, I could not listen to them."

Marius raised her up as he spoke; but she broke from him and rushed towards the little open window. Before

she could utter any cry, however, she was pulled forci-
bly back, and thrown upon the floor.

"This is unpleasant," said Marius, stooping over her;
"but you force me to it."

His three men came in as he spoke, and the woman's
hands were quickly tied behind her, and her mouth
stopped. Then they lifted her up, and bore her out by
a back way into a dense wood which grew near to the
cot. She struggled with all her might; but her efforts
were in vain.

* * * * * * *

In the early evening Prince Bertrand sat in his closet,
wondering how his agents were succeeding. Where
was Pluton? Had he done anything yet? Where was
Marius? Would he bring Marguerite? He was muttering to himself of these things, when Poins came in
and informed him that Pluton was without.

The prince started up, and ordered that Pluton should
be sent in.

The man-at-arms entered with a downcast, troubled
look.

"How now, Pluton? What success?"

"My lord, I hardly dare speak to you the truth. I
would rather that my body were buried in the rough
sands of the sea, than that my tongue should be forced
to the story I have to tell."

Bertrand rose to his feet with an angry gesture; but
before he suffered himself to speak he gained control of
his temper.

"Tell me the truth," he said. "I am prepared for
anything."

"The truth is this, my lord. I had been on the watch
for Conrad du Nord, and this afternoon I saw him walk
down upon the sea-shore with the Duke of Rennes. I.

followed, with my men, being careful to keep out of sight behind the rocks. By and by the duke was called back to his house, and the youth was left alone. I thought the time was now come to strike the blow, and Harold offered to do the work. In fact, he was eager for the privilege. I knew him to be a cool, brave man, and an expert swordsman ; and I let him go. The first part of his work he performed very well. He excited the young fellow to wrath, and got him to draw his sword. But he could not hold a point against the mountaineer. He went down in a very few minutes, with a hole through his body. Upon that the rest of us appeared, and the fellow sprang into a narrow passage between two huge rocks, where he turned as though he would face us. Of course but one could attack him there ; and Michaud, the most powerful of all our men-at-arms, rushed upon him with his heavy blade. But Michaud could not stand before the marvelous skill of that fellow's sword, and he fell dead in less than a minute after the first blow had been struck.

"I did not mean to allow the youngster to do any more mischief ; so I sent two of my men around to attack him in the rear, while Raoul and I held him in front ; but before we could put this plan into execution the captain of the ducal guard appeared, followed by a number of his men, and we made our escape as quickly as possible. Indeed, my lord, we did the best we could. I did not hold the fellow so high as he proved himself, or—"

"You would have made an assassination of it," cried Bèrtrand. "By the mass, that is the way it should have been done. The fellow is a very demon of skill and address."

"I trust, my lord, that you will not suffer your anger to rest against me. Indeed, I did——"

"Go to, Pluton. I am sorry you failed; but I am not angry with you. Perhaps at some time, you may make up for this. I shall hold you to the performance of a bold deed one of these days."

"Anything, my lord. Command me as you will."

The man was earnest and sincere; for he had expected a fall of mighty wrath upon his head. He was just rising from his knees, when Poins made his appearance, with the announcement that Marius had returned.

"Ha!" cried the prince, starting at the sound of that name, "if Marius brings success with him, I shall feel some recompense. Go, Pluton, and keep your own counsel; and also keep your sword sharp."

Pluton withdrew, and shortly afterward Marius entered the apartment.

"Speak, Marius. I have had one note of failure since the night set in."

"The second note will not be sounded by me, my lord."

"Ah—you have succeeded?"

"Yes. The woman for whom you sent me is in one of your ante-rooms, safe and sound."

"You are sure it is Marguerite?"

"Yes, my lord. She is the woman who reared Conrad du Nord. I found her at the Abbey of Saint Aubin; I saw her in company with the old abbot and Francisco; and afterwards she was enticed easily into our power through the influence of Conrad's name."

"Good! good! You shall have your reward, Marius. The woman is under guard?"

"She is."

"Go and keep her until I send for her. See that she has such refreshment as she may need, and be sure that she is treated with kindness and respect."

"Now, my brave Poins," continued Bertrand, as soon

as Marius had gone, "go and bring Father Jerome to me. Let nothing stop him. I must see him this very night."

In less than an hour the old monk presented himself in the prince's apartment. His first look was upon the table, and a shadow crossed his face when he saw that the board was bare. Bertrand noticed the look, and he directed Poins to bring wine.

The shadow was gone from the good father's face; and with a smack of the lips and an extra wink of the little eyes, he turned to business.

"Father Jerome, the woman is here."

"Marguerite ?"

"Yes."

"Have you questioned her ?"

"No. I did not venture. I thought you had better do it."

"You were right, my son. I remember the woman well, and I think she must remember me. But, before we question her, there are some things to be considered."

"Consider well, good father," said the prince, "for upon the result hangs the mitre and crozier of Saint Alban."

The monk nodded his head, and winked emphatically.

"I understand, my son. Do not think I forget Saint Alban. But I was thinking that this woman must be approached very carefully. Evidently her love is all centered in the youth, and if she thought we meant him harm, no power could open her lips. We must make her believe that we are laboring for the fellow's good."

"Certainly. You can manage it as you please. I leave it entirely in your hands."

"Does she know you, my lord ?"

" I think not. At all events, I don't know that I ever saw her."

" Very well. I am ready to see her."

Poins was called, and directed to bring Marguerite into the chamber.

In a little while the woman came, pale and frightened, and trembling at every joint; but when she saw the monk a spark of hope gleamed in her eye, and instinctively she put her hands out towards him. The holy garb seemed to her a harbinger of safety. Father Jerome saw the effect, and he rightly guessed its cause.

" My good sister," he said, rising and extending his hand, " you have nothing to fear. You are safe, and your condition shall be respected."

" Holy father, what means this violence? Why have I been thus dragged from my friends by armed men?" She gave the monk her hand, and her look and tones were trusting.

" Be seated, Marguerite, and I will explain."

" You know me, then?" she said, as she sat down.

" Certainly I know you. Have you forgotten me?"

She looked into his face as he turned it towards her, and presently she recognized him.

" You are Father Jerome."

" Yes, Marguerite. I think it is over twenty years since last we met."

" Three years more than that," said Marguerite.

" Aye—you are right. How time passes away! You and I have both changed; but I trust that the measure of evil has been less to us than the measure of good."

" If it has been so in the past, I pray God it may be so in the future!" ejaculated the dame. Then she looked upon the prince, and a sudden tremor shook her frame.

" You behold a stranger," said Bertrand, smiling.

" Are you not the prince ?" asked Marguerite.

" What makes you think so ?"

" Your face—your dress—your bearing. You are the prince."

" Good sister," interposed the monk, " you are right ; and let me assure you that the prince desires to be your friend. It was at my request that you were sent for ; and if you have been dragged hither, then our servants did wrong. Did you know that Conrad du Nord was in Vannes ?"

" I have learned so since I left Saint Aubin. O, is he safe, good father ?" Marguerite cast a quick, eager glance at the prince, and then bent her gaze upon the monk.

" He is safe and well, my sister ; and we desire to promote his welfare. I will not conceal from you that he is in danger ; but we hope, with your assistance, to save him. If you will listen to me—if you will trust me—I will show you how he can be saved ; or, at least, how I hope he can be saved. I doubt not that you have been tempted to regard the prince as his enemy."

Marguerite's quick glance of fear was answer enough, and the monk continued :

" But you have no occasion to apprehend such danger. That the prince has feared this youth is true ; but I have assured him that he had no just occasion for such fear ; and I have sent for you to confirm him in that assurance."

It was evident that the woman was prepared to trust the holy man ; for she regarded him hopefully, and hung eagerly upon his words. She still trembled, but it was from deep anxiety and concern.

" Speak to me, father, and tell me what is to be done.

The boy is true and good, and he deserves not ill-fortune."

"Marguerite," said the Benedictine, speaking with a show of religious frankness, "the boy's whole danger lies in the mystery that enshrouds his birth."

The good dame turned pale at these words, and trembled like an aspen.

"Be not alarmed," resumed Jerome, persuasively. "I think I know the truth ; and, if I be right, I can save your boy. Will you answer me truly ?"

"Speak on, father."

"Then give me your attention." The monk bent forward, with his hands folded, and continued : "There once lived in Vannes a Count named Marceau. He was a general in the army, and was ambitious. His wife was of gentle blood, and named Marcelline. This count conspired against the life of the king, organizing a band of traitors, and plotting a most fearful rebellion ; and in this plot he was seconded by his wife. The plot was discovered almost upon the eve of its consummation, and the leaders were arrested. Marceau and Marcelline were not only sentenced to death, but their whole family were included in the fatal decree. Marcelline had a young infant, even then upon her breast—a boy—and this boy, the offspring of such wicked traitors and conspirators, was condemned by the laws of the realm. There was no power on earth could pardon him. Even the king could not do it ; for it is written in the book that the children of parents who have conspired against the king's life must die. Marcelline had friends, and her infant's life was saved. It was brought away by the nurse of a powerful lady, and the story was told that the infant was dead. Have I not spoken truly ?"

Marguerite was fearfully convulsed. Her frame

shook, and her bosom heaved as though her heart would leap from its place.

"Have I not spoken truly, my sister?"

"Why—why—have you told me this story? Why do you ask me if it is true?"

"Because I have a purpose. Ah, Marguerite, the story is not a new one to you."

The woman clasped her hands, and once more she turned a frightened look upon the prince.

"My sister, you have nothing to fear for your boy from the truth of this story. Designing men are trying to make use of him, and the prince only desires that he should leave the country. Now answer me: Was not the infant child of Marcelline saved?"

Marguerite did not answer. She gazed with a vacant stare towards the monk, as though some other object stood between him and her.

"Will you not speak, good sister?

"Suppose the child of Marcelline was saved?" said the dame, in a hoarse whisper. "Suppose that child still lived?"

"We would know it," returned Jerome.

"And death would be his portion!"

Marguerite bowed her head, and rested her brow upon her hands.

Bertrand took advantage of the opportunity, and glided noiselessly to the monk's side.

"Remember," he whispered, "we must not lose it now. If you would gain the mitre of Saint Alban, hesitate at nothing. Let no word of promise she may demand stick in your throat."

"My good sister," said the monk, as the prince resumed his seat, "you are laboring under a false impression. If that boy lives he may be saved. If Conrad du Nord is that boy, we will save him!"

Marguerite started up in an instant.

"Do you swear that?" she cried.

The Benedictine would have hesitated; but a look from the prince was sufficient to move him. The golden crozier of Saint Alban was too grand a prize to be lost.

"We do swear it!"

"Aye," added Bertrand; "we both swear it!"

"But how is he to be saved?"

"We will send him from the country."

"Whither?"

"Where no evil influence from Brittany can reach him more."

"O—if you would do this—"

"We swear it by all we hold sacred!" said the prince.

"How is it?" asked Jerome. "Is Conrad du Nord the child of those proscribed and executed parents?"

"Yes."

As the answer fell from Marguerite's lips, she sank back in her chair, with a faint gasp, and in a moment more the monk caught her in his arms.

"God save us!" ejaculated Father Jerome. "She has swooned! Must we push this further? Can you not send the boy away as——"

"Hush! Are you mad?" exclaimed the prince, stamping his foot. "Shall we suffer such a viper to live! By Saint Paul, we should be sinning against the laws of the land. If the fainting of this woman moves you so——"

"Enough, my lord. I am with you to the end."

"Good, my brave monk. See me through with this, and in another year you shall invite the king to sit at your table of Saint Alban."

The Benedictine nodded and winked assent to the proposition, while Bertrand turned to call his servants to come and care for the fainting woman.

CHAPTER XX.

THE CRASH !

Rosaline of Rennes, accompanied by a strong force of her father's guard, reached Vannes early in the evening, where all was in readiness for her reception. The duke smilingly chided her for the haste she had made in leaving the castle ; but the chiding did not grieve her.

"Were you afraid to remain there ?" he asked, with his hand upon her head.

"No, father."

"Ah, you were lonesome, Rosaline ; and your lonesomeness was not wholly because your father was away."

She looked up into his face with an expression of love and of sadness ; and before she spoke, a bright tear gathered upon the long silken lashes, and rolled down the soft cheek.

"Dear father, I have no desire to hide my real feelings. I did wish to see you ; and I wished to see another ;—I missed you both. But it was not wholly that. The old castle is not so bright when you are away as it used to be. When I am left alone within its great walls I feel the weight of mourning settling upon my spirits. I have no mother now to share my thoughts."

The duke bent his head, and imprinted a kiss upon the fair brow ; and then he drew his child to his bosom.

The name of his sainted wife fell with a sigh from his lips, and a tear rolled down his manly cheek.

"I am glad you are here, Rosaline; for your presence is as the sunlight in my path. So make yourself perfectly easy, and assume your position as mistress of the house."

So ended the parent's chiding, and ere long the smiles came back to Rosaline's face. After she had changed her raiment, and partaken of refreshment, she rejoined her father in the drawing-room, where Conrad was waiting to greet her. The duke, when he had witnessed the meeting of the lovers, walked away to an alcove, and commuted with himself. He saw plainly that the love between those two beings was deep and powerful, and he knew that a sundering of the tie would be mortally painful.

"But it cannot be," he soliloquized. "There is no possibility of danger. If he is not already noble, I will make him noble. I will make him noble in station, as God has made him noble in nature. I will not allow the thought of failure to come. He is worthy, and he is true. As for the rest, I leave it in the hands of fate."

He returned and sat down with the youthful couple, and for an hour or more the conversation was earnest and interesting. The duke was more than ever charmed by Conrad's wit and intelligence; and more than once he found himself receiving instruction from his lips. Rosaline, somewhat fatigued by her journey, at length arose to retire; but before she had bidden her father good-night, a servant opened the door and called him out.

"I will see him in the hall," she said, turning, and extending her hand to Conrad.

"Blessed one!" the youth exclaimed, drawing the maiden to his bosom; "should the night come when you are mine no more, I shall remember these moments as the brightest and sweetest of my life !"

"Dear Conrad, why speak you so ? O, do not whisper such thoughts. What can divide us now ?"

" Perhaps—nothing !"

" You are sad. What is it, Conrad ? Surely nothing has—"

" No, no, sweet love. It was but a passing cloud. O, can it be possible that such a heaven is to be mine on earth !" He held the beautiful girl by the hands, and gazed down into her face, and then pressed his lips upon her brow.

"I am yours, Conrad—yours forever !" she murmured, returning his kiss. "Let our dreams to-night be the happy harbingers of a blissful future."

" Heaven bless you, love !"

Rosaline smiled a blessing in return ; and so they separated.

When the duke returned there was a troubled look upon his face, and he regarded our hero for some moments, as though he were trying to frame the language he was to use.

" My lord," said Conrad, noticing the effort, "you have something to say to me."

" Yes," returned Casimir, smiling, and trying to assume a free expression. " Something curious has come to pass. The king has sent for us."

" Sent for us !—the king !" repeated the youth. " What can he want with us at this hour ?"

" Indeed, my son, I cannot imagine ; but we will soon ascertain. His majesty may have found an hour to spare—he may have been busy through the day."

" But, my lord—"

" Let us not anticipate any evil," interrupted the duke.

" While I am with you, you have nothing to fear. We will answer the summons at once."

Conrad had no disposition to oppose the arrangement, and yet he was not easy. However, the assurance of his host gave him something to lean upon, and he prepared for the visit without any show of fear.

Nicolas was called, with a squad of his men, to accompany his master to the royal palace, and when all was ready they set off. In the palace court they were met by Sir Philip de Savenay, who conducted the duke and Conrad towards the king's chamber.

" My dear captain," said Casimir, speaking so that Conrad might not overhear, " can you tell me what is the meaning of this untimely summons ?"

" I cannot, my lord," replied Sir Philip ; " though I suspect," he added, after turning his head to see that their companion was not too near, " that the prince has made some new complaint. Bertrand went into the king's chamber an hour ago, and when he had been there for half an hour, the royal order came forth summoning the Duke of Rennes and Conrad du Nord."

" I have no fears of any complaint the prince can make," said the duke ; " and I think I know what he hath now to complain of. One or two more of his best men are missing. If that should be the case, I shall send out after Nicolas to come in and testify."

When they reached the door of the royal apartment, Sir Philip went in in advance, and presently came back, and bade his companions follow him.

The chamber was well lighted, and the king and the prince seemed to be there alone. When Conrad beheld the bent and trembling form of the aged monarch, and marked the lines of care which had been so deeply drawn upon the pale brow, he was moved with pity ; but when his gaze rested upon the sinister features of

Bertrand, his teeth were shut closely together, and a harsher feeling chilled his heart.

Theobald leaned forward as Conrad approached him, and raised his hand above his eyes, so as to shade them from the glare of the hanging lamps.

"Sire," spoke the duke, "I am here in answer to your summons; and Conrad du Nord accompanies me."

"Is this Conrad du Nord?" asked the king.

"That is my name, sire," replied our hero, advancing another step, and bowing.

Theobald gazed long and earnestly upon the youthful face, and his lips moved as though he were muttering his thoughts to himself.

"This is the man," said the prince; "and I think we had better proceed. It is late, and you are growing weary, my father."

The king roused himself, and turned to his captain.

"Sir Philip, this young man is in your custody for the present."

De Savenay bowed, and drew near to the side of Conrad du Nord.

"Casimir," pursued Theobald, in a tremulous, uneasy tone, "I have a most unpleasant work upon my hands— a work which I would gladly avoid did not the stern laws of Brittany point the way I must go."

"Sire," answered the duke, respectfully, "let the laws of the realm be obeyed. I am ready to bow to them."

"This youth, whom you have taken to your friendship, my good cousin, is also under the law."

"Of course he is, sire."

"Then we will waste no time. You shall quickly know, Casimir, why I have sent for you. Let the monk be brought in."

Bertrand turned towards a side door, which was concealed by a curtain, and presently Father Jerome entered the chamber, and approached the royal seat. The duke recognized the monk at once, and the look upon his face showed that a feeling of uneasiness was beginning to move him. Father Jerome, when he had bowed to the king, turned his eyes upon Conrad du Nord. There was a slight quiver of frame, and his lips were compressed ; but he betrayed no further emotion.

"Good father," said Theobald, "before we make any accusation against this young man, we would hear the story you have to tell."

"Sire," replied the Benedictine, "the laws of the land, and the command of my king, loosen my tongue. What I am forced to reveal is this : Some three or four-and-twenty years ago there was formed in Vannes a most deadly plot against the life of the king. Foremost among the conspirators was Marceau, a count and a general ; and Marcelline, the wife of Marceau, was as deeply implicated as was her husband. Marcelline had formerly been in the service of the queen, and she was thus enabled to lay the plans for the entrance of the conspirators into the royal palace. But the foul conspiracy was discovered before the fatal blow could be struck, and the conspirators were arrested and punished. Marceau and Marcelline were doomed to death, and it was furthermore decreed that all their family should suffer death."

"Remember," interrupted the king, shuddering with the memory of that terrible ordeal, "that this decree was no fiat of mine. The laws of Brittany condemned to death the children of those who raised their hands against the life of the king. You understand this, my lord duke ?"

"Yes," replied Casimir, with an expression of painful anxiety, "I understand that."

Theobald nodded to the monk, who thus proceeded :

"Marcelline had an infant son, only a few months old, in whom her deepest love was centered. This child she desired to save ; and by the assistance of a friend who was high in power, she succeeded in accomplishing her purpose. The infant was borne away, and word was given to the world that it had died. Sire, I was that woman's spiritual comforter and confessor. She confessed to me what she had done, and I saw her infant taken from her arms and borne away. Then the seal of the confessional was upon my lips. The seal is now removed because there may be danger to the king."

"Do you know who bore that child away?" asked Theobald.

"Yes, sire ; I remember very well. It was a woman then in the service of Mary of Anjou. Her name was Marguerite."

"My son," said the king, turning to the prince, "have you this woman in attendance?"

"I have, sire."

"Let her be introduced."

Marguerite was led into the royal presence by the Benedictine, who went out after her. She knew that she was before the king, for Jerome had prepared her for the interview ; still she trembled violently, and when she saw Conrad she would have sprung towards him, had not the monk restrained her.

"Be careful," he whispered. "Offend not the king. If you love your boy, make no demonstration here."

Conrad du Nord, when he saw the woman who had been to him as a mother led into the chamber, grasped the arm of Sir Philip for support. He was weak and dizzy, and objects seemed whirling in mazy circles before him. The crash was upon him, and he felt the quaking beneath his feet.

The Duke of Rennes stood like a block of stone, with his arms tightly folded upon his breast.

"Woman," spoke Theobald, "do you know who I am?"

"Yes, sire," she replied, in a whisper; "I know you very well. I have not forgotten you."

"Look upon the man who stands by your side—him who just led you hither. Do you know him?"

"I remember him, sire."

"Now turn and look upon the youth who stands by the side of my captain. Do you know him?"

"O my God! yes."

"Who is he?"

"He is to me a son."

"You have reared him from infancy?"

"Yes."

"Who were his parents?"

Marguerite clasped her hands over her eyes, and quivered like a storm-riven reed.

"Speak woman; who were his parents?"

"O, spare me, sire!"

The monk whispered something into her ear. He assured her that she need not fear for her boy; and he tried to make her understand that a prompt answer would please the king.

"O, sire, pardon me!" she cried, sinking upon her knees. "I could not refuse the work of mercy. I saved the infant child of Marcelline from the red hands of the executioner. I bore the infant away; and the poor mother died with a blessing for me upon her lips."

"And that child," said the king; "where is it now?"

Marguerite struggled as though she were choking; and the monk was forced to support her.

"Answer," he whispered into her ear. "Excite not the royal wrath."

"Woman," cried Theobold, sternly, "listen to me, and answer. If you speak truly, no harm shall befall you. I will pardon you for the part you took against the weal of the realm. Look upon the youth whom you have reared to manhood. Is he whom you call Conrad, the child you saved?"

"Yes!" burst hysterically from Marguerite's lips; and ere the sound of her voice had died away, she sank senseless into the monk's arms, and was borne from the chamber.

The king started to his feet, and turned his gaze upon Conrad du Nord.

"Young man," he said, "I am almost sorry that I ever saw you; but I am still more sorry that both your parents were traiters of the blackest dye. If you know the laws of Brittany, you know what your fate must be. I have not the power to pardon you if I would. But I will not repeat your sentence to-night. You shall have time for thought and prayer,—Sir Philip, call some of your men."

Thamar was nearest at hand, as had been provided for by the prince; and Thamar answered the call.

"Guardsman," resumed the monarch, as Thamar presented himself, "yonder man is your prisoner. Bear him to a dungeon from which he cannot escape."

As Conrad was taken by the arm, to be led away, he cast a look upon the duke, but he could not catch his eye. Then he called upon him—

"My lord duke!"

But Casimer did not answer, he stood with his head bowed, his face covered with his hands; and his whole frame convulsed.

The unhappy youth made no further effort. With a groan that seemed to burst from the depths of a dying heart, he bowed his head, and allowed Thamar to take away his sword, and lead him from the room.

CHAPTER XXI.

FIDES' LAST MEAL.

Midnight !—cold, dark, and cheerless ! The heavy door shuts with a thundering clang ; the ponderous bolts are shot into their unyielding sockets ; and the dull echoes die away into the stillness of death !

Conrad du Nord is alone—a prisoner. "Great God !" he cries, in shuddering tones, "have mercy upon me !" His fall is terrible ; and for a time he is dizzy and faint. Gradually his memory grasps the things of the past, and he is able to realize the horrors of the situation to which he had been brought.

Dark ! dark ! Not a ray of light. A sealed cavern in the centre of the earth could not have been darker. A narrow cell, with walls of solid rock ; the floor flinty and rough. No chain—no couch ;—what can he want of them ?

By and by the first paroxysm passes, and the youth struggled up to sense and reason. Still he is faint and sick for the blow has been almost mortal, even as it fell upon the heart.

"And thus ends the dream !" groaned Conrad du Nord to himself, as he stood with his hands clasped upon his cold brow. "So fade away the bright pictures of life ; and so opens the tomb, soon to close upon me forevermore !"

He thought of the old home among the mountains ; of the happy hours spent in those wild solitudes ; of the lessons of his old tutor ; of the love of his foster mother ; and of the promises which his young heart had held ere he knew the paths that led to other scenes.   Then came thoughts of the angel that had been thrown in his way. His first whispering of Rosaline's name was with a thrill of rapture ; but in a moment more the icy hand was upon him, and he saw that she had led him to his destruction.

"O," he cried, "if I had never seen her—"

He stopped, as though a pang had pierced his bosom. In a few moments more he bowed his head, and gently murmured,—

"Blessed angel, thou wert not to blame.   Thou art pure and true ; and I will hold the memory of thy love to my heart as the most precious thing of earth !   It is fate ! fate—O, I felt the coming of this blow.   The duke knew that it might come.   He must have known it. And I am the offspring of condemned and executed traitors, and I am myself proscribed !   My blood is tainted ; my name is blasted from off the book of the realm !"

And thus groaning he sank down upon the flinty floor, and bowed his face upon his hands.   He was murmuring the name of Rosaline—bidding her farewell and blessing her—when he heard a sound near his door—a sound as though some one were withdrawing the bolts. He started to his feet, and presently the door was slowly opened, and faint rays of light beamed into the cell.

"Conrad !" spoke a voice.

"I am here," replied the prisoner.   He spoke quickly, for he thought he recognized the tones.

The light grew brighter as the visitor drew the curtain from his lantern; and Conrad soon recognized the duke. Casimer placed the lantern upon the floor, and extended his hand. He trembled violently, and the lines of deep agony were upon his face. For some moments neither spoke. The duke however, at length broke the silence :

"Conrad, I have come to offer you the last token of friendship I may ever have opportunity to extend to you. I hope that you have not cursed me. I know how sadly I have been deceived, and how terribly my mistake has been visited upon yourself. But I never dreamed of this."

" Ah, my lord," said Conrad reproachfully, "tell me not that. I have not cursed you—I will not curse you ; but you must not deceive me longer. You have feared from the first that this blow might come."

" Conrad,—what mean you ?"

" You have, from the first, been fearful that the blasting curse might rest upon my family name."

"My dear boy, you accuse me wrongfully. If you mean that I had any suspicions of this terrible result which has burst upon us, you are entirely mistaken."

" Then why," cried Conrad, " did you hesitate in your promises to me ? Why did you reserve your final word of decision until after this trial ? Why did you put me off with such mysterious words ? Why did you refuse to allow your child to speak my sentence ? Ah, my lord, in all your dealings with me you have had in view the possibility of this awful result."

" Conrad," replied the duke, speaking slowly and earnestly, " you entirely misjudge me. Be calm now, and listen while I tell you the truth. Circumstances entirely beyond my control brought you into the companionship of my daughter. You loved her before my consent could be asked. You remember when you came to me and told of your love. I knew that your affection was deep and pure, and that my child returned it. This was the first appeal you had made to me. How was I to answer? By the laws of our nobility, had you been but a nameless mountaineer, I could not have given you Rosaline's hand. I say that I could not, because the king could have prevented it had he seen fit. But I had a strange hope that you might prove to be of gentle blood. I thought I saw it in your face. I fancied that I could trace lineaments there which were like those of one of my earliest and best friends. I saw Francisco, and from him I learned that your father was a soldier; and he left me to conclude that he was also an officer of rank. Had your old tutor told me that your father died ignominiously; or had he even left it possible for me to suspect such a thing, I should not have held out to you the lamp of hope. But Francisco deceived me. He told me that your father died upon the field of battle.

"Now, my son, reflect calmly upon the subject. You came to me, and told me of your love. I loved you, and I honored you; and it was my earnest desire that my daughter might be blessed with a husband as true and brave as you had proved yourself. I could not refuse you; for I did sincerely believe that you were of noble origin. I had reason to believe so. Still there was a mystery which I could not wholly penetrate, but I had faith to believe that I could penetrate it after a time. You asked me to give the decision of your fate into the hands of my daughter. It seems that a shadow of the coming event even then rested upon your soul."

Conrad shuddered, but made no reply.

"There was no such shadow, upon *my* soul, my son. You look incredulous. What I tell you is true. I refused your request because I have made it a rule of my life not to blindly promise anything. When I hesitated to speak the pledge you sought, I fully believed that you would be my daughter's husband. I never dreamed of this terrible thing which has come to light."

"I believe you, my lord," said the youth; "and I have no wish to blame you. I have almost cursed the fate which led me into this dark pit; but even that curse I wish not to repeat. The die is cast, and all is over!"

"But all is not lost, Conrad. I can place you where I found you. Of course I cannot give you—I cannot link the name of——"

"Hold, my lord! There is no need that you should speak those words. I am not a blind dolt. The name of the noble must not be contaminated. The fate of the angel of light must not be linked with the fate of the proscribed child of condemned and executed traitors! O, my God!"

"Conrad!" cried the duke, drawing the youth's head upon his shoulder, "I pray you give not up to such gloomy fancies. In the years to come you may forget this blow—you may live to outgrow it. You do not feel the blood of the traitor moving in your veins; and under the judgment of God there is no crime upon your hands. In some far-off land, with Francisco and Marguerite still to bear you company, you may once more step forth into bold life, and be free and happy."

"How?" asked the youth, moving back a pace. "Am I not a prisoner? condemned?"

"I have come to set you free. By the utmost exertion of my power I have gained the keys of this dungeon; and I can lead you forth, and set you free. I can send a guard with you as far as the confines of Anjou; and when you are once within the dominions of the duke John, you will be safe. Come—there is no time to be lost. Of course you will accept this last proof of my friendship; for I do assure you that I risk much in the deed."

"Aye," responded our hero, grasping the duke's hand, "I shall accept. I am not afraid of death in a good cause; but I cannot die thus. I will go with you."

"Then follow me at once. You have one other friend in the palace, and he has left the way clear for us."

Conrad supposed that other friend to be Sir Philip de Savenay; but he asked no questions upon the subject.

As he took the duke's arm to leave the cell, he said:

"You spoke of Francisco and Marguerite."

"Yes, my son. They will join you in Anjou."

"Poor Marguerite! how did they drag the story from her?"

"It is a puzzle to me, Conrad. I cannot comprehend it. But you may be assured that she could not help it. I think she would have died for you."

"I know she must have been forced to it."

"Aye—and more than that," added Casimir: "She must have been promised that no harm should come to you. I know that she was so promised. But she can tell you all when you see her. Step carefully. These are dubious ways, and but little trod by the citizens of the upper world."

The duke had picked up his lantern, and led Conrad from the cell; and after winding through many damp, dark passages, they arrived at a landing where stood a guard. The guardsman turned his back, and the duke passed him without speaking.

"Sir Philip helps us," whispered the youth.

"Hush!" returned Casimir. "Speak not the name of one who may be compromised. Philip de Savenay is a good man and true."

Up to another floor—through passages broader than those below—out into a paved court, and at length Con-

rad stood in the open air, with a copse of mulberry
trees between him and the place he had left. The stars
were gleaming brightly overhead, and a gentle breeze,
coming up from the murmuring sea, gave new impulse
to his lungs, and bore to his senses something of returning vigor.

"It is now past midnight—an hour past," said the
duke, " and you must cross the Villaine before morning.
Here is Nicolas with six good men, to bear you company, and you may rely upon them. I think you have
nothing further to wait for. .I have done all I can."

Conrad saw the men who were to accompany him ;
but he did not yet turn to join them. He cast an
imploring look upon the duke, and breathed the name
of Rosaline.

"No ! no !" gasped Casimir.

"You will bear to her one word from me ?"

"I will tell her that you are safe ; and beyond that I
may need all my strength to support and sustain her.
For your own sake, Conrad, turn your thoughts from
her. Do not force me to——"

" Enough !" cried the youth, putting out his hand.
" I thank you for what you have done. Farewell !"

The duke grasped his hand ; held it a moment in
both his own ; and then, with a whisper of blessing, he
turned and hurried away. Conrad was growing faint
and dizzy again ; but the voice of Nicolas called him
back to sense ; and, with a mighty effort, he started
up and threw off the influence that was crushing him
down.

"Come, my brother," said the captain, laying his
hand kindly upon the youth's arm. "We have a long
road before us, and we have need of expedition. Here
is your sword. The duke left it for you."

Conrad first grasped the hand of his friend ; and then

he grasped the faithful sword; and when the honest blade once more hung upon his hip he felt stronger.

"Lead on, good Nicolas. I am ready to follow."

Down by the seashore, where the soft sand drank up the heavy fall of the hoofed feet, they found the horses; and ere long they were speeding away from the city. One last look Conrad du Nord turned upon the turrets and spires of the capital, as they grew dim and indistinct in the gloomy distance; and then, with a blessed name upon his lips, and a faintly murmured farewell, he put spurs to his horse and bade Nicolas to lead as swiftly as he pleased.

. *   *   *   *   *   *   *

The king was weak and hungry. He had not eaten his supper when the prince brought the startling case before him; and he had had no time to eat it since. He had given to Bertrand an order for the private execution of the son of Marceau and Marcelline; and when he was left alone he called his page.

"Ponce, what is the hour?"

"It is past midnight, sire."

"Never mind—I must eat before I sleep."

"Your supper is in your closet, sire."

"I will retire thither and eat it. You may put out these lights, and keep watch here until I call you."

Theobald found a single lamp burning in the closet, and his bread and milk were upon the table. *Fides* heard his master's step, and scratched and whined most anxiously; for he was not used to going so long without his supper. He was quickly admitted, however, and as soon as the meal was prepared, he devoured it voraciously.

"Poor Fides," said the king, as the dog lapped up the last of the bread and the milk, "it may be that you will outlive me. A surer hand than any of earth may be laid upon me—"

Theobald was cut short in his reflections by the dog's leaping up into his lap.

"Down ! down, Fides. I am tired to-night, and feel not like play."

The animal crouched upon the floor ; and presently he began to dig with his claws as though he suffered pain. He groaned and struggled, and started up and ran across the room ; and when he lay down again, there was froth upon his lips, and his eyes seemed starting from their sockets. A few moments more, and then came another paroxysm more severe. It was a painful scene—a terrible scene. The third struggle ended, and the dog crawled upon his side, and rested his head upon his master's feet, and there died !

By and by the king gained strength enough to drag the body of the dead dog away, and to call his page.

"Ponce, this is excellent bread—the best I have eaten for many a day. Do you know who made it ?"

" I think you have a new cook, sire."

" Ah—I was not aware of it."

" Yes, sire. The old cook is sick."

" And who furnished the new one ?"

" The prince."

" Ah !"

" Are you faint, sire ?"

" No, no, Ponce. Get thee gone. I shall want you no more to-night. It is excellent bread !"

The page went away ; and the king bowed his head upon the table, and wept like a child.

CHAPTER XXII.

OLD FRIENDS.

Almost as soon as the day had dawned, prince Bertrand presented himself at the office of the royal guard, with the order for the immediate and private execution of Conrad du Nord. He was to see the deed done. A lieutenant took the keys, and went with him down into the dungeon ; but the place was empty.

"This is not the cell," said the prince.

"This is certainly the cell, my lord."

"Then where is the prisoner ?"

The guardsman was bewildered. He could tell nothing about it.

"How long have you been on guard?" asked Bertrand.

"Since four o'clock."

"How long were those on whom you relieved ?"

"Four hours, from midnight."

"By the gods !" cried Bertrand, stamping his foot, and gnashing his teeth, "if the prisoner has been led away, it must have been done during that time. But let us look."

All the cells in that depth were examined, but no prisoner was found. Then the prince hastened back to the office with the lieutenant, and called for the captain. But the captain was not at hand.

"How many sentinels were there in and about the prison?" demanded the prince.

"The lieutenant said there were ten."

"Let those ten who were on from midnight until four o'clock this morning be instantly summoned."

The summons was sent ; but the men were not found.

"They should be in their beds at this hour," said the lieutenant; "but they are not there ; and their beds have not been touched during the night."

"Then by heaven ! they have deserted !" exclaimed Bertrand, gasping as he spoke.

"It looks like it, my lord."

The prince rushed out, and in the court he met one of his father's ushers, the sight of whom caused him, for a moment, to forget the errand he had started upon.

"Ah—fellow—here ! Have you seen the king this morning ?"

"No, my lord," replied the usher, bowing respectfully.

"I fear my father is not well. He looked sick and faint when I left him last night."

The usher passed on, and Bertrand hurried away to the office of the palace guard, where he assured himself that all the sentinels who had held watch in the prison during the last half of the night had run away. He flew from place to place, like one possessed, and in less than half an hour he had gained considerable information Three things he knew well enough. First : Conrad du Nord had escaped. Second : The Duke of Rennes had assisted him. Third : He had gone with horses and friends.

"I do much suspect," muttered the prince to himself, 'that Sir Philip de Savenay has lent his aid to this ; but I will not accuse him yet ; I will find the fugitives first, and I will deal with him afterwards."

As he thus muttered, Poins came in with a report. He had met some fishermen just beyond the wall, who had declared that they saw, about an hour past midnight, a party of horsemen dashing off over the sands toward the Villaine road.

A few more reports were brought in ; and then the prince sent for Thamar, who quickly answered his call.

"Thamar, how many of the royal guard can you count upon as truě to me ?"

"All whom you have helped to the position, my lord ; certainly a score of them."

"You have your commission as lieutenant ?"

"Yes."

"Suppose I should show you an order from the king commanding the arrest of Conrad du Nord, and that I should bid you to apprehend him ?"

"I should obey you, my lord."

"Then look ye ; The case is ten times more emphatic than that. A prisoner, whom the king had condemned to death for high treason, has escaped. Can you call twenty of the royal guard, and give pursuit ?"

"Yes, my lord."

"Then away at once. You know the man. It is Conrad du Nord ; and I think that some of the duke's guard are with him. If Casimir has directed him to a place of safety, I think I risk nothing in deciding that that place is Anjou. With this clue let your wits serve you. Spare not your horses. Change them as often as you can. Ride for your lives. Aye—my good Thamar, ride for the place of power which Sir Philip de Savenay now occupies ! Do you understand me ?"

"My lord, if Conrad du Nord lives, look to see him back in Vannes when I return ; and I will return as quickly as possible. I will eat and sleep in the saddle, until I find him."

"Good ! Away now ; and if you bring the prisoner back as you promise, the reward I have spoken of may be nearer than you imagine."

Within half an hour from that time, Thamar had placed himself at the head of five-and-twenty stout guardsmen, and was galloping out from the city.

* * * * * * *

Conrad du Nord found good horses in his train, and before daylight he had crossed the Villaine ; and, just as the sun was rising, he reached the hamlet of Chenay, where he concluded to stop and get break-fast.

"We will eat, and change horses here," said Nicolas ; "and then be on our way again. We shall not be long detained."

A small inn was found, where the seal of the duke brought forth promise of the horses, and where a good meal could be readily prepared. While the host was making ready in the kitchen, Conrad threw himself into an easy-chair, and closed his eyes. He had fallen away into a dreamy slumber, when he was aroused by feel-ing a hand upon his shoulder, and hearing his name pronounced. He started up, and beheld Francisco stand-ing by his side.

"My father !" he cried, springing to his feet, and rub-bing his eyes.

"Conrad, my boy !" echoed the old tutor.

"Is it really Francisco ?"

"Certainly it is. By my life, this is a strange meeting. I was just waking from a curious dream when the horses came rattling into the court ; and upon going to the window I saw your very self getting down from the saddle ; and can you wonder, my boy, that I made all haste to meet you ?"

"It was natural that you should. But tell me, Francisco—why are you here ?"

"I have started for Vannes, my boy. Your kind old mother, Marguerite, has been stolen away from us ; and I think she has been carried thither. Ah—I see by your face, that this is no news to you. What have you to tell? I am very anxious, Conrad."

"I have much to tell," replied our hero, motioning his old tutor to a seat.   They were alone, Nicolas having gone to look after the horses, while the rest of the party were in the kitchen.

"I have much to tell," repeated Conrad, resuming his seat. "Listen to me, for I am going to startle you."

And thereupon the youth went on to tell of all that had befallen him since he left the castle of Rennes. He told of the coming of Sir Philip ; of the arrival at Vannes ; of the first interview of Casimer with the king ; of the complaint which the prince entered ; of the attack of Pluton ; of the coming of the last summons ; of the startling disclosures made by Father Jerome ; of the introduction of Marguerite, and of her story ; of his condemnation and imprisonment ; and of the coming of the duke to set him free. At first the old man had been deeply affected ; but he managed to control himself until the narrative reached the disclosures of the monk, and the corroborating testimony of Marguerite. At this point he shook convulsively, and seemed almost inclined to doubt the truth of the story.

"Did Marguerite tell that ?" he asked, when he could control his speech.

"Yes. But, Francisco, I am sure that she had been promised that it should do me no harm. She fainted before the king, and was racked with mortal agony. I cannot blame her."

The hermit asked many questions touching the doings of the prince, the speech of the king, the appearance of Father Jerome, and the movements of the duke; and when he had made himself familiar with all the details, he arose and commenced to pace the room.

Conrad was upon the point of speaking further, when the host looked into the room, and announced that breakfast was ready.

"Let us move quickly," said Nicolas, appearing upon the threshold as the host turned away. "The horses will be ready for us. Ah—whom have we here?"

"This is Francisco,—my tutor and guardian," replied our hero. And then turning the other way, he added, "And this is Nicolas, the captain of the duke's guard."

"Let there be no haste," said Francisco, after he had embraced the captain. "Conrad must not leave this place until he sees another friend."

"But, my good sir," interposed Nicolas, "you know not what you say. We are——"

"I know all," said the old man, interrupting him. "Conrad has told me the whole story; and I must bid him wait. There is one coming who may help him."

"Ah," uttered the captain, shaking his head, "a stop here may ruin all his hopes of escape."

"And yet," pursued Francisco, resolutely, "he must wait. The Abbot of Saint Aubin will be here in a very short time. He must see the abbot."

At the mention of that name the captain's resolution was shaken.

"Is good old Dagobert coming?" asked Conrad.

"Yes. He stopped at Saint Eustace last night, and will join me here this morning. But your breakfast is waiting. Eat, and we will converse afterwards."

Conrad followed the captain to the kitchen, and after

the meal was eaten he rejoined his tutor, whom he found pacing up and down the court in front of the inn.

"I wish much to see old Dagobert; and yet to tarry here is dangerous," said the youth, after Francisco had once more bidden him to wait.

"Conrad," spoke the hermit, stopping, and resting his hand upon the boy's arm, "I would not willingly lead you into danger. Do as I bid you."

"But, father we shall be pursued. Even now the royal guardsmen may be upon my track; and if they overtake us, they will come in a force which may not be resisted. Remember, it is not now the prince who strikes; it is the king !"

"You can tell me nothing which I do not already understand," returned Francisco. "Heaven sent this meeting."

Conrad started at these words, and a wild hope flashed up in his bosom.

"Answer me one question," he cried, grasping the old man by the arm. "Did the monk tell the truth ?"

"In what ?"

"In saying that I was the child of those traitorous parents."

"Dagobert can tell you of that better than I can."

"Beware, Francisco ! O, if you give me reason to hope thus, and the spark should die out——"

"*Wait and see the abbot!*" spoke the old man, slowly, and meaningly. "You must not leave this place until he comes."

"I shall obey you."

At that moment Nicolas came up and announced that the horses would be ready in a very few minutes.

"Let them wait," said Conrad. "I must remain here and see the Abbot of Saint Aubin."

"But, good Conrad, have you counted the cost ?"

"I have counted everything, Nicolas—and I will wait."

The captain turned an inquiring glance upon Francisco, who quickly added :

" The boy is right. He must see Dagobert."

" Then I hold myself above all blame," said Nicolas, not at all reconciled to the arrangement.

" I am responsible," answered Conrad. He spoke promptly ; and yet there was a strange flutter of uncertainty and anxiety in his bosom. When the captain had gone he turned to his old tutor, and asked him if he would answer one more question.

" Ask what you please," replied Francisco.

" If the monk spoke falsely, then Marguerite spoke falsely, also."

" And yet they may both have been mistaken. Wait until you see the abbot."

They waited two hours. Nicolas was in torture, for he knew that the king's guard could readily trace them. He had approached our hero, to remonstrate against tarrying longer, when Francisco came with the announcement that the abbot had arrived.

The venerable prelate entered the room with a firm step, and as Conrad hastened to meet him he smiled benignantly, and invoked a blessing upon his youthful head. The presence of the white-haired old abbot gave great relief to the captain, who pressed forward to greet him with reverence and love ; for the good man upon whose sympathetic heart rested the experience of almost a century, was well known at the castle.

" Now," said Dagobert, when he had taken a seat, " what is this I hear ? Francisco has just been telling me something which deeply interests me. Conrad, what have they been doing to you? Let me have the story."

Our hero related to the abbot the circumstances of his adventures as he had related them to his tutor; and he had just concluded when one of the men-at-arms came rushing into the apartment with the intelligence that a large body of mounted men were approaching the hamlet from the direction of Vannes.

Nicolas started up and hastened out; and very soon came back again.

"It is a detachment of the royal guard!" he said; "and Thamar leads them."

"Hold!" spoke Dagobert, as Conrad started to his feet. "Who is this Thamar?"

"He is a lieutenant of the king's guard," replied Nicolas; "but a tool of prince Bertrand's."

"How many are there? asked Conrad.

"More than a score of them."

"I must not be taken. I will die here—"

"My son," said the abbot, taking the youth by the hand, "you have nothing to fear. If this Thamar has come to take you back to Vannes, go with him quietly. I will accompany you."

"One word," cried Conrad, turning and seizing the old man's hand. "Francisco said you would tell. Did Father Jerome speak truly?"

"*He did not!*" replied Dagobert, calmly.

Conrad du Nord staggered as though beneath a stunning blow.

"O, can you prove it?" he gasped.

"I can prove that, and much more," said the abbot. And then, taking both the youth's hands in his own, and speaking in a gentle, persuasive tone, he added— "I love you as I would love my own child; and yet I say unto thee, go back with me to Vannes!"

The youth was completely overcome by conflicting emotions; but he had confidence in the abbot, and he consented to obey him.

"But how is it with us?" asked Nicolas.

"I answer for all," replied Dagobert.

In a few moments more a loud tramp was heard in the court, and very soon Thamar, followed closely by a dozen of his men, entered the apartment,

"Conrad du Nord," he said, drawing his sword, "I arrest you in the king's name!"

"You may put up your sword, sir lieutenant," returned our hero; "for I shall go with you quietly and unconditionally." The presence of the armed men called him back to conscious pride, and he spoke calmly and bravely.

Thamar was evidently surprised at the coolness of the prisoner, who, he supposed, must know that he was going back to certain death; but he received the token of surrender with a bow, and then turned to Nicolas, remarking.

"And you, too, captain, with your followers, I arrest."

Nicolas bowed, and signified that he should offer no resistance to the king's officers, simply adding:

"Since we surrender unconditionally, I presume that we are to be respectfully treated."

Thamar was a soldier; and he had a respect for brave men; so he had no disposition to be unnecessarily severe. His only orders had been to take the prisoner; and this he would do; and he was glad, too, that he could do it so easily, for he had expected much trouble.

"Sir lieutenant," said the abbot, pointing to Francisco, "this good brother and myself are going to Vannes; and we would ride in your company. I trust that you will have no objections."

Thamar recognized the cross of Saint Aubin, and he bowed respectfully.

"You are welcome, holy father."

"Thank you, my son.   I will go out and see that my horse is in readiness."

In the court Dagobert met a yeoman who had accompanied him from Saint Aubin.

"Pierre," he said, speaking lowly and quickly, "you have a fleet horse, and a stout heart.   Haste thee to Vannes with all speed, so as to get there well in advance of this troop,   Seek Sir Philip de Savenay, and bid him come forth and meet us on the road.   Do you understand?"

"Yes, father."

"Then away with you."

Ere long the yeoman was mounted, and the rate of speed at which he dashed over the road gave token that he duly appreciated the importance of his mission.

———•———

CHAPTER XXIII.

CONCLUSION.

The day was drawing to its close as Thamar approached Vannes with his prisoners.   He turned to one of his men, as he beheld the spires of the city, and remarked that he had not calculated upon so speedy a return.

"The prince will not look for us to-night," he added.

"No," responded the other.   "His highness probably thinks we are still on the pursuit."

"Very likely," returned Thamar ;   "for I told him we

should not probably reach the fugitives until this day had gone. Ha!—who comes there? It is our captain, as I live; and he has a squadron of the guard with him. What means this?"

"Look!" cried the other speaker. "The old abbot is going to meet him."

It was as had been said. As soon as Sir Philip appeared in the distance, Dagobert, who had been riding well in advance of the cavalcade, put spurs to his horse, and soon joined the knight, with whom he entered into an earnest conversation.

Sir Philip had stopped when the abbot reached him, and he waited there until the lieutenant came up.

"How now, Thamar," he said, riding in front of his subaltern, "you have prisoners?"

The officer could not bring himself to offer slight to his captain, however much he may have wished to pass him with his prize.

"I have prisoners, Sir Philip; and I am conducting them to the city."

"Do you conduct them to the king?"

"The order for their arrest was from the king; but I do not report to him."

"Ah,—to whom do you report?"

"To him through whom the order came."

"You mean the prince?"

"Yes," answered Thamar, reluctantly.

"Then," said Sir Philip, with an authoritative nod of the head, "I will relieve you of your charge."

"How! Relieve me?" gasped the lieutenant, blankly.

"Yes," replied the captain, with another nod. "I will take the prisoners directly to the king."

"But, Captain, I have my orders."

"From whom?" demanded Sir Philip, sternly.

"From the prince."

" Does the prince command the royal guard ?"

" But the order was issued by the king."

"And to the king these prisoners shall straightway
be carried ; so rest you easy on that score." And then
Sir Philip added, in a lower tone, and with a look of
deep meaning :

" Thamar, *follow not the whelp until the lion is dead!*"

The lieutenant trembled from head to foot ; and without further remonstrance he resigned his command to
his superior, and fell back with his troop.

Sir Philip, as soon as Thamar had retired, turned to
the old abbot, and asked him several questions, which
were answered in detail and to the point.

"I understand it now," the gallant knight said, smiting his fist upon the pommel of his saddle, while a
bright glow irradiated his features. "By Saint Michael !
it is wonderful ! You were thoughtful, father, to send
for me."

"I had wit enough to see the necessity of that, Sir
Philip. Have you seen the duke ?"

"Not to speak with him. But he is at his house."

" He must be at the palace."

"So he shall be." And thus speaking, Sir Philip
turned to his attendants and beckoned one of them forward.

"Go to the Duke of Rennes, and bid him to repair at
once to the royal palace, and there await my coming.
Also bid him, if he can, to take Marguerite with him.
Hurry away, and let your spurs drip if need be."

It was well into the evening when the King of Brittany was informed by his page that he was wanted in
the audience chamber. He sat by his table, with his
brow resting upon his hands ; and one would have said,
upon first beholding him, that he was dying. All he
had eaten for four-and-twenty hours had been a few

crusts which had been drying and mouldering in his cupboard for weeks ; and his only beverage had been of the water that had been brought to him for washing.

"Who wants me ?" he asked.

"The Duke of Rennes sent me for you, sire."

"Is he alone ?"

"No. There are several with him. Your captain is there, with the young man called Conrad du Nord——"

"Ha !"

"And a white-haired old man, whom I judge to be the Abbot of Saint Aubin."

"What !" cried Theobald, starting to his feet ; "is it Dagobert ?"

"That is his name, sire."

"I will go at once. O, good Dagobert, I have need of thee !"

Without further delay the king repaired to his chamber of private audience, which he found well lighted, and where he saw the duke and Sir Philip, and the young prisoner, and the woman, Marguerite, and several others ; but the one towards whom he moved with quick impulse was the Abbot of Saint Aubin.

"Dagobert ! Dagobert !" he cried, "I am glad you have come !" And as he spoke he fairly sank upon the aged prelate's bosom, as though he expected to find a protector there.

"Sire," spoke the abbot, after he had blessed the king, "if I can be of service to you, you may command me ; but first I have a matter of most pressing moment to present to your majesty. Can you listen to me ?"

"Yes, Dagobert. You may command me, if you please."

"First, sire—do you recognize these people who are with me ?"

Theobald ran his eye over those present, and hesitated not until he came to Francisco.

"Him I know not; and yet I think I have seen him."

"He was for many years in the service of your brother Charles. His name is Francisco."

"Ah—I know him now. And where has he been during this long time?"

"You shall know that anon, sire."

Dagobert led the king to his chair of state, and then continued:

"This youth, whom men call Conrad du Nord, has been once ere this before your majesty; and I am able to inform you that, in the examination which then took place, a most fatal error was committed; and I have now come to reveal the truth. Will you know it, sire?"

"Yes."

"But suppose it should cast a mortal stain upon one near and dear to you?"

"I would not trouble the sleeping dead, holy father."

"I speak of the living, sire."

"Then you mistake," said Theobald, with a sad shake of the head. "I have no near and dear one living!"

A look of relief rested upon Dagobert's face.

"Will you send for the prince, and also for Father Jerome?"

A messenger was despatched, and ere long Bertrand entered the chamber. He stopped when he saw those who were assembled there; and when his eye rested upon Conrad du Nord, he stamped his foot with rage.

"How now!" he cried. "What mockery is this? Why is the condemned traitor here, with his limbs free, and a sword upon his hip?"

"Hold, my son," interposed the abbot, raising his hand in a persuasive manner. "You shall be entirely satisfied that all is right. Ah—here comes our brother Jerome."

At that moment the Benedictine entered the chamber ; and when he saw into what company he had come, he was struck with blank astonishment. But he quickly recognized his venerable superior, and reverently saluted him.

"Jerome," said the abbot, seeming determined to come at the business as speedily as possible, "you have been summoned hither to witness the correcting of a sad mistake, which you have made. Upon your testimony this young man was pronounced the offspring of base conspirators."

" Not upon mine alone, father."

" Your word condemned him, nevertheless."

" The testimony of Marguerite went with mine."

"Jerome," said the abbot, with some severity, " you must not trifle with truth. How came Marguerite to give her testimony ?"

The monk was silent.

" Did you not," continued Dagobert, " solemnly promise her that no harm should come to the youth ?"

" Can that alter the weight of her confession ?" asked Jerome, as though he would defend himself.

" We shall see. Marguerite, come hither."

The woman approached, trembling at every joint.

" My daughter," pursued the abbot, " answer me truly what I shall ask. Circumstances have arisen which render a longer concealment impossible, and I release you from your vows. Why did you tell the king that Conrad du Nord was the child of Marceau and Marcelline ?"

" I did not tell him so."

" How ?" demanded Theobald, with a start of surprise.

"When I was alone with Father Jerome and the
prince," continued Marguerite, quickly and eagerly, "I
may have spoken thus falsely ; for I then hardly knew
what I said. They swore to me that no harm should
come to my boy if he proved to be the child of Marcelline. They said he should be sent out of the country.
So, to save him, I spoke as I did. I was keeping the
oath which I gave to his mother. But when I came
before the king I was more careful of my words. I
said that I bore away the infant child of Marcelline,
thus saving it from the hands of the executioner, which
was true. And then, sire," added the woman, bowing
before the king, "you asked me where that child was.
I did not answer you—I could not. Directly you asked
me if Conrad du Nord was the child which I saved, and
I answered you, yes. I spoke truly, for I saved both
the children."

"Both !"

"Hold, sire," interposed Dagobert, "I must speak
now. Listen to me, all of you, and I will clear away
this mystery. Will your majesty send for your secretary, with instructions that he bring with him the
records of the realm as far back as five-and-twenty
years."

A messenger was despatched, and while he was gone
all was silent in the audience chamber. The prince
chafed and fretted, and tore his fingers into the folds of
his doublet ; but he did not speak. Conrad du Nord
stood by the side of Francisco, his heart throbbing till
its pulsations were distinctly audible ; for the moment
was one of terrible interest to him.

By and by the secretary came, bearing under his arm
two large books ; and when he had saluted the king, he
was directed to attend to the abbot.

"Lepidus," said the prelate, calling the secretary by

name, "I wish you to refer to your records, and inform us when Marceau and Marcelline were executed."

The scribe opened one of his books, and when he had found the record and calculated a while, he answered :

" The event occurred four-and-twenty years and one month ago.'.

" Four-and-twenty years and one month, you say ?"

" Yes, holy father."

" Now look and inform us when Mary of Anjou, the wife of Duke Charles, died."

The secretary again referred to the record, and answered :

" Mary of Anjou died three-and-twenty years ago, lacking two months."

" So that," said Dagobert, " between the execution of the conspirators and the death of Mary of Anjou, there elapsed one year and three months ?"

" Yes, father."

" Sire—Sir Philip de Savenay—my lord of Rennes," pursued the abbot, " you were well acquainted with the household of the duchess. Now tell me—when did Marguerite leave her employ ?"

" Marguerite was with the duchess to the last," said Sir Philip.

" Aye," added the king, " I remember that I found her kneeling by the dead body of the duchess, in the chamber of mourning."

" And thus," pursued the abbot, " we have it clearly proved that for over a year, at least, after the disappearance of the child of Marcelline, Marguerite was with Mary of Anjou."

" Good father," cried the king, with intense eagerness, " what do you aim at ? Keep me not in the dark."

" Sir," replied Dagobert, while a strange shadow

passed over his aged features, "prepare yourself for a wonderful revelation."

"You cannot startle me, Dagobert."

"Be not too sure of that, sire. It is thus that I have to speak."

The abbot moved a step forward, and then continued:

"Four-and-twenty years ago, and two months over, your wife, the Queen Theresa, gave birth to a son. You were filled with joy, and all your people gave thanks unto God. You had waited long years for an heir, and you had even thought of putting away your queen, when this happy event reconciled you to her. But, while all was joy in your heart, a cloud came over the gladness of Theresa. The infant fell sick, and she knew that it must die. She sent for me to come to her. I was her confessor, and I had acted as her physician.

"The child was dying when I reached her; and so I told her. Then she asked me to promise her that I would keep the sickness of her infant a secret. Why should I do that? But she would not explain; only she begged me to promise. I did so. I assured her that I would not speak of it without her consent. On the following day I went again, and found Mary of Anjou, and her serving-woman Marguerite, with the queen. The infant was dead. It had just breathed its last, and even then lay cold and still upon its mother's bosom. Theresa sank upon her knees before me, and prayed that I would keep her secret. I asked what secret she meant. She answered me, that the king must not know his son was dead. At least, she would have me speak no word until she gave me permission. I consented to this, and went away.

"At this same time, sire, the Count Marceau, and his wife Marcelline, had been convicted and sentenced, and

all their family proscribed. Marcelline had been in the
service of the queen, and the queen loved her as a sister.
Even as the infant prince was dying the queen received
a note from Marcelline, containing these words : ' *For
the love of Heaven save my infant child!*' Can you wonder,
sire, that a strange thought presented itself to the
queen's mind ? She feared to let you know that you
had no son. She did not stop to reflect ; she did not
seek my advice ; she only trusted the duchess and Marguerite. Her own dead infant was taken away, and
Marguerite brought the child of Marcelline to take its
place ! A few short weeks after that the queen was
taken sick, and upon her death bed she confessed to me
what she had done. As the matter then stood I concluded to keep the secret. The king knew not that the
child he fondled was of another blood ; and I would not
break the spell.

"Hold !" commanded Dagobert, as Bertrand rushed
forward. "Let me finish the story. Listen a few
moments longer, sire. I will soon conclude.

"A little more than a year subsequent to the events
I have related, your brother Charles, Duke of Nantes,
was slain in the battle of Quimper. His wife, the fair
Mary of Anjou, was then residing in Vannes, and had
just given birth to a son. The news of her husband's
death, coming at a time when she was already weak and
prostrate, gave her a mortal blow ; and when she knew
that she was dying, she became possessed with the idea
that her child—her infant boy—would be in constant
danger if she left him with those who had the legal
right to the guardianship. She had seen so much of
the strife and turmoil of the court, that she dreaded to
leave the little one to grow up under its influence. And
another thing influenced her much. She knew that the
growing child at the royal palace, whom people called

Prince, was not of the royal blood ; and she knew that
her own child, as the heir of Duke Charles, stood next
in line to the throne, if Theobald died childless. All
this frightened her, and she wished that her child might
grow up in some quiet, safe retreat, and be educated for
the Church. She sent for me, and confided to me her
plans. I reflected upon them, and did not oppose them.
I believed that the child would be better off in the Church
than in the court ; and I promised to assist her. Marguerite, her faithful and loving servant, was to be a
mother to the child, and Francisco was selected to act
as tutor and guardian. Francisco had been one of the
bravest and most faithful followers of Charles ; and he
it was who had come home with intelligence of his master's death. Mary of Anjou died, and Francisco and
Marguerite went away with the child.

"Sire, I have but little more to add. The son of
Charles and Mary was not born for the Church. No
power of argument or persuasion could bend his mind
in that direction. His hand itched for the sword and
spear, and his kind tutor finally gave him instruction in
the use of arms. How he has improved under that
instruction you must judge for yourself. I have only
to add, that this noble youth, whom we have called
Conrad du Nord, is your own nephew, the only child of
Charles of Nantes ! Look into his face, sire, and tell
me what you read there. Ask Casimir and Sir Philip
what they read when first they saw him ?"

For a moment all was still, and then the voice of Bertrand broke the spell.

"Fools ! idiots !" he cried, "do you believe this foul
tissue of priestly lies ? Thus shall my sword sunder the
false fabric the hoary dotard would build at my
expense !"

He had snatched his sword from its scabbard ; and, as

he spoke, he sprang towards Conrad, intending to run him through ; but an eye had been upon him from the first, watching his every movement. Francisco drew his own sword, and stepped before him.

" Back, Bertrand !"

" Out, greybeard ! I want not your blood yet !"

Bertrand aimed a furious blow as the words dropped from his lips, and Francisco had but one way to avoid it. He caught the coming blade upon his guard, and would have rested with bearing the point aside ; but he was not permitted so to do. He was before a madman, and his own life was trembling in the balance. The fire flashed in his eye, and the old vigor steeled his arm. Others would have interfered, but there was no time. Blind and furious, and with horrid imprecations upon his lips, the false prince rushed on to his death, for, at the second charge, the blade of the stern old soldier pierced his bosom, and he staggered back, and fell upon the pavement.

" Pardon ! pardon !" cried Francisco, throwing down the dripping sword, and sinking upon his knees before the king. " I could not help it."

" Up, up, Francisco," shouted Theobald, starting from his chair, and seizing the old soldier by the hand. " You have done the State a merciful service ! Wait here, all of you."

Thus speaking the king turned and left the apartment ; and when he came back he brought with him his dead dog, which he laid upon the dais before his chair.

" Behold," he said, shuddering as he spoke, " the dumb companion of my cheerless solitude. This poor animal was poisoned. He died from eating bread which was prepared for the king ! Do you ask me who prepared the fatal food ? Francisco has just saved the State the need of the prisoner's execution."

A startling curse broke upon the air ; and then a cry for mercy.

Dagobert kneeled by the side of the fallen man ; but the prayer which dropped from his lips was for a soul departed !

*　　*　　*　　*　　*　　*　　*

Up, up, from the darkness of despair to a brighter day !

Rosaline heard a step by her side, and a well-remembered voice whispered her name.

"Conrad !"

"Yes, love."

She saw her father standing near by, and her eager, anxious look he well understood.

"All is well, my child," he said.

And shortly afterwards he told to his daughter the wonderful revelation which had been made.

"And now," said our hero, while a hopeful flush suffused his cheeks, and an expectant light beamed in his eyes, "you must allow me, my lord, to repeat the question which once before I asked. Shall the Lady Rosaline speak my fate ?"

"As you will, Conrad. If you choose to trust her, you may rest upon her decision."

Rosaline of Rennes could not throw away the rich treasure of that noble, manly heart ; and when Conrad took her hand, and bade her speak in answer to his prayer, she pillowed her head upon his bosom, and whispered for his hearing the sweetest words that had ever thrilled upon his senses.

Such marvelous things as had transpired could not be kept from the people ; and when they knew that Bertrand was dead, and that the youthful hero of the Nord was heir to the throne, their joy knew no bounds.

But there was no need of haste in furnishing a new occupant for the throne. With the death of Bertrand was removed a fearful incubus from the life of Theobald; and he arose once more to strength and pride, and reigned in peace for many years. But finally the measure of his years was full, and the sceptre fell from his hand.

Then it was that Conrad, in the full vigor of well-trained manhood, stepped upon the topmost round in the ladder of his fortunes; and blessed by the devoted love of his gentle Rosaline, he won the confidence and affections of his people, and honored the crown which fate had placed upon his head.

THE END

AN AMERICAN NOVEL.

Parted By Fate;

OR,

The Mystery of Black-Tor Lighthouse.

By LAURA JEAN LIBBEY,

Author of " Ione," " A Mad Betrothal," etc., etc.

With Fourteen Beautiful Illustrations By Harry C. Edwards.

Paper Cover, 50 Cents. Bound Volume, $1.00.

Miss Libbey's novels appeal to the young, and especially to young women. They are lively and sparkling, abounding in charming sentiment and with incidents connected with courtship and marriage. There are so many complications possible in the relations of lovers that invention would seem to be an endless chain. Miss Libbey's books are among the most popular publications of the present time, and "Parted by Fate" a good example of the very best of them.

For sale by all Booksellers, or sent, postpaid, on receipt of price, by

ROBERT BONNER'S SONS, Publishers,
CORNER WILLIAM AND SPRUCE STREETS, New York.

THE NORTHERN LIGHT.

TRANSLATED FROM THE GERMAN OF

E. WERNER,

BY

MRS. D. M. LOWREY.

12mo. 373 Pages. Handsomely Bound in Cloth, Price, $1.00.
Paper Cover, 50 Cents.

Since the death of the author of "Old Ma'mselle's Secret,"
Werner is the most popular of living German writers. Her
novels are written with great literary ability, and possess the
charm of varied character, incident and scenery. "The Northern
Light" is one of her most characteristic stories. The heroine is
a woman of great beauty and strength of individuality. No less
interesting is the young poet who, from beginning to end, con-
stantly piques the curiosity of the reader.

For sale by all booksellers, or sent, postpaid, on receipt of
price, by

ROBERT BONNER'S SONS, Publishers,
COR. WILLIAM AND SPRUCE STREETS, New York.

OTTILIE ASTER'S SILENCE.

A NOVEL.

Translated From the German

By MRS. D. M. LOWREY.

With Numerous Choice Illustrations By Warren B. Davis.

Paper Cover, 50 Cents. Bound Volume, $1.00.

———

No more charming story of the love-life of a married couple
was ever portrayed in the pages of a novel. Romance does
not end with marriage, and it does not require any demonstration to prove it; but if it did, this novel shows how great
are the elements of romantic interest which exist in the marriage
relation.   There is in it the beauty of family life in a pure
household, and the mother and daughter exhibit all the beautiful
traits which endear women to men and make the charm of the
world.
  For sale by all Booksellers, or sent, postpaid, on receipt of
price, by

ROBERT BONNER'S SONS, Publishers,
CORNER WILLIAM AND SPRUCE STREETS, New York.

The Breach of Custom.

TRANSLATED FROM THE GERMAN

BY

MRS. D. M. LOWREY

WITH CHOICE ILLUSTRATIONS BY O. W. SIMONS.

Paper Cover, 50 Cents. Bound Volume, $1.00.

This is a translation of an interesting and beautiful German novel, introducing an artist and his family, and dealing with the most pathetic circumstances and situations. The heroine is an ideal character. Her self-sacrifice is noble and exalted, and the influence which radiates from her is pure and ennobling. Every one who reads this book will feel that it is one which will be a life influence. Few German stories have more movement or are more interesting. There are great variety and charm in the characters and situations.

For sale by all booksellers, or sent postpaid on receipt of price by

ROBERT BONNER'S SONS, Publishers,

182 WILLIAM STREET, New York

A Sequel to "The Unloved Wife."

By MRS. E. D. E. N. SOUTHWORTH.

With Illustrations by O. W. Simons.

Paper Cover, 50 Cents. Bound in Cloth, $1.00.

In "Lilith," Mrs. Southworth has taken up the fortunes of her heroine from the date of her disappearance in "The Unloved Wife," and created a new and lovely history for her. Each of the novels is perfectly complete in itself, and neither is necessary to the perfection of the other, but they may be read together, and thus they form a more extended and more beautiful development of life and character than either constitutes alone. In "The Unloved Wife" Lilith is a girl; in "Lilith" she is a woman. There are more power and more of the interest and influence of independent individuality and character in the sequel than in the first part of the heroine's strange and tragic history. All who read one will desire to read the other.

A NEW NOVEL
By the Popular Author, Mrs. Amelia E. Barr.

THE BEADS OF TASMER.

BY

MRS. AMELIA E. BARR.

12mo., 395 pages. Handsomely Bound in English Cloth. Beauti-
fully Illustrated by W. B. Davis. Uniform with "A Matter
of Millions" and "The Forsaken Inn," by Anna Katharine
Green. Price, $1.25.

"The Beads of Tasmer," by Mrs. Amelia E. Barr, is a powerful and interesting story of Scotch life. The singular and strenu-
ous ambition which a combination of ancient pride and modern
greed inspires; the loveliness of the Scotch maidens, both High-
landers and Lowlanders; the deep religious nature of the people;
the intense manifestation of these characteristic traits by Scotch
lovers of high and low degree; the picturesque life of the country,
involving the strangest vicissitudes of fortune and the exhibition
of the most loving and loyal devotion, constitute a theme which
is of the highest intrinsic interest, and which is developed by the
accomplished authoress with consummate art and irresistible
power. "The Beads of Tasmer" is certainly one of Mrs. Barr's
very best works, and we shall be much mistaken if it does not take
high rank among the most successful novels of the century.

For sale by all booksellers and newsdealers, or sent postpaid on
receipt of $1.25 by the publishers,

ROBERT BONNER'S SONS,
CORNER WILLIAM AND SPRUCE STS., NEW YORK.

EDDA'S BIRTHRIGHT.

By MRS. HARRIET LEWIS.

With Seven Illustrations.

Paper Cover, 50 Cents.   Bound Volume, $1.00.

———

"Edda's Birthright" is an excellent novel.   Mrs. Lewis has the faculty of making a story thoroughly interesting.   There is, in "Edda's Birthright," a charming girl, who engages sympathy by her spirited behavior in depressing circumstances, and wins the heart of the reader by her truly womanly character. The scene of the story is the great city of London, and the heroine has many strange incidents and episodes in her life. It is her splendid courage which makes her great charm, and which finally wins.   Every one who reads this book will be well repaid.

For sale by all Booksellers, or sent, postpaid, on receipt of price, by

ROBERT BONNER'S SONS, Publishers,
CORNER WILLIAM AND SPRUCE STREETS, New York.

A NATIONAL BOOK.

THE NEW SOUTH,

By HENRY W. GRADY.

With a Character Sketch of

HENRY W. GRADY,

By OLIVER DYER,

Author of "Great Senators."

16mo. Bound in Cloth. Uniform With "Great Senators." With Portrait. Price, $1.00.

"The New South" is a work of national importance. It is an eloquent presentation of the changed condition of the South, the facts of her present growth and prosperity, and the resources which insure her magnificent destiny. Mr. Grady was an ardent patriot. His imagination was aflame with bright visions of the future of his beloved country. He had a mind which was equal to his great heart, and he undertook the splendid task of educating and enlightening his countrymen; and exhibiting the inexhaustible riches of her fertile soil, her beds of coal and iron, her great staple, the cotton of the world's commerce, and her majestic water courses which furnish the power and assurance of empire. His book is his monument.

Mr. Dyer's character sketch of Henry W. Grady is an admirable account of the great orator and journalist. It will be read with enthusiastic approval by every friend and admirer of Mr. Grady in the North as well as in the South. The author of "Great Senators" has grasped the character and presented the spiritual side of his subject with a power and truth which indicate a great writer.

RETAIL PRICE OF "THE NEW SOUTH," $1.00.

For sale by all Booksellers, or sent, postpaid, on receipt of price, by

ROBERT BONNER'S SONS, Publishers,

CORNER WILLIAM AND SPRUCE STREETS, New York.

BERYL'S HUSBAND.

BY

MRS. HARRIET LEWIS.

Author of "Lady Kildare," "Sundered Hearts," "Her Double Life," etc.

WITH NUMEROUS FULL-PAGE ILLUSTRATIONS BY G. A. TRAVER.

Paper Cover, 50 cents. Bound in Cloth, $1.00.

A very charming story.   It opens on the shores of Lake Leman, in the romantic city of Geneva, under the shadow of Mont Blanc. A young English girl, who has been educated at a boarding-school at Vevay, is suddenly left without natural guardians and means of support.   Her beauty and interesting character attract a young English traveller, who induces her to run away with him and marry him.   This is the beginning of a romantic novel of extraordinary vicissitudes and adventures.   To give an analysis of the plot and situations would mar the interest of the reader. It is sufficient to say that it is equal to the best of Mrs. Lewis's novels, not excepting "Her Double Life" and "Lady Kildare."

For sale by all booksellers and newsdealers, or sent, postpaid, on receipt of price, by the publishers,

ROBERT BONNER'S SONS,

COR. WILLIAM AND SPRUCE STREETS, New York.

TRANSLATED FROM THE FRENCH OF

HONORE DE BALZAC. ˙

12mo. 439 Pages. With Twelve Beautiful and Characteristic
Illustrations by Whitney. Handsomely Bound in Cloth, Price,
$1.00. Paper Cover, 50 Cents..

———

Cousin Pons is one of the most interesting characters in the
whole range of Balzac's wonderful creations. Balzac penetrated
human nature to its depth. There is scarcely a type which
evaded his keen eye. His characters are types of the living,
human world swarming at his feet. His creations are as real as
noble peaks standing out against an evening sky. In every one
of Balzac's novels there is a great human lesson. There is not a
volume you can open which does not set forth some deep human
truth by means of characterizations so vivid that they seem to
breathe. So it is with "Cousin Pons." After reading it we
think of him not as a character in a novel, but as a personage—a
sweet and true soul—a simple enthusiast for art and beauty at
the mercy of selfish and vulgar harpies.

THE FORSAKEN INN.

By ANNA KATHARINE GREEN.

ILLUSTRATED BY VICTOR PERARD.

———

Anna Katharine Green's novel, " The Forsaken Inn," is admitted to be her best work. The authoress of " The Leavenworth Case " has always been considered extraordinarily clever in the construction of mystifying and exciting plots, but in this book she has not only eclipsed even herself in her specialty, but has combined with her story-telling gift a fascinating mixture of poetical qualities which makes " The Forsaken Inn " a work of such interest that it will not be laid down by an imaginative reader until he has reached the last line of the last chapter. The scene of the story is the Hudson, between Albany and Poughkeepsie, and the time is the close of the eighteenth century. In writing her previous books, the authoress carefully planned her work before putting pen to paper, but this story was written in a white heat, and under the spur of a moment of inspiration.

" The Forsaken Inn " would have a large circulation even if the author was less well known and popular than Anna Katharine Green. With the author's reputation and its own inherent excellence, we confidently predict that it will prove the novel of the season.

The illustrations of " The Forsaken Inn " are by Victor Perard. They are twenty-one in number, and are a beautiful embellishment of the book.

THE LEDGER LIBRARY.

www.ingramcontent.com/pod-product-compliance
Lightning Source LLC
Chambersburg PA
CBHW030759020726
47499CB00006B/1698